WITH ALL MY HEART

WITH
ALL MY HEART

by

NAN ASQUITH

HARLEQUIN   BOOKS

Winnipeg • Canada   New York • New York

WITH ALL MY HEART

Originally published by Mills & Boon Limited,
50 Grafton Way, Fitzroy Square, London, England.

Harlequin Canadian edition published December, 1968
Harlequin U.S. edition published March, 1969

The Harlequin trade mark, consisting of the
word HARLEQUIN® and the portrayal of a
Harlequin, is registered in the United States Patent
Office and in the Canada Trade Marks Office.

CHAPTER ONE

THE car spluttered and gasped along a further few yards. Then it gave a shuddering sigh and stopped dead.

"That's done it," David said. He got out and tinkered a moment or two under the uplifted bonnet while Stevie and Lisa watched him anxiously.

Lisa, who was crouched under the rug, leaned forward shivering.

"I knew this was going to happen. Ever since it started jerking and backfiring in that queer way."

Stevie turned her head. She was filled with concern as she regarded her sister's pale pinched face and the immense violet-grey eyes shadowed with tiredness.

"We're nearly there," she said reassuringly. "I saw a sign-post a few miles back which said 'Hedburgh 12 miles'."

She broke off as David came back, wiping his hands on his handkerchief.

"I'm pretty sure it's a gasket. Among other things," he added irritably, "it's an unmitigated nuisance."

Lisa shivered again.

"Oh dear, does that mean we're stuck here?"

Stevie pointed ahead.

"I can see a petrol pump, so there must be a garage too. Yes, there's a man, beside that queer-looking car."

David looked round.

"I'll have a word with him. Don't get out in the cold, Stevie. Stay with Lisa."

They watched David walk up to the tall figure beside the battered black car. Saw the two heads jerking in conversation.

"We'll be all right now," Stevie said. "That garage will fix things." She sounded more cheerful than she felt, because she wanted to reassure Lisa, who had been ill and was still virtually convalescent and who was already on the verge of tears with fatigue. Lisa, who was the reason for this seemingly interminable journey from London to Norfolk.

"Don't be such a—a little *Pollyanna*," Lisa snapped. Her usually gentle voice was almost fretful. "Always making the best of things. I can't stand it. I wish we'd never come." She looked through the windows of the car at the landscape beyond, stiffened into the chill austerity of a woodcut under a biting east wind. A landscape that resembled mid-winter rather than early spring. "It's so cold and remote and miles from anywhere. And we're going to live in a strange house with strange people whom we may not even like and—"

She broke off, her voice quavering to a stop.

Stevie caught at the fingers resting on the edge of the seat behind her.

"Please, darling. Don't. You're just tired. I'm not being a Pollyanna. I'm sure we *will* be happy with David's aunt, Miss Arnott, and with his cousin Keith. I can't think that anyone belonging to David won't be as good and kind and—and helpful as he's been to us."

Lisa blinked, her tear-filled eyes more like drenched violets than ever. She squeezed Stevie's hand back.

"I'm sorry. I'm a pig. Especially when it's all my fault we're here in the first place. Because of being ill and Dr. Graham saying I had to get out of London and live in the country or by the sea."

"And that's exactly what Hedburgh is," Stevie said gaily. "In the country *and* by the sea! It couldn't be better. It's the most wonderful thing that David was able to arrange it all for us. And to bring us down in his car like this. I can't think why he should be so kind."

"He's in love with you," Lisa said. "That's why."

Stevie's creamy skin flushed to rose colour. She shook her head.

"We're just friends. Good friends."

Ever since I went to Perringers to work under David, Stevie thought, we've been that. I like him tremendously. He's so clever and capable at his job. So serious-minded and purposeful. Exactly the sort of strong-minded character I most admire.

She could remember the awful pang of regret she'd felt the day she'd told David that she would have to give up her job in the Account's Office, where David, as Assistant Accountant, was her boss. She had hated the thought that this might be the end of their friendship. A friendship that had somehow grown important to Stevie.

It hadn't been the end, because David had stepped right in and helped them. Told Stevie about his cousin Keith, who was a widower and who ran a farm with a riding school attached to it on the Norfolk coast. David's aunt, Miss Arnott, kept house for him and for his small daughter, Judy. Keith wanted someone to help on the farm and with the riding school, which became very busy during the summer months with holiday visitors. And because Stevie was an accomplished horsewoman from those earlier, happier days when both her parents were alive and she and Lisa had possessed ponies of their own, the job was offered to her. Lisa was to rest and convalesce until she was strong enough to help Miss Arnott in the house and with Judy.

David was walking back towards them, a tall figure in brown overalls at his side. He put his head in at the window.

"You'll have to get out Stevie. We're going to push it up to the garage. Lisa can stay inside."

Stevie slid out and as the car started to move forward she helped to push it along. With David guiding the steering wheel they moved it into an open shed alongside the petrol pumps.

"Grand," a voice said from the back of the car. Stevie turned. The man in the brown denims straightened up, seeming to grow taller and taller. Very dark eyes smiled down at her out of an oil-blackened face across which fell a lock of black hair. "It should be O.K. there."

David appeared round the front of the car, his good looking face marred by a frown.

"I don't like leaving it like this. You can't attend to it yourself, you say, and the garage owner has gone to a wedding? When will he be back?"

The young man went on smiling. He had very white teeth. Despite oil and grease and the torn and dirty overalls he was extremely good-looking.

"In about a week's time." He laughed. "It happens to be his own wedding."

9

The other three were too dismayed to see the humour of this. David positively scowled, as though he fully disapproved of the young man's levity.

"Isn't there any other garage? How are we to get to Hedburgh? It's several miles from here."

The young man shrugged laconically.

"Eight, to be exact."

Stevie was staring at the other car. A very shabby, very decrepit black car, immensely high and old-fashioned.

"David—what about *this* car?" She turned and looked at the dark young man. "Could you take us to Hedburgh in this?" She added doubtfully, "I suppose it *does* go?" The bold black stare surveyed her. The casual voice said, "It goes all right. It's been going now for exactly twenty-eight years and never failed me yet." His mocking glance rested on David's small smart car abandoned in the shed.

Stevie wasn't used to such lamentably familiar garage hands, to being stared at with quite such frank appraisal. She said stiffly.

"Then you'll take us to Hedburgh." She looked at David for confirmation. "D'you hear, David? We can go in this car."

David was still frowning uncertainly. He hesitated.

"I hate leaving mine here like this. It might be stolen. Do you think it's safe?" he demanded of the mechanic.

The man grinned, his eyes still on Stevie. Stevie looked quickly away from that easy casual smile. He was almost insolent! Leaning against the car like that: arms folded; wide shoulders propped up against the window; one enormously long leg crossed over the other.

She had a sudden doubt. Perhaps he wasn't a garage hand? His voice sounded quite cultured. On the other hand, in those filthy overalls and with those blackened hands and finger-nails, surely he looked the lowest form of garage hand possible.

"I don't think anyone would go to the trouble of carting it away on a lorry, do you? And it certainly won't go under its own steam. It's safe enough." He looked at Lisa shivering in the chill wind. He added.

"You're frozen. Hop in, won't you?" He gestured towards the high back.

"Thank you," David said coldly. He obviously disapproved of the young man as much as Stevie did. "I'll get our luggage."

The suitcases were stowed safely into the ancient contraption. The young man cranked the engine into noisy life.

"Hold your hats," he commanded, vaulting into the high front seat. "Here we go."

They set off, banging and clattering along the narrow village street, past some low thatched cottages and a tall flint church and on to a stretch of open road, decidedly bumpy.

Lisa gasped despairingly under her breath to Stevie.

"This is the *end*. And I'm so c-cold."

Stevie linked her arm through Lisa's.

"It's only a few more miles. Then we'll be with David's aunt." She looked at David for reassurance.

David was too preoccupied with worrying over his abandoned car to respond to Stevie. His aquiline features were set in lines of rigid disapproval at the whole afternoon's outcome.

Stevie felt suddenly isolated in her own thoughts. She was aware for the first time of tiredness. She had been up very early that morning, seeing to all the last-minute arrangements before their few pieces of furniture were taken away into store. The small flat that had been her and Lisa's home had been sublet and the keys had to be handed over to the new tenants. These last few weeks had been one long rush of organizing and planning, and Stevie had taken on the whole burden of it, as she had done ever since their mother had died and they had been left alone in the world.

Stevie smiled. It was odd to think that actually Lisa was the older of the two. Twenty-six to Stevie's twenty-four. But it was always she who had cherished and protected dreamy impractical Lisa; fought her battles at school, shouldered the burden of their affairs since Mrs. Hylton's death. Lisa had never been strong, and grief and loss had aggravated a natural delicacy. And when Lisa had had to give up working in London, Stevie had relinquished her own job, because Lisa just couldn't get along on her own in some strange place, among strangers.

11

Not quite strangers. David was with them. His presence would help them to feel more quickly at home and bridge that first sense of awkwardness.

I wonder what Miss Arnott will be like? Stevie thought. She had a sudden remembrance of the sprawling handwriting that splashed bright purple ink over thick blue notepaper in the many letters that Miss Arnott had written during the fixing of their arrangements. Letters with every other word underlined and all sorts of haphazard postscripts scribbled upside down and along the margins.

She could remember shaking her head over them and saying to Lisa, "She doesn't sound at all businesslike."

"She sounds kind," Lisa had remarked. "Large, to match the handwriting, and sort of motherly. A round grey bun and a big starched white overall."

Stevie had laughed.

"You make her sound like a cook general, a nice old-fashioned one."

"I imagine her looking like a farmer's wife," Lisa had explained. Adding, "Even if she is a spinster."

There was the nephew, Keith Arnott, too. Stevie frowned, considering. David had said that he was very quiet and withdrawn and that he had never quite got over his young wife's death.

Stevie sat suddenly bolt upright. The car had crested a hill and there below them, in the grey dusk of evening, was the cold North Sea, tossing away in a flurry of foaming white horses. A rim of wet brown sand and dark cliffs edged away into the rain-misted darkness.

Stevie took a deep breath.

"The *sea*, Lisa. Look, here we are!"

Lisa shuddered. The whole prospect appalled her. Only politeness kept her voice to a whisper as she muttered.

"Horrible. It looks cold and dreary beyond words!"

The car stopped with a tremendous jerk that nearly broke their noses on the seat opposite. Stevie looked out and saw a high flint wall and a clutter of grey stone and flint buildings. A creaking sign read, "Whitegates Farm and Riding School."

It was too dark to see more. Only a cobbled yard and the shadowy bulk of a straw stack. David and the driver were having an argument about payment. Then Stevie

12

heard the driver's voice call a casual "Good-night." The thunderous engine clattered into life. The whole preposterous affair jolted away and out of sight.

David picked up the biggest suitcase, shaking his fair head.

"He wouldn't take payment. Most casual. He said I could pay the garage." He shrugged. "Oh, well, come along in. I'll see to the rest of the stuff later."

A door ahead suddenly opened and a beam of light shone out.

"Here you are at last. Hello, David." A small grey-haired woman reached up to greet him, then a firm warm hand caught Stevie's. "Welcome to Whitegates. Come away in." Two of the brightest, most vivid blue eyes Stevie had ever seen flashed a glance round at Lisa. "Is this the one who's been ill? Yes, I can see that. Come along, my dear, you look chilled to the bone and quite worn out."

Stevie was aware of a dark passageway. A cat scuttled mewing from under their feet. A cocker spaniel snuffed at her ankles. Then they were all standing inside a long low room, where firelight flickered a reflection on cream-washed walls, and parchment-shaded lamps cast pools of light on cretonne-covered settee and chairs.

"Sit here," Miss Arnott urged Lisa. "Where it's warm."

"I'll get the other cases," David said.

Miss Arnott's beaming smile embraced the two sisters. Stevie smiled in return, thinking that no one could be more unlike Lisa's pictured notion of an ample farmer's wife than this tiny bird-like woman before them. Grey golliwog hair, feathered into some sort of crazy razor-cut, topped a sharp aquiline nose and humorously turned-up mouth. The vivid speedwell blue eyes echoed the deeper blue of the woollen windcheater above a pair of navy corduroy slacks.

"Now then," she went on, "you must be the one who signed your letters Stephanie—"

"That's me," Stevie said. "I'm called Stevie for short."

Miss Arnott's deep hoarse laugh issued surprisingly from such a small woman.

"I'll call you Stevie too." She thought the boyish abbreviation suited the girl standing before her. It went with the direct glance of the two hazel eyes regarding her. Very clear, very candid eyes. She wasn't beautiful like her slender sister with the delicate colouring and flowerlike air of fragility. But she was attractive. Miss Arnott approved Stevie's shining brown hair and creamy skin. Observed the way the wide cheek-bones curved down to a mouth that looked as if it was used to laughter but which for all its softness was set firmly above a small stubborn jaw. She had an impression of—what? Courage— strength—tenacity?

Miss Arnott looked at Lisa.

"And you're—?"

"Lisa," Lisa answered in her quiet shy voice.

"Pretty name," Miss Arnott pronounced. "Goes with that gazelle look of yours. You can both call me Miss Mabel—everyone else does. Hello—here's David back. Take the luggage up to the big front room, there's a good boy. I'm going to rustle up some tea. It's all ready. Keith is over at Burnham Market, he won't be back until late, and Judy's gone to bed. I thought you'd both feel like a nice quiet meal and a nice quiet sit down by the fire and an early bed." She patted Lisa's shoulder. "We'll see you take things easily for a day or two."

Stevie felt grateful to Miss Mabel for her kindly understanding. She could see that Lisa was fagged out and quite unequal to the ordeal of being sociable her first evening. She thought, "I was right. I am going to like David's aunt. She's nice. Odd, but definitely a darling."

Tea was a sumptuous meal of gammon rashers and fried eggs. Crusty fresh bread and home-made scones and farm butter. Rhubarb pie and cream. The colour began to creep back into Lisa's pale cheeks and she appeared more natural and at ease.

Afterwards Stevie and Lisa sat round the low-set brick fireplace talking to Miss Mabel, feeling as if they were already a part of the family they had come to live with, while David lounged in one of the big arm-chairs smoking his pipe and smiling across at Stevie from time to time, as though he were happy to see her there.

Soon after nine o'clock Miss Mabel insisted on their going up to bed.

14

"No need to be polite," she said. "There's another day tomorrow. You'll settle into things twice as quickly after a good night's sleep." She paused at the foot of the shallow oak staircase. "You know where your room is. I guessed you'd like being together. Sleep well. Breakfast is at eight-thirty."

It was strange. Stevie had thought that both she and Lisa would be too excited to sleep. That they would both have so much to discuss and comment upon. But when they were each lying in one of the two divan beds and Lisa had yawned and said sleepily.

"Miss Mabel—I like her." And Stevie had yawned too and said.

"*Uum.* She's sweet," there was a sudden deep silence before Stevie and Lisa said in unison.

"Good-night—God bless."

The last thing Stevie had a remembrance of was not Miss Mabel's kind bright eyes or David's firm handclasp as he had said good-night to her. It was of a black-haired young man whose lean oil-grimed face creased into a smile as he drawled.

"It goes all right. It's been going now for exactly twenty-eight years." She thought drowsily, "Twenty-eight years. They must be about the same age," and fell asleep.

CHAPTER TWO

THE next morning at breakfast Keith Arnott was present. He had a quiet manner which seemed to go with his serious brown face and grave brown eyes. After a few preliminary remarks he turned to Stevie, who had put on jodhpurs and a navy pullover, and surveyed her with a half smile.

"I see you're dressed ready to go to work. Would you like to come out to the stables with me in a few minutes, and I'll show you round?"

Stevie nodded eagerly.

"I should like to very much."

David drained his coffee cup and stood up.

"I'm going to the garage here to see if they can tow my car back to Hedburgh and put it right. I hope to be in for lunch, Aunt Mabel."

Miss Mabel smiled at Lisa, and at Judy, who was sitting beside Lisa. She was a leggy child of six, with thin brown plaits sticking out somewhat wildly on either side of her small face. Two solemn brown eyes, identical to Keith's, stared up at Lisa.

"Judy will be off to Brownies in a few moments, so you and I'll be able to have a real get-together on our own."

There were only five horses in the loose-boxes. Keith explained that seven others were down on the marshes, where they had been wintering. He intended to go and round them up that morning.

"You could ride Sorrel here, she's steady and quiet, and come down with me," he told Stevie. He looked question-ingly at her.

"I don't know how a good a horsewoman you are?"

Stevie patted the bay and the mare nuzzled a velvet mouth against her outstretched hand.

"It's some years since I rode," she admitted. "My sister and I had our own ponies when we were small, and I used to ride regularly at one time. But not recently." She smiled at Keith. "I expect I'll be pretty stiff for the first few days."

Keith seemed a person chary of smiling in return. He went on staring gravely at her.

"I see. I'll show you the general lay-out of the farm and then we'll go."

The farm was built in an L shape. It was a squat sturdy building of flint and stone with its face turned in the di-rection of the sea. Fields and a roadway lay between the farm and the open cliffs. In the distance a bar of deep ultramarine blue reached away towards the paler blue of sky. Gulls came screaming and calling above the farm-yard and swooped away towards the brown fields lying inland.

It was good to feel a horse beneath her again. Stevie sat very upright in the saddle as they trotted out of the narrow lane on to the grassy verge of the wide road ahead. She sniffed appreciatively.

"What a lovely seaweedy smell. And what a perfect morning!"

She was getting used to the fact that Keith seldom smiled and that his conversation was restricted to essentials. Despite his serious manner, Stevie had decided that she liked him. She felt he was sincere and kind and that his air of gravity was part of the mood of silence that had held him in thrall since his young wife had died.

They skirted some common land and then the road dipped to the grey-green grass of the marshes. On the far side there appeared to be a river estuary. Stevie could see some sails turning gently in the fresh wind from the sea. Where the distant point of land curved away stood the white cone of a lighthouse she had glimpsed earlier on.

Keith gestured with his crop.

"That's Bracklesey, across the river. Sometimes when the tide is low we can wade across the estuary. Otherwise we go up to the bridge further inland."

At Keith's whistle Stevie saw the horses' ears prick up and their bodies stiffen to attention. Two or three started to canter across the mashes towards them.

Keith said,

"Will you go down that side and bring them up, Miss Hylton? I'll round up the others myself—they're the more tricky ones, who try to dodge away."

Stevie turned in the saddle.

"Please call me Stevie. And call my sister Lisa."

Keith nodded gravely.

"Just as you wish. Carry on, will you?"

It didn't take long to bring up the seven horses. Keith had brought along some spare halters. He looked at Stevie as he clipped three of the horses on to his leading rein.

"Do you think you could manage to take these other four back to the stables? Don't worry about remembering the way—Sorrel will do that for you. I have to take these down to the forge for shoeing, and it's no use cluttering up the village street with them."

Stevie hesitated for a moment. But after all, there wasn't much to it. Just to walk them along the mile or so they had come.

"Yes—I think I can manage."

"Old Tom will be about the yard—he'll see them into the stables. Here—take these——" He put some lengths of rope into Stevie's hand. "Sure you're all right?"

Stevie nodded—hiding a nervous qualm or two. These were valuable horses—nothing must happen to them. But what *could* happen to them?

She clicked her tongue and Sorrel started forward with the four horses, two on either side of Stevie, pushing and jostling beside her. She turned and waved to Keith as he set off at a brisk trot along the road leading away from the coast.

Keith was quite right. With hardly any guidance from Stevie, Sorrel set her head firmly in the direction of the farm and the other horses trotted along after her quietly and contentedly enough.

Stevie let out a great breath and felt more at ease. Five horses to cope with, when you had not ridden yourself for several years, was quite a responsibility. But it was wonderful. The whole thing was wonderful. Whitegates Farm and Hedburgh and dear kind Miss Mabel and nice serious Keith. Lisa would soon get well here. This glorious sea air. And what food! Real farm butter and eggs for breakfast and milk *ad lib*.

They owed it all to David. Stevie's heart sang as she thought of lunch-time and seeing him again. He would be back from the garage by then.

The road narrowed past the common. It was difficult to keep four horses abreast. Stevie let out the length of rope and two of the horses fell behind. Their noses pushed against Sorrel's back—her pace quickened to a faster trot.

The next few seconds were an incoherent jumble. Sud--denly, round the bend of the lane, which Stevie had thought led only to the farm, came a car. A huge incredible car. A car all thrusting powerful bonnet and dazzling chromium and massive headlights. A car which came round the bend at a dangerous speed to emit a thunderous "ta-ra-ra-*ruum*."

The horses on the near side reared, backing and plunging like a circus act. The two behind Stevie pulled madly at the rope and broke loose, to go clattering back down the road. Sorrel swerved and side-stepped with a rapidity that all but threw Stevie out of the saddle. As it was, she ended up precariously in mid-air, somewhere above Sorrel's neck.

Somehow she scrambled back into her seat, tugging at the halters of the frightened horses beside her. She called desperately but soothingly, trying to calm them before they broke loose and injured themselves against the car halted so dangerously close to them.

A man appeared out of the car. He managed to grab one of the rope halters and he pulled the two horses to a standstill. Stevie, without pausing to look at him, let the other rope go, crying, "Hang on. Hold them. I must catch the others." She swung Sorrel's head round and went bolting down the road. Her luck was in. The other two horses had stopped and were now cropping at the roadside grass as if nothing had happened.

As if nothing had happened! Stevie's hands were shaking as she caught at the dangling rope and brought the two horses alongside her own. She was thankful to be on Sorrel's back; she was sure that if she had been standing her knees would have given way under her. She was trembling all over from the cataclysmic happenings of the past few minutes. She dared scarcely think of what a disaster it might have proved. And on this, her very first day at the riding school!

She couldn't wait to get back to that monstrous car and the tall figure standing beside the two horses. She said, in a tone of biting rage and fury, without pausing to think.

"You careless *fool!* Coming round a bend like that—at such a speed and making that frightful din. You might have caused a serious accident. You might have injured some of these horses. I—" Stevie broke off on an incoherent breath. She leaned down from the saddle and grabbed the rope out of the man's hand. "Oh—give me that at once. I ought to report you to the police."

There was a long-drawn-out whistle. A tongue clicked chidingly. A deep, somehow maddeningly familiar voice drawled,

"Tut! tut! What a violent outburst! And quite uncalled-for. I might very well ask why, when I'm driving along a road which runs through land that belongs to me, I should find myself suddenly entangled in an absolute Wild West posse of horses? What about the danger of life and limb to me, not to mention an extremely precious passenger?"

Stevie stared. Stared down into laughing dark eyes, in a lean angular sort of face. Saw a smooth cap of blue-black hair above wide shoulders in a superbly tailored tweed jacket. Registered the fact that the hand resting on her reins wore expensive handstitched hogskin gloves.

She almost gasped.

"But—you're—you're——"

He nodded.

"I'm so glad you recognize me. I knew you at once. Even with those charming features of yours distorted with rage."

Stevie couldn't speak for a moment. She just went on staring at the tall figure which yesterday, dirty, oil-grimed and garbed in filthy brown denims, had driven her and Lisa and David to Whitegates Farm.

He looked so different. So well-groomed and sophisticated. So sure of himself. Better looking than ever. Yes, Stevie admitted it, even though this fact seemed to add fuel to the fires of indignation and annoyance.

A girl's voice said plaintively.

"Is everything all right, Charles? Look, I caught my forehead on the windscreen and I'm *sure* it's going to leave a mark."

A figure in pale blue came forward to give Stevie a stare of chilly disapproval before peering with a look of intensest concentration into the mirror of the gleaming gold compact she held in one hand. The other hand, thin, transparent and crimson-tipped, reached up to smooth the unbroken perfection of white skin.

The man called Charles glanced quickly round.

"It's all right, Melanie. Not even a bruise."

The girl shook back waves of shining silver-gilt hair somewhat petulantly.

"You can't tell yet—it's too soon. Anyway, do come on, Charles, we're madly late as it is."

"I'm coming." Charles answered. He looked up at Stevie. "I was just renewing my acquaintance with Miss—er——?" He paused, surveying Stevie with a mockingly enquiring smile.

Stevie shook his hand off the reins, biting out the one word,

"Hylton!" She couldn't bring herself to say anything more. She was still keyed up with the reaction of so narrowly escaping an accident to Keith's valuable horses. And on top of this was the awareness that the man in front of her, with his almost theatrical good looks and his obviously expensive clothes, and that magnificent great car, not to mention the glamorous girl beside him, was in such utter contrast to the figure he had appeared to be yesterday.

No doubt he thought it was very funny. An immense joke. Pretending to be a garage hand! Pretending to own that awful old crock of a car! Stevie felt herself warm with anger and embarrassment at the thought of what perfect fools he had made them all look.

The black eyes, filled with laughter and a devil-may-care sparkle, met Stevie's angry glance. The deep casual-sounding voice said,

"I'm Charles Linmer. And this is Miss Granger. Melanie —Miss Hylton."

Melanie gave Stevie a perfunctory nod before turning back to the car. Charles lifted a crooked black eyebrow at Stevie.

"Don't look so cross! I admit I came round that corner a trifle speedily, but you weren't exactly keeping those horses at a snail's pace—were you?"

Stevie opened her mouth to protest, but she knew that, with the stables almost in sight, the horses *had* quickened their pace, and being fresh and new to the whole business of handling them, she had not had the necessary control. Not for a sudden emergency.

Only there shouldn't have *been* a sudden emergency! Who would expect an enormous monster of a car to come hurtling round a quiet side lane like that? It was really all this man's fault. Standing there with his maddeningly careless manner, his air of nonchalance as if nothing in the world mattered to him.

Charles looked round at the horses, who were tossing their heads and snorting, restive to be on their way.

"Nice bunch you've got here. I take it you're from Whitegates Riding School?"

"Yes." Stevie's answer was a brief monosyllable.

His eyes gently derided her.

"Pupil—or teacher?"

Stevie's voice was stiff with resentment.

"I'm helping Mr.—Mr. Arnott."

"Really?" That crooked black eyebrow shot up another half-inch. "I hope you're more traffic-conscious when you're out with the poor beginners."

Stevie didn't bother to reply. He needn't try to ridicule her, as he'd succeeded in ridiculing them all yesterday with his impersonation of a garage hand. She stared fixedly at some point midway between Sorrel's ears.

Charles' hand reached out to smooth the mare's neck. He addressed Sorrel gently.

"There's a honey." He looked up at Stevie. "Well— having all happily escaped sudden death, we'd better press on."

Stevie inclined her head the merest fraction.

"Good-bye, Mr. Linmer." She gave Sorrel a light kick and the mare moved forward. Charles stepped back against the car as the entire concourse started up at a brisk trot; Stevie glanced neither to the right nor left as they swung past him. In a moment or two she heard the powerful engine roar away round the bend.

Insolent. That was the word to describe him. It was the word she had used yesterday when he had lolled against David's car in that indifferent manner. Infuriating young man! She wouldn't think about him. She hoped fervently she wouldn't encounter him again.

What had he said? Something about the road running through land that belonged to him. But this was Keith's land, surely? These fields and pasture lying so near to the riding school? Here was the high flint wall that enclosed the farm buildings.

The gnarled old man who was called Tom came shuffling out of one of the sheds to meet her. He gave Stevie a suspicious glance from under tufty grey eyebrows as he ran a hand over two of the horses.

"Sweatin'," he said. "Theem hosses a-sweatin'. Reckon you'm hurried 'em a mite too much along they rooods."

Stevie shook her head.

"No, we came fairly steadily. I—we—we met a car rather suddenly. Two of them broke loose and ran off."

She couldn't really explain it all to Old Tom. He was obviously prejudiced against strangers and had yet to be won round.

"Aaah!" Old Tom pronounced. He shook his head disapprovingly. "Bring t'others this way."

Stevie saw them into the loose-boxes and helped brush the horses down while Old Tom whistled and grunted and grumbled to himself. Reluctantly he answered Stevie's questions and showed her where the various things were kept.

"You ain't wun o' they land girls?" he demanded of her. Stevie shook her head.

"No—I've just come to help Mr. Arnott with the riding school."

"Uuum," Old Tom said critically. He stared at her as if about to say more when Miss Mabel appeared at the kitchen door, ringing a small hand-bell and calling.

"Stevie—lunch is ready."

Stevie went into the house and almost bumped into David in the narrow dark passageway. He put out two hands and caught her elbows.

"Steady there!"

Stevie smiled up at him.

"Hello, David. Did you collect the car?"

He nodded.

"I managed to get it towed back to Hedburgh and the garage people here have promised to fix it by this evening."

Miss Mabel's brisk voice said behind them,

"You've both got exactly three minutes in which to wash your hands before lunch. So hurry!"

"Thank you, Miss Mabel." Stevie ran up the wide stairs two at a time. "I'll be down right away."

Keith came into the oak-panelled dining-room with its long refectory table and Jacobean chairs just as Miss Mabel was slicing a knife through the flaky crust of a steak and kidney pie.

"Sorry I'm late, Aunt Mabel." He nodded to Stevie as he slid into his chair. "I see you found your way safely back."

Stevie hesitated.

"I'm afraid we narrowly escaped a mishap, Mr. Arnott. I don't think it was my fault. Someone came tearing round a corner like a madman in an enormous sports car and nearly caused an accident." She went on to explain what had happened.

Keith frowned.

"I ought to have warned you," he said. "That's apt to be a tricky turning. The horses tend to swing round it too quickly because they know they're nearly home. As a rule there's hardly any traffic in the lane. No one uses it except the farm and the Manor people."

Miss Mabel clicked her tongue as she spooned rich brown gravy over the plate in her hand.

"What a nasty thing to happen—your first morning, Stevie. But don't worry about it." She held the plate out. "This is yours, Judy." She looked round at Keith. "You'll have to watch that lane in future. It's bound to take more traffic now the new people are living at the Manor." She shook her head.

"Won't be as quiet as in Sir William's day."

Stevie put down her knife and fork.

"The man who was driving the car was called Linmer—Charles Linmer." She looked at David and Lisa. "Do you know who he was?" She paused. "He was the—the same person who drove us up here yesterday—in that awful old car."

"The garage hand?" David asked.

"That's what he pretended to be." Stevie's voice warmed with indignation. "I can't think why. I suppose he thought it rather funny."

Miss Mabel snorted into laughter.

"But, my dear, it *is* funny. A great joke! Young Charles Linmer happens to be the owner of Hedburgh Manor!"

Stevie stared at her. She thought of the mocking dark eyes, the tantalizing smile that had confronted her a few hours ago. She remembered the greasy overalled figure of yesterday. Her indignation grew.

Lisa giggled unexpectedly.

"Oh, Stevie—that *bone*-shaker of a car. I thought it was going to rattle to bits on the way up here!"

David alone seemed to share Stevie's resentment.

"Owner of the Manor," he echoed blankly. He scowled in remembrance. "But I gave him two shillings. *As a tip!*"

Miss Mabel and Lisa burst into fresh laughter in which small Judy, without fully understanding the joke, joined.

Even Keith's serious brown eyes warmed into a slow smile.

Stevie, glancing at David's affronted expression, felt that they were the only two who failed to see the humour of the situation. What was so amusing about someone who tried to make fools of other people? Humiliating David. Actually accepting a tip from him! That sort of superlatively good-looking young man was always conceited. Thinking far too much of himself.

Miss Mabel was speaking.

"The Linmer family have only recently come to live here. Hedburgh Manor used to belong to Sir William Radlett. He was godfather to this young man, Charles. I understand from the Vicar that Sir William left the Manor to him with the especial wish that it should not be sold but that his godson should live there. Mrs. Linmer is the widow of a wealthy car manufacturer and her son helps to run the business, which is somewhere in the Midlands."

"They make _Limmards_," Judy piped up. "Tommy Coles told me so. He says they're absolutely smashing. He says they go hundreds of miles an hour. That old car is a—a—" She broke off, searching for the word. "Oh dear! I can't _think_ of it. It means something awfully old."

"A veteran car," Lisa suggested.

Judy nodded.

"Yes. A veteran, an' Tommy says it's going to go in a Veteran Car Race."

Miss Mabel smiled.

"There's your garage hand mistake! Probably the young man has been messing about with the innards—trying to make it go or something."

David was not appeased.

"Then why not say so? Why let us assume he was a mechanic? I agree with Stevie—it was a joke in extremely poor taste." He said again on a rising note of indignation, "I gave him _two shillings_."

Stevie looked across at Keith.

"He said something about the land which the lane runs through belonging to him. Does it?"

Keith nodded.

"Yes. Most of the Whitegates land lies west and north of the farm. All the fields east of it belong to the Manor.

Sir William let some of his land off to me—I understand that the new owner is willing to continue to do so."

Stevie didn't answer. She was making a mental note that in future, if that dangerous Charles Linmer was to be in the vicinity, she would take the greatest care when out with the norses.

CHAPTER THREE

DAVID left after supper on Sunday evening. He and Stevie had walked down together to the garage to collect the car the day before, and it was Stevie who saw him finally off, after Miss Mabel and Keith and Lisa had said good-bye.

"I hope you'll settle down all right," David told her. "Keith's a decent fellow and Aunt Mabel, although a bit haywire and haphazard, means well."

"I think she's a darling," Stevie said spontaneously. 'I can't begin to say thank you, David, for arranging everything and bringing us down like this. Lisa and I are terribly grateful."

David smiled down at her through the evening dusk.

"It's a pleasure, Stevie. Don't forget to write and let me know how you get on. I hope to be down for another weekend fairly soon."

"I shall look forward to it," Stevie said softly.

He took her hand, holding it for a long moment in his. Stevie felt her heartbeat quicken. She wondered if David would kiss her. He had never done so yet. He had never made any demonstration of affection.

The moment of expectancy faded. David shook her hand warmly and firmly. Then he released his hold and turned to open the car door.

"Good-bye, Stevie."

"Good-bye, David. Thank you again."

On Monday morning Keith took Stevie to the nearby meadow which he used as the actual school. The grass was worn down to a circular track in parts; some jumps were placed in the centre.

"I always take the beginners here for a time or two," Keith told her as he gave her several explanations and refreshed her own knowledge on riding. "We get quite a few schoolchildren, especially on Saturdays and at holiday times, and this is where I want you to start them off. Also pupils learning to jump. This morning at ten there are two boys of nine and ten coming. Will you saddle Toby and Silver for them? You'd better ride Sorrel yourself."

Toby was a skewbald pony of about ten hands—Silver a decorous old mare with gentle ways and a lethargic trot.

Keith stayed with Stevie to see the two boys under way with their lesson, then he excused himself.

Neither of the small boys was nervous and both were already reasonably proficient. Stevie went through the routine of collecting their horses, walking them, halting and turning and reining back. Finally, they went round and round at a brisk trot.

Stevie enjoyed the morning immensely. At the end of it she was as flushed and rosy-cheeked as the two bright-eyed youngsters beside her. Tendrils of hair escaped out of the neat snood it was tied back into. She felt young and carefree and very glad to be alive.

She glanced at her wrist-watch and saw that it was time to return to the stables.

"Come on—Peter—John. Head up—shoulders back—sit well down into your saddles!" They set off across the meadow to the side gate leading into the stable yard.

As she held open the gate for Peter and John to ride through she heard voices coming from the gateway that opened on to the road. Stevie glanced up. Three people were walking towards her. Two girls and a man. She recognized two of them. The blonde girl, who was called Melanie Granger, and Charles Linmer. The second girl was a stranger.

Stevie stared at them in dismayed surprise.

Peter's reedy voice said.

Peter's reedy voice said,

She turned quickly—swinging off Sorrel's back in one brief movement.

"Yes, of course. Come on—this way, Peter. That's fine, John."

Her hand caught the reins of the two horses in with her own. She looked up at Charles as he came up to her. She said stiffly,

27

"Good-morning."

Charles smiled down at the two boys.

"Hello, Peter—I thought I recognized you. Have you been teaching Miss Hylton to ride?"

Peter burst forth into irrepressible giggles.

"She's teaching *us*!"

Charles grinned.

"Oh, sorry! I wasn't quite sure." He looked at Stevie. "I've come to discuss business. Melanie here—you've met Miss Granger, haven't you?—is anxious to learn to ride." He turned his head. "This is my sister, Carole. Carole— Miss Hylton."

Stevie acknowledged the greeting of the pretty brown-haired girl who was Charles' sister before saying,

"I'm afraid Mr. Arnott isn't here."

Charles' sudden appearance disconcerted her. Once again she had a sense of being abrupt and gauche and definitely unforthcoming. He had that sort of effect upon her.

Charles appeared quite at ease. He nodded casually.

"Bad luck. In that case, perhaps you'll take a booking for us? Miss Granger would like a few lessons to bring her up to scratch: she's not very experienced. The only horse we have at the Manor belongs to Carole here and he's much to highspirited for a beginner. And I'd like to hire a horse for myself, to hack round on with my sister."

Stevie felt somewhat at a loss. She wasn't sure which horses to book and she didn't want to muddle Keith by arranging times that might clash with his own. But she said with an air of calm competence,

"Please come this way," and turned towards the small saddle room where Keith kept an old ledger in which he entered bookings and reservations.

"I'd like to start my lessons tomorrow morning. At eleven," Melanie stated. You could see she was the sort of girl who never wasted time saying "Please" or "May I?" but just said out loud there and then what she wanted.

Stevie flicked through the book of appointments.

"I'm not sure if Mr. Arnott is free," she said slowly.

The smallest frown creased Melanie's smooth forehead. Seen at close quarters she was more beautiful than ever. Baby-fine skin and red lips that pouted in a most beguiling fashion. Big eyes, as round and smoke-blue as a kitten's. And that amazing hair, like a silver curtain swinging above the streamlined perfection of her blue woollen suit.

She made Stevie feel very down-to-earth and ordinary. Very conscious of shabby jodhpurs and a strictly utilitarian navy pullover.

"At eleven," Melanie repeated firmly.

Someone called Miss Nolan was booked for ten a.m. The Misses Raymond at twelve. Did that mean Keith was free at eleven? Or perhaps she, Stevie, might take the Misses Raymond whoever they might be.

She glanced up and encountered Charles' amused stare. He was leaning—no, lolling was the word—against the saddle room wall, just as he had leaned that day against David's car. Arms folded, long legs crossed. Only today the wide shoulders were clad in expensive dog-tooth check tweed instead of greasy denims, and his hands were no longer blackened and stained with oil, but, with their long brown fingers and strong square palms, looked at once oddly fine and sensitive.

"Something wrong?" he enquired of her. "No horses to be had?"

"Yes, of course," Stevie answered quickly. "It's just a matter of fitting in the times."

"Carole and I can come in the afternoon, if you prefer it," Charles said. "Can't we, Carole?"

His sister turned. She was a tall girl with attractive dark eyes and curly brown hair. Not so striking as her handsome brother, but with a look of sweetness in the sudden smile she gave Stevie.

"Any time will suit us."

"No, Charles," Melanie interrupted. "We *must* all go riding at the same time, even if we don't go *out* together to begin with." Her baby blue eyes stared up at Charles. "I'll be left all on my own if you and Carole ride in the afternoons."

Charles smiled down at her, his dark eyes warming into a sort of amused tenderness.

"What a tragedy, darling! To be left on your own. We'll see it doesn't happen."

Darling, Stevie thought. I suppose he's in love with her. She's certainly terribly attractive. She looked across at them as they stood, smiling and very close together, and thought, reluctantly: They both are. To look at, I mean.

A footstep sounded on the cobbles behind her. She swung round to see Keith approaching. It was with a sense of relief that Stevie handed the appointments book over to him and with a murmured excuse said good-morning to the party in the saddle room.

Keith arranged to take Melanie at eleven each morning for a week. A horse was reserved for Charles and he was coming, with his sister, who was mounted on her own horse, to ride at the same time as Melanie.

Stevie was busy with various other appointments. The Misses Raymond proved to be two hearty teenagers, expert horsewomen, whom Stevie had to be quite on her mettle to equal. In between riding lessons there was a lot to do around the stables and Stevie set to to tackle everything, from grooming the horses to helping Old Tom clean out the stables and fork down fresh dry straw.

It was the end of the week when Keith called Stevie over to the saddle room.

"Stevie, would you take Miss Granger this morning, please? I have to go to Aylsham on business and I won't be back in time." He tapped the ledger. "I see you've no other appointments."

She nodded reluctantly.

"Yes, of course, Keith."

The "Mr. Arnott, had been dropped. It was Keith and Stevie and Lisa and Miss Mabel already, in a warmth and comradeship that was very pleasant.

She added slowly,

"And Mr.—Linmer? Is he having Caesar as usual?"

Keith shook his head.

"No—he cancelled his appointment."

Stevie felt oddly relieved. Melanie on her own was someone she could cope with. But Charles? Charles was the aggravating unknown quantity.

This morning Melanie looked like Every Girl's Dream of a Horsewoman. Beautifully tailored covert coat, fitting

30

her slim figure without a crease or a wrinkle. Cream coloured jodhpurs. Silver-fair hair swirled into a smooth shining chignon under the sort of hat that would have been just a plain brown felt on some other girl, but which on Melanie was the most charming and becoming of a head-gear.

It was a pity that with all this outward perfection she was such a poor horsewoman. She had no natural aptitude; she bumped and shook breathlessly in the saddle, despite Stevie's hand under one elbow trying to help her into the rhythm of the horse's trot. The hands in the expensive string gloves were lamentably heavy and sawed unmerci-fully at poor Silver's patient mouth.

Round and round they went in painstaking succession.

"One, two, three—up—down—up," Stevie counted re-assuringly. "That's better. Keep your hands down—one—two—three."

"Oh, *dear*," Melanie gasped. "I'll never get into it."

"Of course you will," Stevie told her. "You've improved a great deal already."

At last the lesson was over. Pink in the face, the brown hat askew, the smooth chignon unwound in silky disarray on her shoulders, Melanie slid off Silver's back.

"Heavens—I feel like the Witch of Endor! Do you mind if I go inside and tidy up?"

"No, please do."

A small downstairs cloakroom adjacent to the side door was put at the use of clients.

"If you'll excuse me, I'll unsaddle the horses."

As Stevie came out of the stable she heard a car turning into the yard. Charles slid his lean length out of the driver's seat.

"Good-morning, Miss Hylton. Is Melanie still here?"

"Good-morning. Yes, she's just tidying up."

He grinned.

"I'm not surprised. You're a remorseless tutor. Very stern and strict, with that fierce 'one—two—three—up—down—up' of yours."

Stevie stared at him, fighting the blush of embarrass-ment that Charles always succeeded so successfully in con-juring up in her.

"You were watching," she said accusingly.

He nodded.

"Over the wall. I couldn't resist it. You certainly put Melanie through her paces, poor sweet. Still, she's improving, don't you think?"

The way he looked at her with that one crooked eyebrow lifted so quizzically. As if he was laughing at her. He *was* laughing at her. It made Stevie furious.

She said sharply,

"You're easily amused at other people's discomfiture, Mr. Linmer. Almost as much as at your own practical jokes."

"My own practical——" He broke off, laughing out loud. "Oh—that. Well, it was rather funny, wasn't it? I've never been taken for a garage hand before." He shook his head at her. "I bequeathed the two bob to charity—alms for the poor, you know."

"I'm not interested in what you did," Stevie said. She moved to pass him. "I'll tell Miss Granger you're here."

He put out a hand to restrain her.

"But you're taking it all so seriously." His voice echoed surprise. "You don't always wear this life-is-real-and-life-is-earnest look, do you? It makes me positively cringe."

Whatever he said only succeeded in making her look more ridiculous. More prim and priggish. He put her in the wrong when it was *he* who was in the wrong. I wish he wouldn't come here, Stevie thought. Why doesn't he buy a horse of his own? He's plenty of money.

She shook off his hand as if it were some irritating insect, and at the same moment Melanie came out of the house, followed by Keith.

Charles turned abruptly.

"Just the man I want to see," he said lightly. "It's about the Point-to-Point Races at Stonham on the twenty-fifth. We expect to have some friends staying with us that weekend and we'd like to book for a party to ride over to them. Say about seven horses? Will that be possible?"

Keith frowned, considering.

"Seven—" he repeated. "Yes—I think so."

Charles looked round at Melanie.

"Miss Granger will be up to the ride by then, I take it?" Keith nodded giving Melanie his brief unfamiliar smile.

"I'm sure she will."

32

"Of course, we'd like you to come along with us," Charles added. "To keep an eye on things. If you will."

Keith shook his head.

"I might be able to ride over with you, but I can't remain with the party, I'm afraid. I happen to be riding in two of the races. But Miss Hylton here will be free to go."

Stevie opened her mouth to protest. To say, "Oh *no!* please, I don't want to go. Not in a party like that. With— with this odious person Charles."

She closed her lips on the words, knowing there was no alternative. It was part of her job. Whether she wanted to go or not didn't enter into it. If Keith said she had to accompany the party, that was the end of the matter.

Charles turned his head slightly. His dark eyes were laughing at her as usual.

"That's fine. By all means let Miss Hylton come. Her presence will add immensely to the gaiety of the occasion."

Stevie didn't answer. She was fully aware that Charles was making fun of her, after he had just commented on what he had termed her "life-is-real-and-life-is-earnest look." She thought resentfully, I suppose he doesn't know what it means to *have* to be serious. To want desperately to make good at a job you've taken on because so much depends on it. Not only for yourself but because of another person. *Lisa*, Stevie thought.

Stevie broke off silent imprecation—suddenly aware of its self-pitying trend. She thought, "I *am* losing my sense of humour!"

In an effort to counteract such a deficiency she forced herself to smile at Charles and say,

"Thank you. I shall be very pleased to come with the party."

That smile caught Charles unawares. Even though a trifle restricted, there was a candid warmth about Stevie's smile that startled him. Come to think of it, he considered, it was the first time he'd ever seen her smile. A frown or an angry stare or a chilly look were about all he had encountered. Stevie's smile and the steady glance from hazel eyes which seemed to be full of changing light and shade were a pleasant surprise.

Charles whistled under his breath. Well, what d'you know, he debated silently—the girl's human after all!

A sharp rapping noise caused them all to turn their heads: Miss Mabel, scattering meal from a large enamel bowl, waved and smiled at them. Around her converged a clucking, pecking, scratching avalanche of hens, followed by a retinue of ducks, their voices raised in querulous concern.

Everyone smiled involuntarily. Keith said,

"Aunt Mabel, I don't think you've met Miss Linmer, have you? And Miss Granger?—my aunt—Miss Arnott. Of course you remember Charles?"

Miss Mabel waved a mealy hand in her brief, friendly way, superbly unconscious of her informal appearance. This morning she was wearing faded blue dungarees over a yellow sweater; her grey hair was fluffed up into an untidy cockscomb above her alert smiling face.

"Yes—I remember Charles." she told him. "Last time I saw you you were a harum-scarum schoolboy of fourteen. Don't think I've seen you since. You came to stay with Sir William one summer. We were living at Bracklesey then and my mother was alive. It was before Keith—" She hesitated abruptly, and Stevie wondered if she had been about to say, "before Keith married." "Before Keith bought Whitegates," Miss Mabel finished.

"I remember," Charles said.

"And how are you liking it at Hedburgh?" Miss Mabel demanded. "Not too quiet for you, is it?" She smiled round at Carole Linmer.

Carole shook her head.

"No—we all like it. My mother knows a great many people in the district and there seems plenty to do."

Lisa and Judy came in through the gate together and Miss Mabel called them over and made fresh introductions. Then she shrugged her thin shoulders and said, "I'd better make tracks for the kitchen. Judy has to be back at school in an hour."

The little group dispersed: Stevie, following Miss Mabel and Lisa into the house, heard the throbbing roar of Charles' car as he turned it in the yard, mingled with the indignant cluckings and quackings of the poultry as they scattered in all directions. Then the farm subsided into its usual midday quiet.

"What a good-looking boy he's turned into," Miss Mabel remarked as, lunch over, they sat down for Miss Mabel's habitual cup of tea. She pushed a chintz-covered cushion into the small of her back and crossed her dungaree-clad legs. She appeared to take it for granted that the others knew to whom she referred. She shook her head. "He has a great look of Sir William." Miss Mabel sighed nostalgically. "Oh, but he was handsome. The handsomest man that ever I set eyes upon. Every girl for miles around fell in love with him."

Keith gave her one of his rare smiles.

"And did you fall in love with him too, Aunt Mabel?" Miss Mabel stirred her tea thoughtfully.

"Yes," she said slowly, "I fell in love with him too." She paused for a long moment, then she gave herself a little shake, smiling across at Keith and Stevie and Lisa. "Not that it did me much good, as you see! Here I am—an old spinster! Pity of it is, I guess William spoiled me for everybody else. No other man ever quite came up to him." She sighed again.

"He married a beauty—Ellen Kershaw, but she was an invalid most of her life. Poor Ellen. And most of all, perhaps, poor William. They never had any children. That's why he left the Manor House and a considerable amount of money to Charles."

Miss Mabel put her teacup back on to the tray, pushing on her glasses and picking up the newspaper.

"Away with you, Judy. Back to your lessons. Lisa, why don't you have an hour's rest? You look as if you could do with it."

"But I'm always resting," Lisa protested. "I don't help you half enough, Miss Mabel."

"Nonsense!" Miss Mabel said, peering over the rim of the blue-framed glasses that matched her vivid eyes. "You help me plenty. Take her upstairs with you, Stevie. Then she'll be fresh to come out visiting with me later this afternoon."

Stevie and Lisa went arm in arm up the stairs to the big bedroom from whose low-sashed windows they could glimpse the sea, blue and wind-tossed in the far distance.

"Miss Mabel's so sweet to you," Stevie said, "So thoughtful and kind." She added, "To us both. I can't believe we haven't known her always—can you?"

Lisa folded back the green candlewick bedspread and sat down on the low divan bed.

"No—she's a pet." She stared up at Stevie. "D'you realize it's just a week—one short week—since we came here? It's incredible."

Stevie crossed over to the mahogany chest and began to brush her hair before the quaint antique mirror which stood upon it.

Lisa's voice went on behind her.

"Do you really think Miss Mabel was in love with Sir William? Seriously, I mean. Perhaps that's why she never married. She must have been pretty when she was younger. Her eyes are beautiful still. And she has lovely skin." She added. "He *is* terribly good-looking, isn't he?"

Stevie's head was bent down as she brushed her smooth hair vigorously. Lisa's voice sounded indistinct and she scarcely heard what she was saying.

"But we've never seen him," she protested.

Lisa laughed.

"I don't mean Sir William, I mean his godson. I think he's terrific. Like a film star or something."

Stevie straightened up. She was rather glad of the curtain of hair falling over her face. She said carelessly,

"If you admire that type. I don't. I expect it's a case of Sir William all over again. Every girl for miles around falling in love with him." She brushed her hair back into its accustomed shining smoothness. I prefer someone who's good-looking without being superlatively so and who's clever and sensible and understanding. Someone who has a—a goal in life, if you like."

"Like David?" Lisa interposed mischievously.

Stevie stared at her reflection in the mirror.

"Yes, perhaps," she admitted. "David adds up to all those things."

The reflection in the mirror looked unwontedly serious. Was this what that hateful Charles had meant when he'd made his remark about her "life-is-real-and-life-is-earnest expression"? No doubt he would sneer at David, too.

David, who was ambitious and hard-working and who had a purpose in life.

Why do I bother about what he thinks? Stevie reprimanded herself. Except that he's an irritating sort of person and we keep bumping into one another. Now there's this wretched Point-to-Point affair.

In the ordinary way it would have been fun. Stevie had been to such meetings before and loved every moment of them. They were full of that cosy informality most characteristic of country living; horses and riders were known to the throng of local bystanders in a friendly way that the average racegoer could never experience. But she wasn't at all anxious to accompany a party that was made up of Charles and his friends. Keith, however, took for granted Stevie's acceptance of the matter and went ahead with the arrangements, deciding which horses, out of his stable of twelve, should go on the ride.

CHAPTER FOUR

ON the following Thursday Stevie, coming into the kitchen just before milking time, found Lisa and Judy busy together before the cream enamel kitchen cooker. Lisa was stirring something in a big pan, while Judy hovered at her side, peering into its bubbling brown depths and jumping up and down excitedly at intervals.

"It's nearly done now. I'm sure it is. Gosh! What a scrummy smell!"

Lisa turned her head at the sound of Stevie's step.

"Toffee," she announced. "Treacle toffee. I hope!"

Judy looked up at Stevie. Her two thin plaits stuck out more wildly than ever on either side of a small pointed chin ornamented with sticky brown smears.

"It's for the Fair. Lisa's making it for me to sell at our stall on Saturday." She added, "We mustn't eat any of it. 'Cept perhaps a *tiny* bit. But Lisa's going to give me the pan to scrape."

"Lucky you," Stevie said. She smiled down at small excited Judy, who had talked of nothing but the Guide and Brownie Fair, which was being held on Saturday, for weeks.

"Would you like a cup of tea?" Lisa asked. "The kettle's nearly boiling." She pushed it further forward on to the hotplate.

A voice spoke behind them.

"I wouldn't say 'No' to a cup."

It was Keith. He dumped a sack of grain beside the scullery door and walked into the kitchen.

"That's for Aunt Mabel's hens." He sniffed. "What's happening in here?"

"We're making toffee," Judy told him. "At least—Lisa's making it an' I'm helping her. It's for the Fair."

Keith straddled a corner of the kitchen table.

"What Fair?"

"The Guide and Brownie Fair, of course," Judy cried indignantly. "You never listen to *anything*." She tossed her head, turning her back on him. "I don't care if you don't come, 'cos you didn't come last year either." She added in a small voice. "Everyone else came but you didn't."

There was a sudden silence. Stevie was filled with a quick sense of sympathy as she saw Judy's small mutinous face flush to scarlet and her mouth tremble when she swung away from her father. She was aware that Judy had justice on her side, for it was apparent, in the short while she and Lisa had been at Whitegates, that Keith took small interest in his little daughter and that it was only to Miss Mabel that she could look for outward love and affection.

Lisa broke the pause, turning to pour a stream of rich brown liquid into the greased tins, and saying gently but matter-of-factly,

"Perhaps Daddy was too busy, dear. He has to work hard, you know." She looked across to Keith. "But this year Stevie and I are here to help, and he may be free to go."

Their glances met. It was as if in Lisa's beautiful grey eyes there was a plea—a question. Keith stared at her in the set fixed way he had, and then he nodded abruptly as if answering some request.

"I'll be able to manage it this year." His voice was stiffly awkward, as if he scarcely knew how to address Judy. "Saturday afternoon, did you say?"

Judy half turned. Her eyes glanced sideways at him. She looked like a small shy animal which is uncertain of accepting some overture of friendship.

"Yes. It's at the School. You have to come an' buy something."

"I'll buy a lot of things," Keith said.

Judy's solemn brown eyes never left his face.

"It would be nice if you'd buy some of the toffee," she suggested hopefully.

For the first time something like a smile lightened Keith's brown face.

"That's a good idea."

"Lisa's helped me make some simply darling things," Judy went on, gaining confidence. "There's mats—they're kind of raffia in little rounds all sewn together, an' she's shown me how to make some cases an' they hold brushes and polish for your shoes, you see. An'—an' then we've sewn some velvet into a sort of glove and you use it for picking up coal. It keeps you hands *quite* clean. And—" Judy broke off, frowning, while she considered what other wonders Lisa had performed.

"Lisa seems to have been pretty busy," Keith said quietly. He looked across at her and Stevie was startled to see her sister's face tinged with pale rose.

Judy flung herself at Lisa, clutching her round the waist with two thin arms.

"I *love* Lisa," she declared. "Better'n anybody in the whole wide world."

Lisa put one hand gently on Judy's rough brown head and with the other hand held out the spoon she had used to scrape the pan with.

"You love toffee," she said smilingly. "Come on—here's the pan."

"Oh—scrummy!" Judy cried, and plunged away with it.

Stevie had moved to the stove to brew the tea. As she filled the cups Aunt Mabel came into the kitchen.

"What a gathering of the clans," she declared. "And what a delicious smell! Tea too. Pour me a cup, Stevie dear." She looked round at Keith, pulling a letter out of the pocket of her ancient tweed suit. "Letter from David. It came by the second post. Says he can come down on

39

Friday for the weekend. If it's all right we're not to bother to reply."

"It's up to you, Aunt Mabel," Keith answered. "You're in charge here."

"Thank you," Miss Mabel said. "But it's your house, my dear."

"Of course he can come. Nice to see him again so soon."

Miss Mabel's bright blue gaze moved from Lisa to Stevie. Her tone was dryly amused.

"Very nice. I wonder what the attraction is."

Stevie looked away from the keen eyes which missed so little. She finished drinking her tea and said,

"I'll go and help Sam with the milking."

She was pleased and excited at the thought of seeing David again. Was he coming to see how she and Lisa were getting along? Was he coming also, perhaps, to see *her*? She very much hoped that he was. Friday. That was tomorrow. He would be here tomorrow evening.

It was a little after eight o'clock when they heard the sound of a car turning into the yard and guessed that David had arrived. Miss Mabel had delayed supper so that they could all eat together, and within a few minutes of his arrival they were sitting down in the oak-panelled dining-room.

"You're both looking very well," David told Stevie. "I can see Hedburgh suits you." He smiled at Lisa. "I believe you're putting on a little weight, Lisa."

"I hope so," Lisa replied. "I've been much too thin for too long!"

"It's Aunt Mabel's cooking," David declared. He helped himself to more salad with the rosy slices of home-cured ham that Keith had carved for him. "By Jove—this food is different from my digs." He shuddered. "Sometimes I have appalling meals."

"Why don't you change them?" Stevie asked. She thought David looked paler and thinner. Or was it in contrast to Keith's tan and Miss Mabel's healthy bloom?

David shrugged.

"It isn't worth the effort. They suit me in other ways. They're very economical and convenient."

40

It was a family evening. After supper they all went into the pleasant sitting-room to sit round a cosy log-fire which crackled gently in the low brick grate. Conversation ranged from work on the farm to plays which David had seen recently in London. Stevie had no opportunity of being on her own with David, but she did not mind. She was happy just to see him sitting there—his fair head glinting in the lamplight—a pipe between his long firm lips.

Next morning after breakfast David sought Stevie out. She was busy feeding Keith's pigs.

"Hello—you look awfully busy." He smiled down at her. "I can't quite reconcile this version of the Complete Country-woman with that neat capable figure who used to sit in my office taking dictation!"

Stevie smiled back at him, resting the empty bucket on the wall of the sty.

"Nor can I. But this is much more fun. Except that—" She broke off, conscious that she had nearly said, "Except that I miss you." She added, with pardonable curiosity, "I hope my successor is proving satisfactory?"

David nodded.

"She's a phlegmatic young woman named Miriam Palmer, whose efficiency is indisputable." He shook his head. "But she can't take your place, Stevie. No one can."

Stevie met his look. The blue eyes usually cool and detached, expressed a warm appreciation. She said slowly, "That's very nice of you, David."

"I'm not just being polite," David said. "I mean——" He broke off, as if hesitant to say more. He added, "What I really came out to say was—how about coming into Norwich with me this afternoon? It will give us some time on our own together. I'd like very much to show you the Cathedral. It's really beautiful, with one of the finest Norman towers in England. We could have tea somewhere afterwards and perhaps go to a cinema."

Stevie's face lit up with pleasure.

"I'd love to, David. Thank you very much. I haven't explored Norwich at all yet." She paused abruptly. "Oh, David—I *can't*! I'm awfully sorry. I'd much rather come with you, but, it's Judy's Guide Fair. We've all promised to go."

David frowned quickly.

"Guide Fair? Oh—that kid stuff. You can easily miss it, Stevie." He added, "After all—I'm not down every weekend."

Stevie hesitated—torn between a longing to accept David's invitation and spend a happy afternoon together on their own and the feeling that the Fair meant so much to Judy.

She shook her head as she moved away from the sty carrying the empty bucket.

"I don't know, David. It's very difficult. Poor little Judy has counted so much on us all going. She was awfully hurt because her father didn't put in an appearance last year, and I'm afraid if we don't rally round Keith may not go again this year either."

David kicked aside some muddy straw.

"What a place! You need to wear gumboots permanently, as Keith does. Stevie, do try and get out of the wretched thing." He looked sideways at her. "Otherwise I shall feel you prefer these fearsomely parochial gatherings to my company."

"You *know* I don't—" Stevie began unhappily, when Miss Mabel called from the kitchen door.

"David, dear—do a little errand for me, will you? Mrs. Linmer promised Judy's Guide Mistress some flowers and fruit for the Fair this afternoon, but they haven't arrived. Miss Burton doesn't like to worry her too much, but they want to finish arranging the hall. I said you or Keith would run up in a car and collect them."

David shrugged resigned shoulders.

"You did, did you? All right, Aunt Mabel, I'll go. On condition Stevie here can come along and help me."

"Of course she can," Miss Mabel said. "Have you finished the pigs, dear? That's right. Slip your overall off and go with David and put poor Miss Burton's mind at rest."

"The way everyone enters into these absurd little village goings-on amazes me," David said as he and Stevie drove up the lane towards the Manor House in David's car. "They assume a ridiculous importance. I can't understand it."

"In a way it's nice," Stevie said slowly. "People in small communities like Hedburgh seem to join in and work together at everything. I like it. You feel you belong in a way you can never possibly do in a huge place like London."

David heaved a sigh of relief.

"Thank heaven for that!"

Stevie smiled, shaking her head at him.

"I don't know. It makes for a sense of personal responsibility. Look at little Judy. She's worked like a Trojan for her Guide and Brownie Fair. When she's older she'll work even harder at something else that perhaps will help other people too."

"Oh, I approve the principle," David agreed. "It's just that—I suppose I prefer the wider, more impersonal life of cities." He swung the car up a long tree-lined drive. "Here's Hedburgh Manor. Do you know, I've never been here before. Aunt Mabel was the only one of us on visiting terms with Sir William and Lady Radlett."

The Manor House looked very beautiful in the morning sunshine. It was a Queen Anne building of soft faded pink brick. Not large, but a graceful and gracious-seeming house. Stevie had been so wrapped up in David's company and conversation that she had overlooked the fact that she might meet the tiresome Charles again. She tilted her chin unconsciously. "It's not very likely," she decided. "He's probably out somewhere with Melanie."

To be quite certain she said aloud,

"I'll wait here in the car for you, David."

"Nonsense!" David answered. "Come and help me. There might be a lot of flowers and stuff to carry."

A pleasant-faced parlourmaid opened the door to them.

"I'll tell Madam you're here. Please come this way." She led them into a circular cream-panelled hall. Here a curved stairway rose the height of the house. Light from an immense dome above it shone down to pick out the glowing colours of the Persian rugs scattered on the polished floor.

The maid opened a rounded door set into the curve of the wall.

"If you'll wait in here, please."

It was a small sitting-room with cream satin-striped paper and chintz-covered furniture. There were many vases of flowers and several pieces of superb china. On the mantel-piece stood an exquisite Sèvres clock.

David cocked his head sideways.

"Listen! Someone playing the piano. Beautifully, too."

Stevie listened. From a doorway leading obviously into a second room came the liquid rippling notes of Greig's Concerto in A Minor, played with a depth and feeling that seemed to flow right through the closed door and swirl around them, a tide of rich nostalgic music.

Stevie sighed—closing her eyes for an instant. She thought, "It must be Carole," and was aware of surprise that pretty Carole should be capable of evoking such beauty.

The door to the hall opened and a tall woman with deep-set dark eyes came into the room.

She held out her hand.

"I'm Mrs. Linmer. You've called for the few things I promised the Guides?" She shook her head as they introduced themselves. "I feel very guilty not to have sent them down yesterday, but Carole was out for the day and Charles"—she hesitated—"Charles was—not able to use the car. He *was* to have brought them down this morning. However, you're here instead, and it's most helpful and kind of you to have come for them."

She smiled at Stevie, and Stevie felt a little shock of recognition as the dark eyes, so reminiscent of Charles Linmer's, surveyed her. Mrs. Linmer was a beautiful woman and perfectly dressed in a grey wool two-piece which seemed to set off the sweeps of iron grey in the otherwise still-black hair. Her manner was friendly and kind and charmingly informal.

She turned to David.

"If I take you to the conservatory and show you which ones they are, perhaps you can put them in your car?" She gestured to Stevie, who had turned to accompany them. "No—please don't trouble, Miss Hylton. Ottoway, our gardener, will help Mr. Arnott to carry them. If you'll wait here a moment, I'll send Carole in to talk to you." She smiled at Stevie. "You've been teaching Melanie to ride, I hear. Charles says she has made great progress."

David and Mrs. Linmer left the room together.

CHAPTER FIV E

STEVIE stood there, looking at the beautiful china. She moved to the long window and stared out at the smooth lawn stretching away in front of her, shaded by one magnificient cedar tree and leading to a distant ha-ha where the garden dropped away to the park beyond.

The music had changed. Stevie recognized the clear limpid notes of Debussy. She listened hard—trying to remember what the piece was called. It came to her suddenly. *"Jardins sous la pluie."* She thought, "But it's sad. How can anyone feel so sad?"

Equally suddenly the music broke off. A step sounded. The intervening door opened.

Stevie swung round expecting to see Carole.

Charles—tall, dark, and, for once, curiously unsmiling, stood there.

He said abruptly,

"What on earth are you doing here?"

Stevie was conscious of embarrassment. She stammered,

"I—we—we called for some flowers and fruit. Mrs. Linmer promised them for the Guide Fair."

He lifted one black eyebrow. His expression altered. He was suddenly the casual smiling Charles again.

"The Guide Fair," he echoed. "A worthy cause. I might have guessed you'd be embroiled in Guides and Good Works."

The way he said it warmed Stevie's blood. David had expressed a criticism of village get-togethers. Charles was implying a criticism of herself.

She said coldly,

"I'm afraid it doesn't concern me at all. Miss Arnott asked David and me to come up and fetch the things." She gave him a level look. "I believe you were to bring them. I suppose such errands are below your dignity. Or are you too busy playing the piano?" she added.

Charles whistled.

"You don't pull your punches, do you? Do you disapprove of my music too?"

Stevie didn't reply. Honesty would not permit her to offer criticism of the music she had just heard. Music at once so superbly played, so deeply expressed—she found difficulty in reconciling it with the flippant smiling Charles.

The pause was broken by the reappearance of Mrs. Linmer. She walked lightly into the room.

"Ottoway is carrying the things to the car for Mr. Arnott. Oh—Charles has discovered you. That's nice. Of course you know each other quite well already?"

Charles turned to smile at his mother. He put an arm about her shoulder in an affectionate protective way. Mrs. Linmer smiled up at him out of dark eyes identical to her son's. They were amazingly alike. Stevie was suddenly aware of a deep bond of sympathy, of affection, between them.

Charles said,

"Miss Hylton and I have met several times. In fact Miss Hylton is coming on the ride to Stonham with us next weekend." He added, "The Point-to-Point, Mother."

Mrs. Linmer's expression changed. The smile seemed to fade out of her eyes and a shadow took its place. She said anxiously, "Oh, Charles—is it wise to go?"

Charles frowned, as if in warning.

"When do I do anything for wisdom's sake, Mamma?" he answered lightly.

Stevie saw Mrs. Linmer move away from Charles' encircling arm. She seemed to square her shoulders a little as she did so, as if unconsciously bracing herself to meet some threat. She said very quietly,

"Of course, Charles. You must do as you wish." She half turned her head to smile wistfully at him. "I don't mean to be silly."

Charles didn't answer his mother but as he smiled in return his dark eyes held an expression of loving reassurance.

Stevie was aware of being both puzzled and touched at the evidence of such close accord between them. Charles' quiet courtesy, his air of deep concentration for his mother, seemed to be in absolute contrast to his usual flippant manner.

They seemed to become conscious of her standing there in the same instant. Mrs. Linmer smiled with a trace of apology at Stevie.

"I'm afraid Carole must be out with Melanie." She gestured with a thin white hand. "Charles, you had better come along and help Mr. Arnott and Ottoway with the plants."

The three of them moved towards the doorway.

"I hope the grapes will be ripe enough," Mrs. Linmer went on. "And I do hope that the Guides will have a successful Fair. I understand that Mr. Pollitt the Vicar is opening it for them. I shall hope to look in myself." She glanced round at Charles. "You too, Charles. We must support these local affairs."

Charles nodded.

"Definitely." His black eyes regarded Stevie with mock gravity. "You'll be there, Miss Hylton?"

Stevie wished with all her heart that she had been able to accept David's invitation to go to Norwich and so escape any further meeting with the exasperating Charles. She said, as politely as she could,

"I expect so."

David was stacking the last of Ottoway's cherished pot plants on to the floor of his car. He turned, wiping earthy hands on a handkerchief, as the others came down the steps of the house. When he recognized Charles his face stiffened. He replied to Charles' greeting with studied aloofness, and avoided looking at him directly, confining his remarks to Mrs. Linmer.

They said good-morning to Mrs. Linmer and Charles and drove away.

David was frowning.

"So that's our young Squire," he remarked. "I suppose he rather fancies himself in the role."

The queer thing was that when David criticized Charles Stevie couldn't bring herself to join in. He must be conceited, of course. How could anyone as handsome—oh! she acknowledged his superlative good looks—and so rich and favoured of the gods as Charles appeared to be, *not* be conceited? He would have to be an exceptional person.

"Don't you agree?" David said. He turned his head to look at Stevie in some surprise at her silence.

"Yes. Yes—I suppose so," Stevie said quickly, unthinkingly.

"We'd better leave this stuff right away at the School," David went on. He added, "Are you coming to Norwich with me this afternoon, or must we be sacrificed to make sport for a Brownie's holiday?"

"I feel I must go," Stevie said reluctantly. "Miss Mabel—Lisa—everyone is putting in an appearance."

David's thin mouth curled a little.

"Even the Squire! I'm surprised he doesn't open the silly thing." He shrugged resignedly. "Oh well, I suppose I'll have to go too. Anyway, Stevie, shall we make it a definite arrangement to run over to Norwich this evening? We can get away early. Perhaps have dinner there, if we don't go to a film."

"That will be lovely, David," Stevie said eagerly. "Thank you."

David mentioned their project to Miss Mabel after lunch. She was sitting by the fire as susual drinking her invariable cup of tea. Miss Mabel didn't look up from the copy of the *Eastern Daily Press* she was reading.

"Good idea, David," she remarked. "Are you taking Lisa and Keith along with you too?"

David looked blank.

"Well, to tell you the truth, it hadn't occurred to me," he said. "I mean—Keith's always so dug in around the farm, and—and Lisa—" His voice trailed off. Obviously, he did not wish to seem impolite, but the presence of Lisa would make an unwanted third in David's estimation.

Miss Mabel went on reading her column with undisturbed placidity.

"Keith's too much around the farm. And it's dull for Lisa always being left with me. Make a nice foursome if you all went. Why don't you suggest it, David? Of course, I don't want to interfere——"

For the first time she glanced up. The blue eyes regarding David above the bright blue frames were so keen and alert, it was so obvious that Miss Mabel fully intended to interfere if she possibly could, that Stevie was forced to smile.

"Well—I'll put it to Keith, if you like," David said slowly. "He probably won't want to come, though."

Whether Miss Mabel had been busy with more suggestions no one knew, but, surprisingly, Keith agreed to go. They were all walking up the road to the School House when David mentioned the idea.

"I can't leave until after milking," Keith said. He looked thoughtfully at Lisa. "But if Lisa would care to go, right! David, we'll come along with you."

"I'll see to the milking," Miss Mabel said. "As soon as you've had a good look round here and bought some things, I should slip away—the lot of you. No need to hang on all afternoon."

Judy was wildly excited as she presided over her stall with a Brownie friend who had bright red hair and a snub nose. She whispered hoarsely to her father,

"I've saved you some of the toffee. You said you wanted to buy some."

The School Hall was full of people—peering over the various stalls—dipping in the Bran Tub—taking a chance on throwing rings round objects, and so on.

At first it was difficult to draw Keith into things. He stood about in an awkward, constrained fashion, staring above the heads of the chattering parents and friends of the schoolchildren as if he were wishing himself far enough away. But Lisa gently and unobtrusively drew his attention, first to one item, then to another, and Judy skipped to and fro at intervals, so obviously pleased and proud to have her father present that gradually Keith seemed to unbend and his rare smile appeared a little more frequently.

Stevie glimpsed Mrs. Linmer, elegantly beautiful in tweeds and a mink stole, with Charles and Melanie, talking to the Reverend Mr. Pollitt. David caught sight of them too.

"Our young Squire's condescended to appear, I see. Come on, let's go this way. We don't want to become involved with the Linmer party." He added, "Who's the Show Piece?"

For a moment Stevie was puzzled.

"Oh, you mean Melanie? She is a friend of the family, I think. She's been staying with them for several weeks. She *is* very attractive looking, isn't she?" she finished generously.

David shrugged.

"Too synthetic for my taste. I hate glamour girls." His expression softened as he smiled down at Stevie. "You know the type I admire."

Stevie met his meaningful look. She said slowly, "Do I?"

"You should do," David answered. "I like a girl who's sweet and sensible and level-headed and who has something in her. In short, a girl like you, Stevie."

Stevie felt her heart warm at David's compliment. It was the first real one he had ever paid her. He wasn't given to flattering speeches or easy gallantries.

Her smile held a sudden trace of shyness.

"That's very sweet of you, David. Thank you."

David inclined his head.

"Oh, it isn't a snap judgment, I assure you. I don't mind admitting that when we were working together I had plenty of opportunity to assess your character and I did exactly that. I've watched you, Stevie, and I consider your good qualities far outweigh any defects."

For a moment Stevie felt somewhat dashed at the way David had considered her so analytically. There was a cold-water quality about his acceptance of her defects as well as her virtues.

She had a sudden impulse to enquire what her defects were but hastily dismissed it, lest David should think she were poking fun at him.

She was about to make some answer when an eager voice broke in on them both.

"Now come along, you young people. You mustn't stand about like this when there are so many things you should be joining in at. Have you tried the Bran Tub? You *haven't*?" Mrs. Pollitt's round brown eyes regarded them questioningly. "This way, this way. Here is Edna simply longing to let you try a lucky dip. Only a shilling, you know, and it's all in *such* a good cause!"

Stevie and David found themselves shepherded towards the Bran Tub where, admist a smiling, murmuring press of people, they each extracted a small parcel. Stevie's proved to be a tablet of soap and David's a large india-rubber. Urged on by Mrs. Pollitt they moved up towards the Leathercraft Stall. Here a display of really attractive hand-made leather objects was on show.

David reached his hand out.

"I'll take this," he said. He paid out some money. Look, Stevie, this is for you."

It was a small case of stamped brown leather, hand-stitched, and holding a writing pad and matching envelopes inside.

"Now you'll have to write to me every week," he said smilingly as he handed it to her.

"Oh, David." Stevie glowed with delight, as much at David's thought for her as for the actual gift. "It's lovely. And it will be awfully useful. I've just never possessed one. Thank you very much indeed."

"It's all in such a good cause, to quote Mrs. Pollitt," David observed. "Whenever you use it, you'll spare me a thought, won't you?"

"Of course I will," Stevie promised. "And I shall use it next weekend to tell you all about the Stonham Point-to-Point. It's next Saturday." She looked up at him. "I wish you were here to come with us."

David shrugged.

"I can think of pleasanter things. It sounds drastically energetic. I'm afraid I'm a townee at heart."

"Don't say that," Stevie protested.

"Why not? Aren't you?"

Stevie shook her head.

"No, not really, David. We had to live in London when my father was alive. I had to have a job there later. But my heart wasn't in it."

David looked down at her.

"Suppose you married a man who preferred city life? Who wanted to live and work in town always. How would you feel about that?"

Stevie met his intent look and then glanced away. She had a sudden awareness that David was putting his question deliberately. Did he mean if she married *him*? Was this the sort of cautious roundabout way David would use to discover a girl's preferences before committing himself? I like David, she thought. I like him tremendously. But to marry? To live with for always in some flat in the heart of a city? She couldn't visualize it. But if you loved someone, it wouldn't matter where you lived. Town or country, Tennessee or Timbuctoo . . . your heart made its own Paradise.

She said as lightly as she could,

"If you loved someone, it wouldn't matter where you lived, would it? I was only speaking of a personal preference."

David's voice was suddenly non-committal and matter-of-fact again.

"Of course. Circumstances alter cases, I agree. Look, there's Keith and Lisa, let' go over and see what they have been up to."

In a little while the four of them were able to take their leave and depart for Norwich, where they had arranged to spend the evening together.

CHAPTER SIX

ON the morning of the Stonham Point-to-Point Stevie and Keith, with the aid of Old Tom, were busy before breakfast brushing and grooming the horses. The party from the Manor House were due to arrive at ten o'clock. It was a little after the hour when two cars pulled up in the yard. Stevie recognized Charles at the wheel of his own big one, while behind him came a wide sleek American car, driven by a stranger.

Keith came forward at once and introductions were made.

Stevie found herself shaking hands with a tall, sandy-haired man called Captain Dennis, and his striking auburn-haired wife; a pretty girl called Renée Hartley and her brother Tony, and, lastly, a heavily built young man, dressed somewhat incongruously in a check lumber jacket and narrow trousers fitted into short leather boots. His dusty brown hair was crew cut; he had a full pale face and rimless glasses.

Charles gestured towards him.

"This is Irving Darrell. He looks like a fugitive from 'Hopalong Cassidy' but he's quite harmless. He comes from Canyon City, Colorado."

A powerful hand gripped Stevie's.

"Sure am pleased to meet you, Miss Hylton, if you're the girl who's taught little Melanie here to ride. When she was over in the States last year I couldn't get her near a horse. It's a real pleasure to me to see her rarin' to go, as we say back home."

Keith came forward leading a big black stallion named Sultan on one side of him and Shannon on the other.

"This is Miss Granger's mount," he said. "And yours, Charles."

"Thanks. I'll see her up."

"Pardon me," Irving interposed. He put a big square hand on either side of Melanie's slim waist and lifted her up on to Shannon's back. He stood back, blinking up at her through his thick glasses. "You sure look pretty up there."

Charles swung up on to Sultan. At almost the same moment Trixie, Miss Mabel's tortoiseshell cat, came scuttling out of the barn after a real or imaginary mouse. Sultan, who was given to showing off in company, skidded sideways in mock alarm, then reared in spectacular display.

Charles' voice said,

"Steady there!"

Stevie looked round. The big black horse and the tall blackhaired man riding him were like a piece of statuary outlined against the brilliant sunlight. A masterpiece in bronze carved by Rodin or Carl Milles.

Her heart seemed to miss a beat. Afterwards she thought that queer sensation must have been fright. Now she simply stared until Sultan's front legs came down to earth again and he stood blowing gustily through flaring nostrils at Trixie, who had sprung up on to a shed roof out of harm's way.

The momentary tension eased itself in laughter and sudden talk. In a few minutes the party was mounted and assembled. Miss Mabel and Lisa waved from the back door as they all set off, the gay jingle of bridles mingling with the creak of leather and the clip of hooves. Keith led the way with Captain and Mrs. Dennis, while the others followed on behind. They were to meet Carole at the cross-roads, as she was riding her own horse, Diamond.

It was a fresh March morning. The wind was not off the sea today. It came from inland, bringing with it the indefinable but delicious scent of earth and grass and growing things. The sun, bursting through the scurrying clouds, lit up the landscape ahead. Hedgerows, trees and fields pin-pointed with spring wheat were suddenly flushed into the first bright green of spring, and in the cottage gardens primroses and polyanthus rioted in royal hues down pink brick paths.

Stevie was filled with a sharp sense of happiness. This was so beautiful. So very different from the past few years living and working in London. Perhaps after all, she thought, as the horses broke into a trot and they all went clip-clopping up the dusty road, she was glad to have come on the ride!

It took them a good three hours to reach Stonham. Charles had arranged for the party to have lunch at the George Hotel in the town. It was a pleasant, whitewashed building, homely but comfortable. The meal was excellent and everybody had keen appetites to do justice to it after the long ride.

Stevie found herself seated between Tony Hartley and Captain Dennis. Tony was about twenty-two and an extremely lively conversationalist. He had the inestimable gift of making any new acquaintance feel like an old friend. Stevie couldn't help but chatter away with him and laugh at his absurdities. Tony's congenial influence removed any sense of shyness, so that it was easy, too, to talk with Captain Dennis.

Charles had taken the head of the table. Melanie sat on his right, and on Melanie's other side sat Irving Darrell. Irving never seemed to remove his serious spectacled stare from Melanie's beautiful face throughout the entire meal. It was quite apparent that he admired her intensely.

Charles heard Stevie's low laughter, a deep-throated chuckle that was somehow attractive. He glanced at her in some surprise. Today there was colour under the creamy skin from the recent fresh air and exercise. The hazel eyes, which were neither brown nor gold but the colour of a stream that used to run bubbling over the stones of the Highland burn where Charles had gone fishing in past holidays, were sparkling with mirth. He watched small white even teeth flash between lips as firm and red as cherries, and was startled into the admission that today Stevie looked extremely pretty.

He felt a trifle piqued that so much charm and animation had never been revealed to *him*. Then he shrugged philosophically, deciding that he and Stevie were definitely not *en rapport*. Whenever they met the sparks flew and some disagreement ensued.

After luncheon was over the party set off the few miles to where the races were held. It was on a stretch of land with a slight slope to the south. Along the bottom of the course ran a roadway and here groups of people stood, or perched on car roofs, all ready to catch a good view of the riders circling round and taking the jumps which were placed on the level ground at the foot of the slope. On various other points of land people stood watching and the Whitegates party soon found an excellent place where the horses could be tethered while they watched the scene before them.

As the afternoon wore on the colour began to fade out of the landscape. It was suddenly all greys and browns where a little while ago it had spread itself in the green and gold of spring. There was frost in the air. The hint of it was in the midst of the blue distances and in the pearly rose of the sky.

"Time to go," Keith pronounced, knowing that a three-hour ride home lay before them.

Captain and Mrs. Dennis and Carole began to pull ahead on the way back. Their horses were faster and all three were experienced riders. Stevie and Tony Hartley rode alongside one another, with Keith and Renée following behind them. Lastily came Irving Darrell with Charles and Melanie. Melanie, the least expert of them all, found it hard to keep pace and Charles was constantly pulling in Sultan to remain level with her.

The ride home seemed longer. They were all tired after the long day and even conversation began to flag after a while.

They had been riding some time when Stevie became aware that her saddle was slipping. It was a most uncomfortable sensation. Evidently Trigger had been a little more artful than she had been aware of, and cunningly blown himself out when she had adjusted the saddle girths before leaving Stonham.

She turned to Tony.

"I'll have to stop and adjust this saddle. Don't wait for me—I'll catch you up farther along the road."

Tony hesitated.

"Sure you can manage? Right-ho, then."

Stevie slid off Trigger's back, calling out to Keith what had happened as he rode past. He waved his crop in a gesture of assent and trotted on with Renée to catch up to Tony. Charles and the other two drew level, but Stevie averted her head.

There was some trouble with Trigger's girth. In the dusk of evening Stevie had to feel rather than see what she was doing. At last she adjusted it satisfactorily, saying with a warning pat,

"Blow now if you dare, Trigger."

It had taken her longer than she had thought. She looked up the empty road but there was no sight or sound of the others.

Stevie swung up on to Trigger's back.

"Come on, boy, hurry up."

Trigger made good speed up the road and in a minute or two Stevie saw someone on horseback ahead. For a second she thought it was Tony waiting for her, then she decided it must be Keith—the figure was too tall for Tony. It was only as she drew level that she saw, with something of consternation, that it was Charles.

She said abruptly,

"Where are the others?"

He gave her a curious smile. A rather lop-sided smile, entirely unlike any expression of his that Stevie had ever seen before.

"They're ahead somewhere."

Stevie listened for the sound of hooves on the hard road; for the echo of voices or laughter on the quiet air. All she could hear was the voice of a thrush singing his evening anthem.

"We'd better hurry or we shall lose them." Her tone was offhand.

She gave Trigger a light kick and he set up immediately into a brisk trot. She didn't wait to see if Charles was following. Suddenly, through the grey light ahead, Stevie glimpsed the white arms of a signpost. She reined Trigger in sharply, staring down at them.

The printed signs read "Stonham, Windingham, Bassett" and "Couldon St. Mary". Stevie frowned in dismay. If only she knew the district better. She looked round at Charles, suddenly conscious that he had only just caught up with her. She stared at him in surprise—knowing Sultan's powerful stride.

"It doesn't say 'Hedburgh'. Do you know which way they would go? There's no sign of them ahead, so I feel they must have turned here."

Charles shook his head slowly.

"I haven't a clue." He gave Stevie that queer rather strained smile again. "I'm a stranger here myself!" He shrugged. "Your guess is as good as mine."

"It's absurd," Stevie said. "They can't be far."

She stared in puzzlement at the signs. Wasn't Bassett somewhere near Hedburgh? It had a familiar ring.

She swung Trigger's head to the left.

"I think this road leads home through Bassett."

Charles drew up alongside.

"I'm in your hands."

Stevie turned her head to look at him.

"How did you come to fall behind too?"

Charles smiled, but this time he didn't look even like himself when he smiled.

"How did you?" he countered.

"Trigger's saddle slipped," Stevie explained briefly.

Charles didn't speak. He didn't even try to explain why he had been left behind.

Stevie felt annoyance rising within her again. Really, he was the most casual, uncaring person she had ever met. And now she was stuck with him for the rest of the way home. A way he couldn't even bother to try to fathom out.

"Don't scowl so," Charles said. For some reason his voice sounded remote and far away. "You make me nervous."

"I'm not scowling," Stevie said coldly, aware that she was doing just that.

"It's not my fault we're lost," Charles went on in mild reproof. "*You're* lost too, you know. The careful Miss Hylton is just as unlucky in that respect as the careless Mr. Linmer."

Stevie rod on in silence. It was blue dusk now. The first evening star pricked the rose stained west. The trees whispered gently in the night air. She strained her ears, trying to hear above the horses' walk the sound of other horses, other voices.

Charles said,

"I'm sure you disapprove of me terribly. I can't imagine why. But you have the same chilly look in your eye my governess used to have, when I was a small boy and had done something particularly heinous. Come to think of it, you remind me a lot of Miss Wurple. I *think* her name was Miss Wurple."

He was laughing at her again. Stevie, tired, and now beginning to feel taut with anxiety as to where they were going or likely to end up, turned her head sharply. She said,

"As you're so very clever, Mr. Linmer, I'll leave you to find your way home alone. I'm sure you're more than capable."

She gave Trigger a smart rap and he set off up the raod, breaking into a gallop as Stevie urged him on. She was so angry she wasn't quite aware of what she was doing. Only so furious that she was determined to get away from that odious Charles. *Miss Wurple*, indeed! Oh, he was hateful!

Across the low-lying hedgerows she saw a light. A light that turned slowly—disappeared—came on again. Stevie felt her heart leap. The Bracklesey lighthouse! Then she was nearly home. Hedburgh couldn't be far now. She saw a low gate ahead—a stretch of brown fields leading away towards the turning light. In an attempt to leave Charles far behind—to prevent him following her—she set Trigger's head at the gate and he took it in one clean smooth leap.

Stevie turned her head. She wondered if Charles had seen her jump the gate. She heard the sound of a horse coming up the road and smiled. He was going past. She was just going to set off across the fields when she pulled Trigger up so abruptly that he reared back.

A horse was going up the road. A black horse—Sultan. But he was riderless.

Stevie went on staring. Slowly, almost reluctantly, she turned Trigger's head and rode back to the gate. She leaned down and undid the catch and then fastened it again as soon as she and the horse were through.

She stared up and down the dark stretch of road. The first thing to do was to catch Sultan and then go back to see what had happened to Charles. She swung Trigger round and they trotted up the road and discovered Sultan nibbling at the hedgerows in an aimless sort of way. His reins had fallen down over his neck and, tangling between his feet, had halted his runaway progress.

Stevie looped them back over his head and, pulling Sultan round alongside her, set off in the direction she had just come.

CHAPTER   SEVEN

SUDDENLY, through the glimmering dusk, she could see the figure of Charles. He was leaning against a tree with his head in his hands. At the sound of the horses he looked up—staring in a queer unfocused sort of way at Stevie. In the half light his face looked very white and strained.

Dismay quickened in Stevie. She swung quickly down from the horse's back. She forgot her resentment and the fact that she had just rushed away from Charles in a fit of anger.

"What happened?" she asked anxiously. "Did you come off?"

Charles went on staring down at her. Stevie had the extraordinary feeling that he wasn't really seeing her at all. He said slowly and with difficulty,

"I must have done. I'll be—all right in a jiff."

He was still holding his head with one hand.

"You must have knocked yourself when you came off," Stevie went on worriedly. "Perhaps——" she hesitated, "if you'd let me see——"

59

She put out a gentle hand and Charles let his arm fall to his side. There was no sign of cut or bruise. Stevie's soft fingers, passing through the thick dark hair, could feel no trace of knock or swelling.

She gave him a tentative smile.

"You don't seem to have banged yourself too seriously."

Charles shook his head quickly to and fro, as if testing some reaction. The black eyes blinked spasmodically.

"It's—nothing," he said again. For the first time he looked at her with some sort of awareness. He smiled unexpectedly. "Thanks for coming back."

Stevie hesitated. She nearly said, "I'm sorry I lost my temper." But, even incapacitated, Charles was still the enemy. If he hadn't provoked her she wouldn't have ridden away so suddenly, and Charles himself might not have met with this accident. She looked at him with a sense of puzzlement. How *had* the accident occurred? She knew that Charles was a first-rate horseman and it was difficult to imagine how Sultan had managed to unseat him. Perhaps he had just felt queer in some way. Faint? He had certainly seemed unlike himself when they had met on the road a short time back.

She said slowly,

"We're not far from Hedburgh. I've just seen the Bracklesey lighthouse flashing on and off. Do you think you could manage the ride back?"

Charles seemed to take a deep breath.

"Yes. I'm fine." He took a step forward. "Here we go—"

His voice trailed off. He stumbled against Stevie. She put her arms out towards him in a sudden fear, conscious that she couldn't possibly support Charles' tall weight if he was about to collapse on her.

His hands came down heavily on Stevie's shoulders. He seemed to steady himself as he clutched at her. His black head stayed low against her own.

"Sor—ry," Charles muttered, his face pressed against Stevie's neck and shoulder.

For a long interminable moment they stood there in a queer sort of embrace. Stevie could feel her heart pounding against Charles' tweed jacket. With apprehension and distress: with consternation and alarm. With some other entirely different emotion, unaccountable and un-defined.

Charles jerked his head upright. He rubbed a hand across his eyes several times as he pulled away from Stevie.

"Sorry to scare you," he said. He smiled ruefully. "Can't think what's come over me."

It was a smile very unlike Charles. Diffident and un-certain. A smile that didn't quite reach the strained stare of the dark eyes.

Charles' smile had a peculiar effect upon Stevie. She was filled with a sense of bewilderment and compassion. She wanted to put a hand out to Charles—to say consolingly, "Don't worry, please. I'm sure it's going to be all right. Whatever it is."

She gave herself a little shake as if to throw off the strange emotional impulse.

"If you could give me a—a hand up," Charles went on, "I think I can make it."

Stevie frowned anxiously.

"Are you sure?"

He nodded.

"Yes. That was just a—spot of dizziness." He moved towards Sultan and gathered up the reins, reaching with the other hand towards the saddle.

Somehow Stevie managed to help him on to Sultan's back. He sat there, looking white and breathing rather quickly. His voice was oddly embarrassed as he said,

"Thanks." He added, "D'you mind if we take it easy?"

"Of course not," Stevie said. "We'll walk the horses."

It was a queer ride along the deserted country road, dark now with night and with the shadowed trees whis-pering and sighing above them. Charles didn't speak and Stevie, feeling that silence was easier for him, remained quiet too. Sultan and Trigger, tired with their long day, were content to plod slowly along side by side, their heads drooping, as they contemplated thoughts of supper and a warm stable ahead.

Stevie recognized a round flint cottage that at one time had been the toll house on the old turnpike road. The way ahead was suddenly familiar. She broke the long silence to say,

"I expect everyone will be wondering what has happened to us. Your sister will be feeling anxious and—and your friend Melanie."

Charles said abruptly,

"Stevie——"

Stevie swung her head round. It was odd to hear him calling her for the first time by her Christian name.

"Yes?"

"I'd be—grateful if you wouldn't make too much of a song and dance about what happened. My spill—I mean." She was aware, without actually being able to see, that he was frowning. "I don't want to—to worry Melanie."

"I shan't say anything," Stevie answered gently, "except that we lost our way."

This time she saw him smile. The flash of teeth—the gleam of black eyes.

"Thanks."

Another five minutes brought them into Hedburgh's main street and the first turning left took them to Whitegates Farm. The horses pricked up their ears and broke into a trot to go clattering through the gates and into the yard.

Almost immediately the back door opened and in the beam of light Stevie saw Keith. He strode quickly across to them as Stevie slid to the ground.

"We were beginning to worry about you both," Keith said. "Did you have an accident?"

Stevie answered before Charles could speak.

"We lost our way. After I stopped to fix Trigger's saddle I caught up with Charles and then—I don't know how it happened—we must have taken the wrong road. We came back through Bassett."

"And we came home via Couldon St. Mary." Keith clicked his tongue. "Never mind, you're back safe and sound. Take Charles in, Stevie—Aunt Mabel's kept some coffee hot for you both. I'll see to the horses."

"Oh, thank you, Keith."

Miss Mabel's sprigged sitting-room seemed to be overflowing with people. A tray with cups and saucers and some glasses stood on the side table—there were sandwiches and biscuits beside them.

"My dear child, we thought something had befallen you," Miss Mabel exclaimed. "Come along to the fire. Charles, you look positively *grey*. Get this hot drink inside you."

Tony pushed a chair forward for Stevie. Melanie was sitting on the couch between Irving and Mrs. Dennis. Charles bent down behind her to say something.

Melanie's voice was low, but very distinct. Stevie could not help hearing her answer.

"What do you mean—you got lost? It's absurd. I thought it was most queer the way you suddenly dropped behind like that. I'm not such a good rider as you are and I managed to keep up with everyone." Stevie was amazed to see Melanie's kitten-blue eyes dart a sharp and distinctly feline glance in her direction. "Are you sure you didn't get lost on purpose?"

For a moment Stevie felt only amusement at Melanie's fantastic notion. The idea that Charles should have manoeuvred to get himself lost with her! But amusement changed to something like indignation as she saw Charles move abruptly away and almost flop down on to a chair against the wall. The chair was out of the glow of lamplight and almost hidden in shadow. But before he sat down Stevie had glimpsed the set expression, the tightening of the firm jaw as if in some sort of determined effort.

Compunction stirred in her. Can't Melanie see that he's not himself? That he's hurt, in some way? But that was exactly what Charles didn't want Melanie to know, Stevie amended. She observed, as Miss Mabel had, the grey tinge under his tan. The silent figure in the shadow was suddenly someone quite different from the smooth self-confident Charles who always seemed to have everything so perfectly under control.

Keith came in from the stables. There was more conversation and explanation in which Stevie found herself joining with more volubility than usual. The last dregs of coffee were drunk; the last sandwich eaten.

"Well, now our host has been safely restored to us we needn't inflict ourselves any longer upon Miss Arnott's hospitality," Captain Dennis said, standing up and looking round.

Charles uncoiled his lean length.

"I'm afraid I—" He caught Stevie's eye, and added, "We seem to have rather crabbed the evening's plans." He turned to Miss Mabel. "I'm sincerely grateful to you, Miss Arnott. I'm afraid we've imposed on you."

"Nonsense," Miss Mabel gave him her brilliant smile. "Loved every moment of it. It's been like a party. Come again." Her bright blue eyes swept the room. "All of you."

Everyone laughed. The party began to break up in a spate of talk and expressions of thanks.

Stevie stood back with Lisa as the others pressed forward to take Miss Mabel's hand and say good-night. She heard Charles speaking to his sister,

"Will you drive, Carole? I'll sit in the back with Melanie." He tucked his arm through Melanie's and bent his head to hers. "If she'll let me."

Melanie pouted, then smiled a charming forgiveness.

"Oh, I suppose so! Though you don't deserve it."

From the doorway Charles looked across the room towards Stevie. He gestured with one hand.

"Good-night, Stevie," he said. "Thanks—for everything."

It was a casual enough remark. It could have meant anything. Only Stevie was aware of its real intention. Her answering smile was more formal than she realised. She was suddenly very conscious of the two people in the doorway: the tall dark man and the slender blonde girl tucked against his side.

"Good-night," Stevie said.

The thought of Charles kept coming back to her all evening. She kept remembering that strange moment under the tree, when she had stood with her arms about Charles, helping to support him, while his cold brown face had been close against her own. But superimposed upon this would come the remembrance of his mocking voice saying, "You remind me of Miss Wurple, my governess. I *think* her name was Miss Wurple," and that slanting sideways glance of laughter.

One moment she was feeling sorry for Charles and the next she was disliking him as much as ever.

CHAPTER EIGHT

AFTER the excitement of the Point-to-Point the stables settled down into a sort of jog-trot routine. Keith began to leave Stevie virtually in charge of the riding school while he busied himself with the work of the farm. Several times Lisa went out riding with Stevie and it was like old times to jog-trot along lanes green with spring trees and sweet with the scent of lilac and blossom.

One afternoon as she and Lisa were setting out on a ride, Carole arrived at the stables. She gave Stevie her warm friendly smile.

"Hello. I've come to borrow a horse. Diamond has a shoulder lameness. The vet thinks that rheumatism is causing it and he has to rest for a week or two. She looked up at Lisa, who was seated on Tess. "Are you going out now? Because I'd love to come along if it's possible."

"Of course," Stevie said. "You can have Shandy or Jupiter. I'll saddle one of them for you."

"Jupiter, please," Carole said.

"Miss—Miss Granger didn't want to come with you?" Stevie asked, as the three girls set off in the direction of the common.

"We haven't seen her at the stables for a week or so."

"Melanie's gone up to London," Carole answered. "Didn't she tell you she was going away?"

Stevie shook her head.

"No." She added, "Is that where her home is?"

Carole laughed.

"Oh no: her parents live in Washington. Mr. Granger's something fearfully important at the British Embassy. I suppose you'd say that Melanie's home is really with us. She's a sort of terribly vague cousin—something like a second-second-second one removed, and while she's over here in England she's staying at the Manor."

"I see," Stevie said. That explained a lot of things. Melanie's protracted stay at the Manor House and the way Charles and Carole made so much of her.

"What do you think of Irving?" Carole went on. "He's one of her beaux. She knew him in Washington and I believe he's come over here specially this spring in order to track her down. He's fearfully smitten, as you can see. Not that he has the ghost of a chance," she added lightly. "Charles is top man around Melanie. He's in love with her himself." Carole giggled. "And when brother Charles goes after a girl, no one else gets her—believe me!"

Lisa smiled round at her.

"He must be like his godfather. Miss Mabel told us every girl for miles around was in love with Sir William. Perhaps it's the same with your brother." She added, "He is terrifically good-looking."

Carole laughed.

"Oh, Charles is a charmer all right. I'm his sister, so I should know. You'd be surprised how extremely popular the sister of a handsome and eligible young man finds herself. I collect *masses* of invitations to parties that aren't meant for me at all. I'm the decoy to get Charles along!"

"But don't you mind?" Stevie said slowly.

Carole shook her head.

"Of course not! Why should I? It amuses me. I expect it amuses Charles too. I'm sure he's quite aware of all these eager mammas and their equally eager daughters who hurl themselves at his head!"

Stevie didn't answer. It's true then, she concluded silently, what I thought in the first place. That Charles is much too good-looking and rich and—and fortunate not to be spoilt into the bargain. Conceited too. How can he help being?

A *charmer*, Stevie thought, in a sudden spasm of irritation. Well—he doesn't charm me, for one!

She was aware of being childish. It's Melanie he's bent on charming, she reprimanded herself. Don't be silly. He doesn't concern you.

Carole was speaking again.

"This *is* fun. Can I come again tomorrow? I feel awfully lost, all on my own. Charles is away as well as Melanie."

"Yes, of course, come again tomorrow," Stevie said. "We'll ride on the shore—the tide will be out later in the afternoon."

But tomorrow found the rain coming down in a heavy deluge. It was something more than April showers. It was the sort of rain that sometimes comes so unexpectedly in the midst of bright spring weather. Rain that fell intermittently for three long days, splashing on to the cobbled farmyard, on to the tin roofs of the barns and sheds; rain that went gurgling down gutter spouts and drumming into the water tubs.

Miss Mabel and Lisa tood advantage of being housebound to catch up with the tag end of spring cleaning. They spent two days emptying and sorting out the vast and commodious cupboards in the old-fashioned kitchen. Their example inspired Stevie to have a blitz on the harness room, much to Old Tom's consternation.

Suddenly, the rain was gone again. Stevie woke to a warm sunny day escaped out of May. The rain had washed the landscape into a more breathless green, the sea was as calm and blue as the Mediterranean. She took the horses, on Keith's instructions, down to the marshes as there were no rides booked for that day, and then raced back on Sorel to help with the farm work. Keith was busy up on the fields—harrowing and rolling his spring wheat with the aid of his men.

He shook his head at Stevie when after lunch she suggested helping him.

"There isn't much you can do," he said. "Fred and I are managing nicely." He gave Stevie one of his rare smiles.

"I'd much rather you took the afternoon off." He shook his head at Stevie's look of surprise. "I don't believe you've had as much as that since you came here."

Stevie smiled in return.

"Of course I have. "Besides—I never feel I *am* working when I'm with the horses. It's so exactly what I'd do for pleasure."

"Never mind," Keith answered firmly. "My instructions are—take the afternoon off. Go out with Aunt Mabel and Lisa. They're always tea-partying somewhere or other."

Stevie went almost reluctantly back to the house, only to find when she got there that Miss Mabel and Lisa had gone, in Miss Mabel's rickety little car, to Norwich for the afternoon. She remembered now that Lisa had mentioned the project, asking Stevie if there was any shopping she wanted done.

Taffy, the golden cocker spaniel, wagged his tail and smiled ingratiatingly up at Stevie.

"Didn't they take you?" Stevie commiserated. "Never mind—I'll take you out. I expect you feel like a good run after being cooped up indoors with the rain. Come on, Taffy, which way is it to be?"

Taffy's mind was made up in advance. He raced ahead through the gates and stood waiting for Stevie to catch him up, and when she did so, dashed off again heading down the road in the direction of the shore.

The sands stretched away firm and golden in either direction. Stevie turned along the shore towards Bracklesey Point. It was too far to walk to it, but the distant lighthouse and the small white sailing ships and the green rim of marshes looked very inviting.

Taffy was in a seventh heaven of delight. Dashing into the sea, barking at seagulls, scrabbling at stones and returning to Stevie to deposit various ones at her feet. It was hard to say who was enjoying the walk most. Stevie thought it an absolutely perfect day. She stood by the water's edge a long time, gazing out at the dancing expanse of blue water, watching the plume of smoke from some trawler turn and disappear over the horizon, while the small waves curled gently in towards her feet with a quietly soothing "swish—swoosh."

Taffy dug at her toes as if to remind her to throw yet another stone. Stevie turned away and walked on. At first glance she had thought the shore was deserted, but now saw with surprise that someone was seated on a wooden breakwater below the cliffs, apparently painting the seascape ahead.

She stared disbelievingly. It wasn't possible, surely, that it was *Charles* painting. Taffy, filled with eager curiosity, settled the matter for her. He raced ahead to sniff and snuffle at the figure sitting there. The man turned his head, said reprimandingly as Taffy seized a paint-brush in his mouth,

"Hi-drop that—"

He bent to retrieve the brush. Looked up and round. He saw Stevie.

"Well—" He smiled. "Hello."

"Hello," Stevie said slowly, almost reluctantly. Now that she was standing within view of Charles she was filled with the most contradictory of emotions. A sudden impulse to turn on her heel and walk away: an equally strong impulse to remain exactly where she was. Again there was the remembrance of that queer moment together, under the tree. But in the amused glance of the black eyes regarding her there was no trace today of the other diffident, uncertain Charles.

She said abruptly,

"I didn't know that you painted."

Charles put his head on one side, screwing up his eyes as if assessing the perspective of the scene before him. He made a great to-do with paint-brush and palette before answering.

"Didn't you? It's one of my unsuspected talents."

As usual, his voice held a note of hidden laughter. Stevie glanced quickly at him, but his face was gravely absorbed as he worked away at the canvas before him. She was filled with a sudden curiosity.

"May I see what you're painting?"

Charles waved a careless hand.

'Why not?"

Stevie moved round behind him and looked over his shoulder. She stared in bewildered surprise. The scene depicted before her was scarcely recognizable. It was a hotchpotch of colour—an impressionist daub. The splash of white in the centre of the canvas could possibly have been the lighthouse ahead.

"What is it supposed to be?" Stevie asked unkindly.

Charles glanced round at her. He shook his head reproachfully.

"The remark of a Philistine! You're obviously no judge of art. Must I explain in words of one easy syllable that this is a view of Bracklesey Point?"

Stevie looked at him. She was very conscious of the turn of the well-shaped dark head; the clean-cut features that resembled some profile on an ancient coin, and the firm yet sensitive mouth that spoke of a drive and purpose Stevie found it impossible to associate with Charles.

No man had a right to be so good-looking! Stevie thought of Carole's phrase and her mouth curled. "A charmer!" That was exactly what he was. And no more! A charmer who had nothing to do all day but drive around in a huge expensive car, and ride a horse, and play the piano and—and fool about painting.

Her glance was caught and held by the brightly coloured jacket of a book lying face downward on the sands. It read: *Landscape Painting for Beginners*.

The sight of it added fuel to the fire of Stevie's disapproval. It seemed to epitomize all that Charles stood for. His dilettante attitude towards life. His casual laughter. His inconsequent idleness.

She shrugged her shoulders, answering his last remark.

"You don't expect anyone to take you seriously, do you? The only thing it looks like to me is a fearful waste of time."

Charles lifted one black eyebrow at her.

"You're in your governessy mood again today," he said chidingly. "I detect the authentic note of Miss Wurple herself speaking. I can't think why my humble striving to become a painter should meet with such firm disapproval. After all, it's a fashionable hobby. Look at all the famous people who go in for painting on the side.

His mocking tone and the reference to Miss Wurple stung Stevie to fresh resentment.

"You're forgetting one thing," she said coldly. "Most of those famous people do a worthwhile job of work in addition."

Charles turned his head to look at her. He said evenly, "And what makes you think I don't work?"

"Do you?" Stevie demanded. "I can't imagine when. You always seem to have all the time in the world on your hands. It's surprising really. Because everyone works today. Even the most wealthy and privileged of people."

Charles gave her a quick glance before turning back to his painting. His voice was smoothly agreeable when he spoke. Only a tightening of his jawline, a flash in the depth of the black eyes, told Stevie that her words had had any effect on him.

"I'm sorry I can't offer you a soap-box," he said. "It would go splendidly with your somewhat aggressive tirade. But I'm afraid you'll have to run away now and find someone else to reform. I'm allergic to interfering and bossy-minded females!"

With serene unconcern Charles started to mix up fresh colours.

Stevie turned on her heel. She walked away across the sands at a breakneck pace that would have been a run if she hadn't clung so desperately to the last shreds of her dignity.

Stevie was out of sight and earshot of Charles before she began to slow down. She felt quite breathless and her heart was thumping quickly, but not entirely because of her swift pace. It was beating an angry tattoo against Charles.

Hateful person. Calling her "interfering" and "bossy-minded."

Stevie stopped dead in her tracks. Taffy paused abruptly too, staring up at her with head cocked and silky ears erect.

"I'm *not*," Stevie protested aloud to Taffy. "I'm *not* bossy or interfering."

Had she been overwhelmingly rude? Implying that Charles was a useless idler? For a moment compunction seized her.

"But he started it," she told Taffy in extenuation. "Telling me I was like—like Miss Wurple. Telling me I was governessy."

And after all, he doesn't *appear* to do any work, Stevie went on to herself. I mean, why is he in Hedburgh all the time? Why doesn't he go to his factory in the Midlands instead of hanging about here? Naturally, people get the wrong impression.

Stevie tilted her chin obstinately as she started to walk on again. If it is a wrong impression, she argued. I doubt it very much.

Despite her resolve not to be affected in any way by the remarks of so inconsequential a person as Charles, Stevie found herself questioning his criticism. When she and Lisa were getting ready to go to bed that night she said suddenly, unexpectedly,

"Lisa, do I seem to you an—an interfering sort of person?"

71

Lisa was lying stretched out on the divan bed, her hands underneath her head. She turned her big grey eyes slowly round to Stevie.

"Interfering? Of course you're not interfering, darling. Whatever gave you that idea?"

Stevie screwed the lid back on a jar of cream.

"I just wondered. I mean, I've always sort of taken charge of things, haven't I? Perhaps to—other people it makes me seem, well"—she hesitated over the word—"bossy?"

Lisa shook her head.

"You're not a scrap bossy. You're capable and self-reliant and you take everything in your stride, just as it comes. You've a sort of courage I haven't got, Stevie." Lisa's voice was wistful. "I wish I had. Everyone admires you. Miss Mabel—David—" She paused before adding, "Keith."

Stevie smiled wryly.

"You're seeing me through the rose-coloured glasses of sisterly love! I don't think anyone admires me. In fact—some—some people would find a great deal to criticize in me."

'What people?" Lisa demanded loyally.

Stevie didn't answer. For some reason she couldn't bring Charles' name into the discussion. Lisa saved her from replying by continuing to speak. She said slowly,

"I saw a photograph of Lois today. She was awfully pretty." Lisa frowned, staring up at the ceiling. "She reminded me of someone."

"Lois?" Stevie echoed. "Oh, you mean Judy's mother? Miss Mabel told me she was a very sweet person. Doesn't it seem sad that poor little Judy can't remember her at all? She was only a year old when her mother died."

Lisa nodded.

"Yes. It's sad for Judy. And for—Keith." She went on staring up at the ceiling with a far-away look in her grey eyes. "Do you think he will ever get over it? I mean—" Her voice was so low Stevie could scarcely hear the last few words. "I mean—enough to marry again?"

Stevie wasn't really thinking as she answered. She shut the drawer of the tall chest and turned towards the bed.

"Oh, I expect so. Some day. After all, he's quite young, isn't he? I know he loved his first wife very deeply, but I think Miss Mabel would like him to marry again. She said something the other day, about not always being able to help run the house and farm herself, and said that she would belong too much to an older generation for Judy, as she grew up."

Lisa turned her head to look at Stevie. Her voice was flat and expressionless.

"I think you'd suit Keith nicely. You get on so well together, and you could help him marvellously with the farm and—and everything. And he likes you. I know he does."

Stevie laughed as if Lisa were joking.

"He likes you too, darling. We'll have to toss up for him." Lisa stared up at the ceiling again.

"No, I wouldn't be any good to Keith. I'm not capable or practical and you need to be strong physically to be a farmer's wife—" Her voice faltered and broke off.

Stevie stared at her across the space between the two beds.

"But, Lisa—" she began in a sudden consternation.

Lisa stretched out a hand and snapped off the bedside lamp.

"I'm tired," she said in a muffled voice. "Let's go to sleep. Good-night, Stevie."

"Good-night, Lisa darling," Stevie answered automatically. She lay in the darkness aware of Lisa's wakefulness in the other bed. She was hesitant to intrude upon her with questioning or remark. "Lisa's fallen in love with Keith," she thought in deepening dismay. "Oh dear, is it really serious? And can anything come of it?"

She was sure that Keith liked Lisa. And she was conscious that something in Lisa's gentle manner softened his reserve and taciturnity in a quite unexpected way. But that his regard was more than the ordinary friendliness of a host and employer she was uncertain.

Stevie's sense of doubt increased. Lisa was right in one thing. A farmer's wife should be someone more robust in constitution than Lisa was; someone more vigorous and active.

It wouldn't really be suitable, she thought. Even though Judy loves Lisa, and from that point of view things would be easy, Lisa ought to marry someone with plenty of money, so that she could live a sheltered easy life, without much care or effort.

Stevie smiled ruefully. Charles Linmer. Now *there* was the sort of rich husband Lisa ought to have. At least—materially speaking. Of course, he was in love with Melanie, but it would be nice if Lisa could meet one of Charles' friends—someone who was as well off and fortunate as he was. Only not so flippant and uncaring.

Stevie turned over and pushed her face into the pillow. She thought wryly. "I suppose Charles would say I was trying to interfere again."

CHAPTER NINE

IT was suddenly summer. Stevie thought that she had never seen anything quite so beautiful as the way this countryside, which a few short weeks ago had seemed bleak and bare, warmed into the unsurpassed richness of May. The hawthorn trees, which had bent in stunted submission away from the chill sea winds, were transformed, overnight it seemed, into a scented glory of cream and crimson. The young larches were like a painted emerald frieze, and across the common the gorse bushes rioted in yellow sweetness. Everywhere there were rhododendrons; heady masses of purple and rose and white and pink. For once, the east winds subdued themselves and the whole coastline shone and sparkled in a symphony of blue and gold.

David was coming to spend the Whitsun holidays at Whitegates, and on top of this news came an invitation to Carole Linmer's twenty-first birthday party on the Whit-Saturday.

"We're all invited," Miss Mabel said, pushing her glasses on and then peering over the rims of them in her invariable fashion. "Gracious me—I can't think what I shall wear. Haven't an evening dress to my name."

Keith frowned, looking up from reading the *Farmer's Weekly*.

"No need for you and me to go, Aunt Mabel. Stevie and Lisa can go and David can go in my place. I'll be only too glad to get out of it."

"We're *all* invited," Miss Mabel repeated with brisk emphasis. "David's included. And I don't know what you mean by saying 'no need for you and me to go.' I *want* to go very much indeed." She shook her head. "I want to see if they've altered the house much since William's time. And you'd better get your dress-suit out of moth-balls, Keith. You're coming along with us."

Keith smiled reluctantly.

"How such a tiny person as you, Aunt Mabel, can combine the force of a bulldozer with the drive of a United States President, I never cease wondering. But you do!" He shrugged. "All right, if I have to. Only I hate dancing."

Stevie and Lisa were not quite in the same predicament as Miss Mabel—without an evening dress to their names. But they both decided that what they had was scarcely adequate for such a grand occasion as a twenty-first birthday dance at the Manor House. Both—for separate reasons that neither admitted to the other—were anxious to appear at their best. Stevie on account of David: Lisa because her thoughts were centred on Keith.

Lisa was extremely clever with her fingers, and she and Stevie got busy with paper patterns and material. Miss Mabel surprised everybody by making the splendid gesture of going off to Norwich in the car one day and returning with a charming and undoubtedly expensive dress of grey lace.

It was an elegant party which finally assembled in Miss Mabel's sitting-room on the Saturday evening. Keith, brown and rugged of face, with his dusty brown hair unwontedly sleeked down, nevertheless looked very distinguished in his newly pressed evening suit. David's fair, handsome good looks had never appeared to better advantage than set off by the well-cut black and white tails. Lisa had made for herself a skirt of floating lilac tulle, worn over one of almost violet taffeta. The bodice was of the same taffeta, and round her slender shoulders she wore a tulle stole. She looked very beautiful—the violet grey eyes deepened by the colour of her dress, her dark hair waving softly about her oval face.

Lisa had helped to chose and make Stevie's dress, insisting on a heavy cream-coloured satin, cut very slim and straight to give Stevie height. It was a simple dress— it's beauty was in the soft lustrous material, which made a perfect setting for Stevie's flawless creamy skin. Lisa, with a stroke of genius, had set Stevie to sewing an edging of gold sequins to the bodice and slim shoulder straps. The light from them seemed to reflect into Stevie's hazel eyes. Above the simple perfection of the cream silk her smooth brown hair shone as sleek and satiny as her dress.

As for Miss Mabel—Stevie and Lisa scarcely recognized her. For all her tininess she looked as regal and upright as a duchess in the cobwebby lace dress, and for once her untidy grey hair was chicly smooth. Crystal and garnet ear-rings shone and sparkled at Miss Mabel's ears and round her neck glittered a superb antique necklace of crystal and garnets. It was difficult to reconcile this splendid vision with the gypsy-like figure who fed the hens in worn corduroys or shabby dungarees.

They clambered into Keith's ancient car to drive the bare quarter of a mile to the Manor House.

The Fates had been kind to Carole. It was a fine May night, unexpectedly warm for that bracing coast. The grounds of the Manor House were hung with fairy lights and Japanese lanterns. The lilt and fall of a dance orchestra could be heard sounding through the double french windows that opened on to the terrace at the side of the house. The long drive was lined with parked cars.

David caught and held Stevie's hand as he helped her out of the car—keeping it in his own as he said,

"You look lovely tonight, Stevie. What a beautiful dress."

Stevie glowed. With pleasure—with happiness—with anticipation of the evening ahead.

Carole was standing beside Mrs. Linmer, waiting to receive her guests and thank them for the presents that they had sent. She looked very pretty in an exquisite dress of crimson faille.

Stevie stiffened involuntarily. Inside the doorway of the long drawing-room, which had been cleared and decorated for the dancing, stood Charles—waiting to say good-evening to his sister's guests. He shook hands with

Miss Mabel and Keith, smiled and half-bowed to Lisa, and turned to face Stevie.

Stevie had made a firm resolve to herself. This evening there should be no opportunity for Charles to criticize her. Nothing she would say or do should bring forth the adjectives "bossy" or "interfering" or "governessy." She had made up her mind to avoid Charles as much as possible, without being obviously impolite, but if she *had* to speak to him she would mask all resentment and disapproval with a pleasant smile and manner.

The effect of all this disconcerted Charles. After their last encounter on the shore he was prepared to greet Stevie with grim courtesy; prepared to meet an aloof and chilly stare in return.

Instead, the girl standing before him in the shimmering cream dress looked up out of shining hazel eyes and smiled suddenly, radiantly. It was a smile that went right under Charles' guard. A smile that seemed to set the seal on some feeling or emotion within him. He thought in amazement,

"But—heavens!—the girl's lovely."

It was gone like a flash. Stevie had moved away. She was just a brown-haired girl in a pretty evening dress. Charles was aware of acknowledging David's reserved greeting. He watched David step forward—bend his head to Stevie—put his arm about her waist as they danced away.

He thought "That was odd," and turned away to find Melanie.

A voice hailed Stevie as the dance finished.

"Hello there! Remember me?"

It was Tony. He and his sister were staying at the Manor House for Carole's party. He quickly claimed Stevie for a dance. As they moved round the floor, chatting like old friends, Stevie also recognized Irving Darrell. He caught her eye and smiled and waved one hand in a circular gesture.

Stevie's smile deepened. So Irving was here too. That should provide a little competition for Charles with Melanie! Although it was difficult to see how Irving, so large and cumbersome and solemn, would provide much competition for Charles.

77

It was difficult indeed to think of *anyone* who would provide much competition for Charles. Stevie, looking over Tony's shoulder, saw him suddenly in the centre of the room dancing with Melanie. She had to admit, reluctantly, that as usual he looked outstandingly handsome. That long lean height and the small well-shaped head—so sleekly blue-black under the glittering chandeliers. Wide shoulders in immaculately cut evening tails. And to crown it all, a superb dancer.

"He *would* be," Stevie thought on a spasm of irritation. "Lounge lizard!"

She had to retract the unspoken words. No one could possibly term Charles a "lounge lizard." He was too emphatically masculine for that. Stevie watched him and Melanie sweep across the room and thought that it would be hard to find a more striking-looking pair.

Tonight Melanie was wearing white. A frosty white dress that shone and sparkled as if she were Hans Andersen's Snow Queen herself. Her only jewellery was a wide diamanté necklace above which the fabulous silver-gilt hair swung in gleaming perfection.

Charles bent his head to speak to Melanie. Melanie's wide blue eyes smiled up at him. Her shining head turned against his shoulder.

"I suppose they're in love with one another," Stevie thought. Well—why not? They were well matched. They had known each other a long time. What could be more suitable?

Stevie looked away quickly as if she did not want to look at them any longer. Her glance fell on David dancing with Carole. How handsome David looked. And how pretty Carole was in her lovely dress. Like a rose. An Etoile de Hollande rose.

Carole had arranged several surprise items for the evening. She was anxious that the occasion should be a real birthday party and not merely a dance. The dancing was therefore interspersed with one or two amusing guessing games and there was a spot waltz with prizes. After the delightful buffet supper Carole clapped her hands and announced an "Upside-Down Scavenger Hunt." Some of the guests looked a trifle puzzled until Carole explained that it was like an ordinary Scavenger Hunt, but that the twenty objects chosen were all deliberately put out of place throughout the house.

"Here are paper and pencils for everyone," she called. "David, will you give them out? Don't touch or move anything, but just make a list of each object as you find it. I'll give you a clue. If you discover an onion in a bowl of fruit, for instance—well, that's the sort of 'upside-down' thing I mean. Does everyone understand?"

Stevie was standing beside David.

"It sounds fun, doesn't it? Though I can't think where we'll begin."

"Will everyone hunt in couples, please," Carole went on. "There are rather a crowd of us and it's much simpler if you do." She pulled a face. "Oh dear—I wish I hadn't arranged it all—now I can't join in!"

Everyone commiserated aloud.

"Oh, poor Carole!"

"What—our hostess not playing. Bad luck."

Carole smiled.

"Any volunteers to keep me company?"

There was an instant outcry from several of the male guests.

Carole put up her hands protestingly.

"I'm in danger of being submerged. I think I'll choose." She looked across to David and Stevie.

"David, I did hear your voice, didn't I? Will you stay with me and help judge the winners?" She smiled at Stevie and then round at Charles who was standing beside her. "Charles hasn't a clue about the game. He was out when mother and I planned it. So you can partner Stevie, Charles."

Stevie stared up at Charles with something like dismay before her glance followed David as he walked over to Carole.

Charles shook his head at her.

"Sorry about that," he said in a low voice. "I'm afraid the Birthday Girl beat you to it." He grinned unexpectedly. *I* didn't hear David's voice, did you? I rather suspect a spot of well-placed cheating in that direction."

She made herself smile.

"At least I won't suspect *you* of cheating. It wouldn't be very likely, would it?"

79

Charles looked at her. He was aware for the second time that evening of Stevie's charm. She wasn't a beautiful girl. Nor a glamorous one. She couldn't hold a candle to Melanie, for instance. But there was something about her that appealed to him in an odd fashion. It wasn't anything to do with looks or clothes, although he admitted that she had a beautiful skin and an attractive figure. Nice hair too, Charles decided. Smooth and brown and shiny. Little girl's hair.

No, it was the way she had of looking at people that he liked. Very straight and direct, with that candid honesty. As if she were a person who—who belonged to herself, Charles thought. A person who had the courage to make decisions and who would stand or fall by them.

He was surprised at this penetrating analysis. He said quickly,

"You never know, I might. Especially when you look as you do at this moment." He lowered his voice to a discreet whisper. "Not a sign of Miss Wurple. What happened to her?"

Stevie refused to be baited. She said lightly,

"I thought you knew. Miss Wurple never attends birthday parties."

Charles laughed out loud.

"So you have a sense of humour! You know, I doubted it when we first me." He lifted a black eyebrow questioningly. "We'd better get cracking. Everyone's rushed forth to scavenge for all they're worth!"

They went out into the hall, where two other couples were peering up and down and round at every available object. In the small sitting-room where Stevie had waited that Saturday morning Keith and Lisa were standing scribbling busily with their pencils. At Charles' entry they stopped writing and walked away with ostentatious carelessness.

Charles glanced about him.

"Must be *something* here. Let's see. Mantelpiece—cabinet—chairs—"

Stevie stared hard at everything. She started to laugh. "Look—there it is!"

She gestured with one hand, but Charles stayed her.

"Quiet! Here comes someone. Where? Oh—!" His black eyes twinkled as he stared at the celery stalks reposing gracefully inside the flower vase, in place of conventional blooms. He whispered, "That's it, all right. Come on—we'll jot it down in the other room, away from these people."

The room he led Stevie into was a long room obviously furnished as a music-room. In the window stood the beautiful grand piano which Stevie had heard Charles playing upon. Here they found another misplaced object. A pile of cookery books in place of the usual volumes of music.

Couples ranged over the entire house—chattering—laughing—scribbling on slips of paper. Breaking off into abrupt silence at the approach of another pair lest they should reveal the presence of a further clue. Stevie found herself whispering and giggling in entirely unexpected harmony with Charles as they discovered such incongruous items as a jar of split peas among the coloured jars of perfumed bath salts in one of the gleaming bathrooms; an inverted saucepan shading a bedside lamp; an old shoelace tying back a brocade curtain.

"We're making progress," Charles announced. "Sixteen objects found. Four more to go."

"Let's try downstairs again—" Stevie began.

"Shh!" Charles said. He caught her hand in his as voices sounded on the landing, and pulled her back behind the door. "Don't let them hear us. They'll know we've found something in here."

They stood quite still and quiet. Stevie was suddenly very aware of Charles' firm hand holding her own. She was conscious of him standing so close beside her—his shoulder pressed tightly against hers. The room was in darkness except for the chink of light shining through from the wide landing. Charles turned his head slowly.

"Foiled!" he whispered. "They've gone into the next room. Wait a second and then we'll slip out."

He was so near Stevie could feel his breath on her hair. In the gloom his dark eyes stared down at her. His handclasp was warm and hard on her own.

For some unaccountable reason her heart gave a great jerk and raced on in double-quick time. Stevie was sure Charles would hear it bumping against him in the tiny constricted space in which they stood together. It was somehow like that moment under the trees the night of Stonham Races. Only more strange, more exciting.

Stevie swallowed. She must speak and break the tension.

"We'd better—" she began uncertainly.

"Shhh!" Charles said again. He put one finger against her lips. He moved his head slowly from side to side, close above Stevie's hair. "You smell delicious," he whispered. They stared at one another through the darkness. Then Charles smiled. He released his hold of her hand.

"Make it snappy," he said. "Before they hear us."

Stevie hurried out of the room, on to the brightly lit landing. She seemed to fly down the wide staircase, passing Tony and a girl named Betty on the way, but scarcely seeming to see them or to hear Tony's cry of,

"Hi—Stevie! Any luck up there?"

Charles followed more slowly after Stevie. He caught her up on the threshold of the big drawing-room.

"What's the hurry?" he enquired lightly.

Stevie couldn't have answered him. She didn't know herself. She was filled with a strange and obscure confusion.

Melanie and Irving came across the room towards her. Melanie's face puckered into a babyish scowl as she said,

"Bill and Anna have won. They found every single one. Irving and I had awfully bad luck. Only eleven." She added. "It was Irving's fault—he's so slow."

Irving gazed down at her with the utmost contrition.

"I'm real sorry, honey. I just don't seem to have got the hang of this game, I guess. It's foxed me completely."

Melanie turned to look up at Charles.

"*You* should have partnered me, Charles. We might have won."

Charles smiled at beautiful sparkling Melanie without speaking.

Admist a lot of laughter and cheering Carole proclaimed the winners of the Upside-Down Scavenger Hunt and presented them each with a prize. The music started up for dancing. The couples who had been partnered in the game started to dance with one another. Irving put his arm about a reluctant Melanie and danced her away.

Charles said,

82

"This is us, Stevie."

His arm encircled her waist. Stevie felt as if she were in some sort of dream. She and Charles danced round in an unbroken silence. She saw Carole dancing with David —her head thrown back as she looked up at him and spoke with animation and vivacity. She was aware of Melanie's glances in Charles' direction as they passed and repassed.

Charles said,

"Carole's doing a heavy line with your young man. You'll have to keep an eye on him."

Stevie felt a sudden unexpected irritation at the remark.

"He's not my young man."

Charles' black eyebrow shot up.

"Really? I thought he seemed a very attentive admirer of yours." He shrugged. "I'm sure he's Carole's unwilling victim, you know. Don't hold tonight's defection against him."

"You're being absurd," Stevie said. Against her intention her voice sounded short ."David and I are merely very good friends." She added somewhat defensively, "He has wonderful qualities. No one could help but admire David."

Charles inclined his head solemnly.

"I agree. He's a thoroughly worthy fellow. Pity he has a tendency to be a bit of a 'stuffed shirt,' as our American friend Irving would say."

All Stevie's good resolutions fled to the four winds.

"David isn't in the least bit a stuffed shirt!" Stevie exclaimed. "But then, I could hardly expect a"—her voice sharpened with contempt—"a rich playboy like you to understand the attitude of a man who is serious and hard-working and ambitious!"

They stared at one another in open dislike. Once again they were at loggerheads.

The music ended with an abrupt clash of cymbals. The sound seemed to express the angry flash of feeling between them.

Charles said in a bitingly even voice,

"Miss Wurple seems to have gatecrashed an entry, doesn't she? Will you excuse me, please," and turning on his heel walked across the floor in the direction of Melanie.

Stevie was thankful to hear David's voice at her shoulder.

"I'm sorry you didn't win the prize, Stevie! What about the next dance?"

CHAPTER TEN

IT was good to be with David again. To dance round in pleasant accord, without that sense of tumult and conflict that Charles engendered in her. No matter how firm Stevie's resolve, the sparks seemed to fly between them! She had meant to remain calm and polite this evening, and ignore any provocaton, but she hadn't succeeded.

That strange moment in the Scavenger Hunt had been the cause. Somehow it had unnerved her, set her on edge in some queer fashion. It was a pity that Carole had requested David to stay behind with her. If that hadn't happened David would have partnered her, Stevie, and all would have been well.

David was referring to the game and Stevie made an effort to concentrate on the conversation.

"Rather childish, don't you think?" he said. "I really wasn't sorry to be left behind to make a little intelligent conversation with Carole instead."

Against her will Stevie had the impression of David's smile seeming slightly superior. She fought the idea. Fought back the echo of Charles' words, "stuffed shirt." How absurd. How unjust. David was the type of person who had a natural dignity and reserve. It wasn't easy for him to abandon constraint and enter wholeheartedly into party games and such-like things.

"I think most people found it fun," Stevie said, unable to bring herself to criticize Carole's party.

David shrugged.

"Most people are very easily amused." His voice was faintly condescending. "Still—I suppose it's a party." He added, "By the way—where's Aunt Mabel got to?"

"She's palying bridge with Mrs. Linmer and Mr. and Mrs. Pollitt," Stevie answered. "They were sitting together in the library a little while ago."

David looked appraisingly about him.

"It's a handsome house, isn't it? I like this room immensely. That row of tall arched windows all down one side and those pale green walls. Adam green, don't they call it?" He clicked his tongue. "Imagine it being left to our young Squire just as it stands. He's certainly been fortunate. And he doesn't seem to have to work very hard for it all, does he?"

Stevie shook her head slowly.

"No, he's at Hedburgh most of the time." For some unaccountable reason she added, as if defending the idleness which she had condemned so openly to Charles himself. "Perhaps he—he has to attend to the estate and the land."

"There's no need for that," David said. "The land is let—to Keith and another farmer. There's only the house and the garden and the acre or two of parkland that surrounds them." He shook his head. "As far as I can see, Linmer's a gentleman of leisure."

Lisa came past, dancing with Irving. Against his broad bulk she looked very slender and fragile. The tulle skirts of her lilac-coloured dress floated out petal-wise as she drifted by.

"Lisa looks very charming tonight," David observed. "Who is it all in aid of? The American fellow?"

Stevie shook her head.

"He's Melanie's admirer." She hesitated, reluctant to betray Lisa's secret, even to David. She said, "Lisa always looks beautiful, no matter what the reason."

"She is pretty," David admitted. He smiled. "And Melanie or nor Melanie, I'm pretty certain Irving's noticed it!"

Stevie turned her head in sudden curiosity and saw Irving beaming down at Lisa through his thick glasses and speaking with, for him, unexpected animation.

She said slowly,

"I don't know, David. Americans are very polite and attentive to all girls. It's probably just his manner."

David shrugged.

"Maybe. But you know, someone like Irving would suit Lisa. America's a woman's country and from what Carole said he's an extremely wealthy chap. His father manufactures chewing-gum! Lisa would have a nice easy life of it if she found someone like Irving."

Stevie didn't answer for a moment. She was filled with a sudden dismay at David's remark. Imagine Lisa in love with an American and perhaps marrying him! Going away to live in America. For ever. Oh—she couldn't bear for them to be parted.

But Irving was in love with Melanie. Carole had told them so. And Lisa—? Stevie's hazel eyes clouded. Unless she was utterly mistaken Lisa was in love with Keith. Not that that helped matters. It wasn't at all suitable. David was right there. Someone like Irving would suit Lisa much better. She glanced across the room and thought, "But I can't imagine Lisa in love with him. He's not at all romantic looking."

That didn't matter. Sometimes plain people had wonderful qualities of mind and spirit. "Handsome is as handsome does," Stevie thought with an unconscious tilt of her chin as she saw the tall black head and the clean-cut profile of Charles moving past.

No matter whom Lisa loves, or where she had to go and live—if that is for her happiness I'll be glad, Stevie vowed.

The evening was nearly over. It ended in a whirlsome riot of "Sir Roger de Coverley" and afterwards everyone singing "For she's a jolly good fellow" to celebrate Carole's birthday.

The last cup of hot punch was drunk and the party from Whitegates set off home.

Keith was silent as usual and Lisa seemed tired. Stevie felt pleasantly sleepy, but Miss Mabel was an alert and wide awake as ever.

"Mrs. Linmer's improved the house. Yes! I didn't think anyone could. I've always loved it just as it was, but her taste is charming." She shook her head sadly. "William let things go a bit towards the end. Natural enough. He wasn't getting any younger and poor Ellen was dead." Miss Mabel's voice brisked up again. "Oh well—nice to think that handsome lad Charles is going to settle down

there. Is he going to marry the pretty fair girl—Megan—
Melissa—whatever her name is—Melanie?"

Keith smiled his rare smile as he opened the front door
for them.

"You're an incorrigible old gossip, Aunt Mabel. If you
don't know, how should we know?"

Miss Mabel turned her bright blue gaze on him.

"Well, it's done *you* good to have an evening out, once
in a while. I'm sure you looked almost handsome dancing
round with Lisa here. What a lovely evening it's been!
Oh—here's Mrs. Kett! Have we kept you up *very* late,
Mrs. Kett? It's good of you to come to sit in with Judy."

Mrs. Kett smiled drowsily. She looked as if she had
just woken up from a sleep by the sitting-room fire, where
the logs still gave out a cosy red glow.

"That's all right, M'm. Been a pleasure. Old Taffy here,
he's kep' me company and Miss Judy's never woke at all."

"I'll walk down the road with you, Mrs. Kett," Keith
said. "And see you safely to your cottage door."

"You reely shouldn't trouble, sir," Mrs. Kett protested,
but Keith would not hear of doing otherwise.

Lisa and Stevie said good-night to Miss Mabel, refusing
an offer of tea. Lisa trailed slowly up the stairs while Miss
Mabel bustled off into the kitchen to brew herself a cup
of tea as if it were six o'clock at night instead of half-past
one in the morning.

David lingered at the foot of the stairs. As Stevie turned
away to follow Lisa he said softly,

"Stevie!"

Stevie paused, one hand on the rail.

"Yes, David?"

He came and stood close beside her, smiling down at
her.

"I just wanted to say, it's been a grand evening and
you—you looked lovely in that dress."

Stevie glanced up to meet his intent stare.

"Why—thank you, David."

He laid his hand over hers as it rested on the balustrade.

"We don't seem to have had much time together on
our own, do we? I thought perhaps—we might go sailing
tomorrow. Over at Bracklesey."

Stevie was aware of the restraining clasp on her fingers. Once before this evening someone had held her hand in his. In a firm warm clasp. And her heart had raced and she had been filled with a most strange confusion and disturbance. She had felt herself tremble with an emotion that was half fear, half excitement.

How queer. Now, with David's hand upon her arm, she was as calm and normal as if she were with Miss Mabel!

She said,

"I'd love to, David, but tomorrow and Monday we shall be awfully busy at the riding school. On account of it being Whitsun weekend Keith is booked up with visitors from the Cliff Hotel and the Ship." She added, "Perhaps we could go in the evening?"

David frowned.

"It's a question of tides. I'll have a word with Keith. If not—we might go on Tuesday. I'm staying on an extra day and you might not be so busy then."

Stevie smiled gently.

"I'd like that. Thank you." She moved her hand as if to pull free from David's hold. "Good-night, David."

David's grip did not loosen. He leaned forward and before Stevie realized, his firm mouth came down on her own.

She remained quite still under his kiss. Still and—what? Expectant? As if a part of her were waiting for something to be released within her. Some feeling—some response?

David let go her hand and stepped back a pace. He said in a voice not quite so steady as usual,

"Good-night, Stevie, my dear."

Stevie hurried quickly up the stairs. She laid the back of her hand against the lips which David had just kissed. She was conscious that David was not the sort of man who went around kissing girls indiscriminately and he had never kissed her before. Or called her "my dear" in quite that tender tone of voice.

Was David in love with her? Or on the way to being so? Am *I* in love with David? Stevie thought. Could I be?

Lisa was in bed. She opened one eye.

"What a time you've been, Stevie. Do hurry. I'm absolutely dead."

"Sorry, darling," Stevie said apologetically. She unzipped the cream dress and hung it carefully up. In a few minutes she was undressed and washed and into bed.

Lisa was asleep. Stevie switched off the light. For a moment or two she lay in the darkness, thinking of David. Remembering his kiss. And mingled with that remembrance was the touch of Charles' finger laid against her lips and the way he had almost rested his face against her hair and breathed in her perfume and said—so softly, "You smell delicious!" And something within her had seemed to leap and surge in the most extraordinary way.

"I can't understand it," Stevie thought in sleepy puzzlement. And puzzling, drowsed off.

CHAPTER ELEVEN

STEVIE was quite right. The next two days she and Keith were extremely busy with the school. The hours seemed to flash by with the various appointments and there seemed scarcely time to snatch lunch or tea in between. All the horses were in use and as fast as some were rested for an hour others had to be saddled to go out on fresh rides.

In consequence, she was not able to enjoy much of David's companionship. He accompanied Stevie on a ride or two, but the horses were needed for clients and Stevie was usually busy with some beginner, so that her attention was divided. In the evening she felt too tired, after all the fresh air and exercise, to do anything more energetic than potter about the farm or walk down the road with David and Keith and Lisa to the Ship Inn for an hour, where David and Keith played darts with some of the holiday people, while Stevie and Lisa watched them and chatted with other guests.

The arrangement for the Tuesday afternoon was a little confused. David was uncertain about the loan of the boat and Stevie was booked up all morning with pupils. A somewhat casual plan was made for Stevie, if she was free by two o'clock, to take some of the horses down to the marshes in order to rest them after their full-time weekend, and then walk from there across the estuary to Bracklesey—tide permitting. David would go by car the long way round earlier on, to see about hiring a boat.

It was half-past two by the time Stevie closed the gate on Sorrel and four other horses and set off down the narrow rutted track edging the marshes in the direction of the muddy sweep of the estuary below. The tide was coming in fairly quickly. If she were to get across and save the necessity of a long walk up to the bridge she would have to hurry. She was wearing a pair of navy blue linen jeans in which she had been able to ride Sorrel bare-back. She rolled them up high above her knees and tied her rope-soled sandals round her neck and set off across.

It was a glorious day. A perfect day to go sailing, Stevie thought, as she lifted her head to look at the expanse of sparkling sea on her right. The sky was blue, almost cloudless. The fresh wind, blowing through her hair, flattening down the grey-green grass of the marshes, seemed scarcely to ruffle the surface of the water.

Stevie picked her way up the mud-bank on the other side and, after drying her feet on the springy grass, pulled on the sandals again and set off down the track to where the dazzling cone of the lighthouse and the cluster of fishermen's cottages denoted Bracklesey.

She looked about her for David, shading her eyes against the brilliant sunlight. There was no sign of his familiar tall fairness. Only an old man in a fisherman's jersey cleaning some nets, and another younger man mending a lobster pot.

Stevie frowned. It really had been an awfully vague arrangement. If only she could see David's car parked somewhere? There were a small blue two-seater and a sports car standing off the cobbled runway, but no glimpse of David's car. She glanced at her watch. Three o'clock. She was late, but surely David would have waited?

There were some boats beached farther along the shore and a man's figure moving among them. She walked a little way towards them in case he was David.

She recognized Charles immediately, although he looked so different in a loose grey sweater and stained navy linen trousers turned up at the knees. There was no mistaking that sleek black head and tanned profile.

It was extraordinary the way they were always running into one another. On a day like this, when she had come to meet David, there was no David to be seen but there was Charles.

Stevie fought the childish impulse to run and went on the few more yards until she was level with him.

Charles saw her. For a second he seemed to stiffen—straightening upright to await Stevie's approach.

"I'm sorry to bother you," Stevie begain in a formally polite voice, "but have you seen David anywhere?"

That quizzical black eyebrow lifted. Charles smiled his mocking smile.

"Superman?" He shook his head. "Not since this morning, I'm afraid."

Stevie frowned. The jibe "Superman," with reference to David, had not gone unmarked, but she had other things on her mind at that moment.

"Do you mean you saw him here this morning?" she asked. "We had an arrangement to meet at Bracklesey—to go sailing. But it was for the afternoon."

"Superman appears to have mixed his dates," Charles said lightly. "Carole brought him home unexpectedly for lunch and I understand he's gone with her, Irving and Melanie, to Norwich."

Stevie stared at him blankly.

"But—are you sure? I mean—" She broke off.

Charles shrugged. His voice was sardonic.

"I told you to keep an eye on him," he remarked. "Young Carole's taken a fancy to him."

Stevie gave him an angry glance before turning on her heel. She had gone six paces when Charles' voice said at her shoulder,

"I'm sorry. Don't go off in a huff. Look—why not come sailing with me? My boat's all ready. I've only been waiting for the tide."

Stevie turned her head reluctantly. Charles' black eyes stared down at her. He smiled with a sudden charm and warmth.

"We might as well console one another. Melanie's forsaken me for Irving—she can't stand boats at any price—

91

and Carole's decoyed David away, so why shouldn't we have an afternoon's sailing? It seems bad luck for you to have to go back now." His dark gaze took in Stevie's blue jeans and the blue striped linen blouse and the navy sweater over her arm. "Especially as you're all dressed ready to go."

Stevie hesitated. Charles seemed suddenly so apologetic and friendly. Ahead of her the blue sea danced and sparkled in the bright May sunshine. The freshing wind tore at her hair and clothes, giving her a quickening sense of zest and excitement.

She nodded quickly.

"All right—I'll come. Thank you. Only—" She paused and shot him a warning look. "No Miss Wurple."

Charles flashed into laughter, his teeth very white against the brown tan of his face.

"No Miss Wurple. I promise! Come on—this way."

Charles' boat, the *Petrel*, was lifting on the incoming tide. He helped Stevie scramble aboard. The mainsail was already hoisted—Charles busied himself with the jib as he said,

"Have you done much sailing?"

Stevie shook her head.

"Very little. I just about know which is fore and which is aft. What kind of a boat is this?"

"It's a sloop," Charles said. He started to cast off. The sails of the boat were rattling and shivering like a flag waving in the breeze. Stevie glanced up at them and Charles caught her look. "She's Bermuda rigged—what they call a jib-headed rig."

He took hold of the leech of the jib and swung it to one side and the bow of the boat turned slowly in the opposite direction. He let go the jib and went aft to take the tiller and sheets in hand.

"All set?" he called. "Better put that sweater on—the wind is strong today."

The boat was soon moving quite fast. In no time at all, it seemed to Stevie, Bracklesey was merely a muddle of white houses under the lee of the lighthouse, and the marshes and coastline were fading into a line of grey-green under the afternoon haze.

Out at sea the wind was strong. Much fresher and stronger than Stevie had expected. But it was wonderful! Brilliant blue sky, and dazzling blue sea, and the whip and crack of white sails in the breeze. Stevie felt her heart lift with the thrill of it as the boat raced and danced across the water. She was unexpectedly grateful to Charles for his offer to take her. She would have hated to miss this experience!

Charles' brown face was intent and absorbed as he manoeuvred the boat. Stevie found herself watching him. He didn't appear to mind that Melanie had gone out with Irving. Was he so sure of her—so sure of himself?

He turned his head unexpectedly and met Stevie's stare. He gave her a friendly grin.

"Enjoying it?" he called.

Stevie smiled.

"It's marvellous."

"Come and sit up here." He looked round at her as she scrambled over. "Like to take the helm for a bit?"

Stevie frowned.

"Can I? I don't understand a thing about sailing."

"Just hold it here—like this. Now let her go. That's right. Watch her come closer to the wind—d'you notice? Wait a second—steady there!" Charles' firm hand came down over her own on the tiller—he held it in a tight grip before letting go. "That's better. This wind is terrifically strong."

Stevie's heart seemed to be pounding with the same force and velocity as the racing seas tearing across the bows. She couldn't speak. She was too much aware of the lean brown face close to her own—the pressure of the wide shoulder against hers.

Her voice sounded breathless as she stammered,

"It—it is—awfully—strong. The wind, I mean."

The boat was cutting across the blue water. The coast-line had dropped out of sight. There was just *Petrel* and Charles and herself in a world of open sea and sky.

"It's an offshore wind and it's rising," Charles said frowningly. "I think I'd better take over, Stevie. These sudden gusts and overblows of wind are much more dangerous than a strong steady breeze."

93

Stevie clutched at the gunwhale as the boat heeled steeply over. She gave a gasp.

"It—it does sort of catch us suddenly."

Charles' smile was reassuring.

"It's all right. I wanted her to do that. It's what we call spilling the wind. The important thing is not to lose headway, because these sudden puffs can come from another direction next time and catch us unawares."

"I wish I could be of more use," Stevie said. She was aware, with Charles, that the wind appeared to be blowing in every direction and that it was certainly becoming more heavy.

Charles put the helm down as the wind seemed to veer to the same side as the mainsail. He said quietly,

"I'm going to reef. Can you hold the helm for me, Stevie? Like this—try to keep her steady. I want to keep the boat headed into the wind all the time, so watch for these sudden gusts. D'you understand?"

Stevie nodded.

"I think so."

Charles' sudden smile flashed.

"Sorry about this. We seem to have caught a spot of heavy weather. Not nervous, are you?"

Stevie, clutching tightly at the helm and aware of a seemingly endless expanse of racing sea around her and a boat that kept threatening to heel right over, swallowed.

"No—of course not."

Charles dropped the jib and then the mainsail. Stevie was too intent upon her own part of the proceedings to watch what he was doing. She heard the sail fall to the side of the boom. Charles struggled to make the reef cringles fast to the tack and clew. Singlehanded he managed somehow to roll the sail up between the boom and the reef band.

Once, during Charles' struggles, the boat seemed to lose headway. He leapt over to Stevie's side and seized the helm and somehow headed *Petrel* into the wind again. He whistled through his teeth.

"Near thing that time! We almost had a knockdown. We shall be all right when I've finished reefing and fixed the storn jib. Can you hang on?"

Stevie nodded breathlessly. She hung on to the helm as best she could until Charles had finished. As he came aft he seemed to stagger with something more than the swift movement of the boat. He fell on to the seat beside Stevie in such abrupt fashion he almost came down on top of her. Stevie turned in amazement to look at him and saw that Charles' mouth was set in a grim white line and his eyes were blinking in an unfocused way at her.

She said quickly,

"Charles?" with a sudden remembrance of the time before when he had stared at her like that. Under the trees the night he had come off his horse.

His hand came out—groping into mid-air, and clutched at her arm. From Stevie's arm his hand slid down to grasp her hand.

"I can't—see a thing," Charles gasped. "Can you—keep her into the wind? She'll be all right now." He said very slowly and carefully, "Won't—point—as—closely, that's all."

"*Charles!*" Stevie cried again.

"Hang on," Charles muttered. "Don't—let—go—the—helm." His head came down on to his knees and his voice broke off.

Stevie went on holding the helm with both hands while her mind whirled at the sudden catastrophe that had befallen them. What had happened to Charles? Had he fainted?—was he ill? The wind tore at them—the boat seemed to plunge into the long steep troughs of the waves before rising to each new and frighteningly windy crest. She didn't know what to do. She had never sailed a boat before. There wasn't a chance for either of them unless Charles would lift his head and look at her and speak and tell her what to do.

Stevie had never been so frightened before in all her life. She hadn't the slightest idea of what she was trying to do, except to hold the boat into the wind, so that the rigged sail remained firm and taut, and somehow, despite everything, the boat kept steerageway.

Charles lifted his head slowly.

"I'm—all right." He stared at her. "Everything's a blur, but it's coming back." The unfocused black eyes gazed past her. "You've been a marvel, Stevie."

"But—what happened?" Stevie whispered. "Are you ill? Is there—a flask, some brandy somewhere?"

Charles shook his head.

"There's no time for that. Or for—explanations. Which way are we heading? Towards land?"

Stevie stared at him in a sort of terror.

"Yes. But—can't you—can't you *see*?"

Charles shook his head.

"Not well enough to be of any use. You'll have to be my eyes, Stevie. It's a question now of getting back as best we can. We'll probably have to tack." He scowled. "Oh, my God!—to be so helpless."

Stevie's heart turned over at the despairing note in his voice. She made herself say very calmly,

"Tack? What does that mean? I'll do whatever you tell me."

Charles' voice was as steady as her own.

"I'll direct you. Tell me which way the hawk is pointing. That's the weather vane set in the masthead. Keep telling me all the time. I can work out then which way the wind lies and in what direction land is. Can you see the shore?"

Stevie screwed her eyes up, trying to determine if the hazy blur on the horizon was land or not.

"Yes—I think so."

"Good girl. Now listen—this is going to be dashed tricky, but somehow we've got to try and do it. We've got to keep crossing the path of the wind and yet make headway all the time. I can see dimly, enough to use the helm if you'll keep repeating to me all the time the position of the hawk."

It didn't seem possible. How on earth could a temporarily blinded man and a girl who didn't know the first thing about boats succeed in sailing to safety, under the treble handicap of a heavy offshore wind?

It wasn't possible—but it was achieved. Slowly but surely the blur of land ahead edged into clarity. Became the green-topped cliffs of Hedburgh; levelled to the grey of the marshes, and Stevie could see the silver arm of the estuary reaching inland, and there was the lighthouse again.

All speech had been reduced to the mechanical repetition of the weather vane's position—to answering Charles' sudden questions as to direction.

As they came in to the coast the wind dropped a little. The boat nosed more sluggishly ahead. For the first time Stevie turned to look at Charles.

"How are you feeling?" she asked gently.

Charles rubbed one hand across his eyes.

"Better." He gave her a sudden crooked smile. "You've turned into a girl again instead of a white-faced blur! Sorry about all this, Stevie. It's enough to make a landlubber of you for life." The dark eyes stared directly at her. "And before I forget—thanks. For saving both our lives."

Stevie felt herself colour.

"But I didn't do anything. Only what you told me to."

Charles shook his head.

"You did a bit more than that. You hung on like grim death and kept us steady, and you didn't flap or panic." He paused before adding slowly, "Somehow, I don't think you ever would." A sudden awkwardness crept into his manner. He looked away as he went on. "I feel I owe you a bit of an explanation, Stevie. I hate talking about the whole business, but this is the second time you've been up against this sort of thing. You must be wondering what on earth's got into me."

"I imagine it's some sort of—faintness. Or illness," Stevie said in a low voice.

Charles stared at the coastline ahead.

"Not quite that. It's—look—you're the only one I've ever told—except my mother. Even Carole doesn't know. I don't need to ask you not to repeat it, do I?"

Stevie shook her head.

"Of course not. But—if you'd rather not? I mean—it doesn't matter, Charles. You don't have to explain anything to me. I shall understand—and forget—about the whole thing."

Charles turned his head to look at her.

"I believe you would. You know—you're rather an exceptional person, Stevie. Different from the ordinary run of girls. Perhaps that's why it's really quite easy for me to tell you. The fact of the matter is—I had a smash up.

In the last motor trials when I was driving one of our sports cars. It happened in the South of France. I was in hospital for a couple of months—fractured wrist and broken collar bone. Also concussion. It—affected my eyes. Some pressure on one of the nerves. I get bad vision at times and I've had a black-out or two. That's what happened just now. And what happened to me that night on the way home from Stonham. I didn't come off the horse in the ordinary way. Everything had been dimming for the last few miles—I dropped behind and you caught me up. Then you dashed away and I was about to follow when—a black curtain came down on me." He broke off abruptly.

Stevie hardly knew what to say. She was filled with an inexplicable emotion. Distress—sympathy—compassion. A sense of compunction at her unthinking behaviour towards Charles the night he spoke of. And underneath it all some stronger, fiercer emotion crystallizing into awareness.

She said quietly,

"I'm sorry, Charles. I wish I'd known. And I wish I could help in some way." She stared at him gravely. "It it—are you getting better?"

Charles smiled. A queer, twisted smile. He said,

"That's the trouble, I'm afraid. Unless the pressure on the nerves of the eyes clears up it seems I'm likely to go blind."

Stevie stared at him in a sort of blank horror. A cold hand seemed to clutch at her heart.

"*Blind!*" she whispered. "Oh *no*, Charles. It isn't— possible. You—of all people—to be blinded."

Charles looked at her.

"Why not me—of all people?"

Stevie couldn't answer. She couldn't say to him, "Not you, Charles. With your charm and good looks. With your strength and superb physique and your wealth and good fortune. Surely you were meant to be favoured by the gods."

She said instead,

"Can't they—the doctors—specialists—cant' they do something to help?"

"I'm hoping so," Charles answered. "I'm under a man called Walderbroke—the top eye-man in Harley Street.

I've been ordered six months' complete rest. No reading, no writing, no eye-strain of any kind. I'm supposed to laze around for a while and then there's the possibility of an operation." He gave Stevie a rueful smile. "I'm afraid the lazing around part got in your hair a bit, didn't it? Quite understandably."

Stevie didn't know how to answer him. She felt horrified at the recollection of the way she had jibed at Charles. Baited him—sneered at him. And all the time he had been under doctor's orders; struggling against the threat of disaster that hung over him.

"Please forgive me. I—how could I realize?"

"Forget it," Charles said lightly. "But I couldn't explain and I'm afraid I got riled in return. You see, the reason I haven't told anyone except my mother is because of Melanie. I haven't even told Carole, in case she let it slip to her. It would distress Melanie unbearably. She's so gay and lighthearted and she has a horror of illness and ugliness and all the morbid and depressing things in life. I expect you've guessed I'm—by way of being very much in love with her? I haven't been able to do anything about it under the circumstances. I've got to wait until this thing is licked before I can ask her to marry me." He shrugged. "If it licks me—that's that. At least Melanie won't be tied up to a blind husband."

Stevie had the sensation of walking on a tight-rope over a deep chasm. It was there below her. Waiting for her to slip and fall—down, down, into a hopeless abyss. If only she could get over to the other side she would be all right. She knew she would.

It was the most extraordinary feeling. A sort of mental hallucination.

She looked at Charles and she thought of how she had misjudged him. His flippancy and his gaiety—that attitude of nonchalance and uncaringness which had so irritated her. They had been only a mask. A cloak of gallantry to hide the fear and despondency that must have very often seized him when he comtemplated the future.

Charles said,

"Well—we made it. A few more minutes and we'll be safe ashore."

Stevie looked up at the rising beach and the white cottages of Bracklesey. She hadn't realized how near in to shore they had come.

Charles turned his head.

"I don't like to think of where I'd be now if you hadn't come along this afternoon. Down in Davy Jones' locker, maybe." He smiled. "You're by way of being my guardian angel, Stevie."

It was that warm steady smile that did it. The friendly look in Charles' dark eyes. They were on land again. They were safe. The danger was all over.

But not for Stevie. It was as if with that smile the imaginary tight-rope snapped. She seemed to go hurtling down into the pictured chasm. Into desolation and despair and hopeless heartbreak.

I love Charles, she thought. There wasn't a doubt in her. Anywhere. She was wide open to the impact that came crashing in upon her. The conflict of emotion had crystallized into this one inescapable fact. Her love—impossible, unattainable, quite without hope of return—for Charles.

I think I loved him all along, Stevie thought desperately. Right from the beginning. I've tried to disapprove of him, but there's nothing left to disapprove of. Only to admire and respect. He's been so courageous and so gallant. So thoughtful for Melanie.

Melanie. He's in love with Melanie and he's going to marry Melanie. If—if he gets over this. And please God, he will, Stevie prayed.

It was terrible to be praying for something that would mean the end of all your hopes and dreams.

"Look, lend a hand," Charles broke in reproachfully. "You're just standing about day-dreaming now you're on terra firma again. Belay there!"

"I'm sorry!" Stevie started forward to obey Charles. She was too self-conscious to meet his glance. She helped him to moor *Petrel* safely and then they walked slowly up the cobbled runway together.

Charles paused beside the blue car Stevie had seen earlier on.

"I came over in Carole's little car. They used Irving's. Can you——" He hesitated. "Could you drive, Stevie?"

Stevie was only too thankful to do something. To have to concentrate on a definite task.

"I think so. If you'll show me the gears."

Charles looked somewhat shamefaced as he slid in beside her.

"I don't like to risk running someone down. Everything's still a bit foggy." He glanced at her and Stevie, without looking up, was aware of his smile. "I take it you're still with me? I can sort of see you, but you sound very far away."

He put a hand out to one of Stevie's resting on the steering wheel. "I'm dim at making pretty speeches, but— thanks again, Stevie. I don't know why, but I find you a very easy person to talk to. D'you think now we've sort of cleared the air a bit we might get around to being— friends? Good friends."

Stevie felt herself tremble at Charles' touch. She had to make a tremendous effort to steady the awful surge of emotion that swept through her. The bitter-sweet awareness that for some reason or other Charles liked her. In a friendly platonic way.

Her voice was quite steady.

"I should like to be—just that, Charles."

"Good." He started to explain the gears.

Stevie's foot came down on the accelerator as she changed into top. The car leapt forward along the open road.

Charles whistled.

"Hey—steady there!" But Stevie scarcely heard him. She had to drive fast. She had to keep moving. She didn't want to stop or to hear Charles' voice or to have to talk. She wanted to race away from the pain and the unhappiness that threatened to engulf her. She loved Charles and Charles loved Melanie and if he didn't get better and marry Melanie the reason would be that he had gone blind. What an awful muddle life was, Stevie thought.

She eased her foot off the accelerator. It wasn't fair to Charles to go tearing along the road like this. He probably still felt queer and giddy. His vision hadn't cleared yet. He'd just said so.

Oh, *Charles!* Stevie's heart whispered. Poor Brave darling Charles.

The last thing in the world Charles wanted was her pity. Or anyone else's. It wasn't his way. That was why, by the very effort he made not to seem ill or handicapped, he was apt to make other people underestimate all he had gone through.

The car dropped to a steady twenty-five miles an hour. Stevie turned her head and distress weighted her heart again as she saw the rigid lines of Charles' mouth and the greenish pallor under the tanned skin. Aware of her glance, he relaxed a little and gave her a twisted smile.

"That's better. I'd hate to think we've escaped a watery grave only to end up a couple of road casualties!"

I can't bear it when you go on joking, Stevie thought miserably. Making light of everything. Once it annoyed and irritated me. Now it almost breaks my heart.

The tall iron gates of the Manor House lay ahead of them. Stevie swung the car round and went slowly up the wide drive. She stopped at the foot of the shallow steps.

"Thanks," Charles said. He slid out of the car. "Ottoway will run it round to the garage later. Come on in, Stevie. I'll get someone to rustle us up some tea."

Stevie hesitated.

"Perhaps—your mother—" she began.

Charles shook his head.

"Mother will love you to stay. And—it will help me, Stevie. I don't want to flap her and she's got eyes like a hawk. Having you around will ease the situation tremendously."

"Then I'd love some tea," Stevie answered gently.

CHAPTER TWELVE

MRS. LINMER was coming down the curved staircase as they stepped into the hall.

"Tea?" she echoed in answer to Charles' query. "Of course, dear. Ring the bell for Parsons. You're very late, but it doesn't matter." The dark eyes seemed to regard Charles with a sudden sharp scrutiny.

Charles moved away.

"We had rather a set-to with the wind and were delayed. Stevie here helped enormously. This way, Stevie."

"Are you a sailing enthusiast, Miss Hylton?" Mrs. Linmer asked as they sat down in the pretty little sitting-room that led off the music-room.

Stevie shook her head.

"I think it's great fun. But I haven't done very much sailing."

Mrs. Linmer's smile was abstracted. She seemed scarcely to hear Stevie's reply. She said slowly,

"Charles—you look tired. I hope—" She hesitated.

She was interrupted by the sound of footsteps and voices in the hall. Parsons, entering with a laden tea-tray, stood aside for Carole and Melanie to come into the room, followed by Irving and David.

"We've had tea," Carole stated. "Hello, Stevie." She turned to her brother. "Did you go sailing, Charles?"

"Yes. It turned a spot choppy, though. Stevie came along with me."

Stevie was aware of David's guilty look. He came and sat down in a chair beside her, and said in a low voice,

"Did you—er—go over to Bracklesey then, Stevie? I went out myself, but I couldn't see the man who had the boat for hire, and I was coming back to tell you when I met Carole. It was rather difficult—I was sort of involved in lunch—" He glanced at Stevie in the midst of this somewhat confused preamble. "I'm really awfully sorry, Stevie. I ought to have let you know."

Stevie was too engrossed in her own thoughts of Charles to pay much attention to David's excuses.

"It's all right, David. Don't worry. It was only a vague arrangement, anyhow." She gave him an absent-minded smile.

Melanie spoke, her voice dropping clear and smooth into the circle of conversation.

"Of course, Charles asked *me* to go sailing with him, but I wouldn't. It just bores me to death. I expect *you* found it a pleasant change from those horsey sessions of yours, Stevie."

Her smile was pleasant enough, but it only curved the full red mouth: it didn't reach Melanie's eyes. There was a sharpness in the look that rested on Stevie.

"It was most enjoyable," Stevie answered. She was aware of some sense of antagonism between herself and the other girl, and for a moment wondered if the others present were also conscious of it. She chided herself instantly.

It's my fault. Melanie doesn't mean anything. You'd better face it, Stevie, she told herself, you're just plain—jealous. You're resentful of Melanie and you're looking for faults in her because she's the girl whom Charles loves. But if Charles cares for her, she must be just as lovely a person inside as she is outside.

I want her to be, Stevie's silent voice affirmed. I want her to be warm and loving and kind. I want her to love Charles with all her heart, if that is what *he* wants. And to help him through all this awful trouble of his.

Oppression and sadness were like a heavy weight upon her. She gave an involuntary sigh, which caused David to turn and look at her.

He said persistently, "I'd no intention of missing our date this afternoon. I meant to let you know there was no boat available before you left—I'm sorry I forgot, Stevie."

Stevie shook her head quickly.

"It doesn't matter, David. It wasn't a definite date."

"I thought you seemed annoyed with me. You're so quiet. Something is on your mind," David said in an aggrieved voice, suddenly piqued by Stevie's very real indifference.

"It's nothing to do with you—with us." Stevie managed a reassuring smile.

She glanced at her watch and saw that it was a quarter to six. They would be milking now at Whitegates. If she hurried she might be able to lend a hand. And if she and David left, the party would probably disperse and Charles might be able to go and rest. She glanced at him and saw the strained expression on his lean face.

As she said good-bye Carole broke in.

"Oh—Stevie—Irving has an inviataion for us all to go over to a concert and dance at the big American camp at Ellingham. Some friends of his are stationed there. Could you come?" Her glance went past Stevie. She smiled. "David promised to come if you are able to, and we'd love Lisa and Keith to join us too."

Stevie hesitated, remembering that David had to return to London in the morning.

"Do you mean—tonight?" she asked slowly.

Melanie answered for Carole.

"Yes—won't it be fun?" She slid her arm through Charles. "You too, Charles."

Charles' dark eyes encountered Stevie's quick glance of concern, before they smiled down at Melanie. He shook his head.

"Sorry, darling. I don't think I can manage tonight."

Melanie frowned.

"What nonsense! Of course you can. We've no other arrangements made."

Charles took her hand in his.

"I'd rather not—tonight, poppet. Some other time."

Melanie freed her hand and arm in quick annoyance.

"I want to go *tonight*, Charles. Really—you're awfully stuffy these days. I can't think what's got into you. You used to be ready for absolutely anything."

Charles seemed to waver, reluctant to disappoint Melanie, yet obviously in no fit state to drive miles to some gay and noisy camp concert.

Stevie turned to Carole. She thought—Perhaps if we don't go either the whole project will fall through. She said, with a pleasant firmness,

"I'm awfully sorry, Carole, but I'm afraid I shan't be able to go. And—I doubt if Lisa and Keith are free tonight—Keith has a riding appointment at seven." This was true, and it was more than probable that he would want Stevie to give him a hand at the riding school. She turned to Mrs. Linmer. "Thank you so much for tea, Mrs. Linmer. Please forgive my hurrying away."

David's face fell. It was apparent that he had hoped to make one of the Manor House party for the evening.

Mrs. Linmer held out her hand. The dark eyes regarding Stevie held a curious expression of—gratitude—relief?

"Good-bye, Stevie. I'm so pleased Charles brought you home for tea. Come again soon, my dear." She turned to Carole. "As Stevie and her sister and Keith and David are unable to go with you to the camp concert, I suggest you postpone your visit until you can all go together." She smiled at Irving. "I'm sure Irving's friends won't mind?"

Irving inclined his head.

"Surely, Mrs. Linmer. Whatever you say. I guess you'd like us all to stay home tonight with you—huh?" He gave her his slow smile. "Suits me vurry well. I've got a pile of correspondence to wade through."

Melanie pouted. She had set her heart on going over to the camp and being fêted and admired by a crowd of handsome American Air Force officers. She had looked forward to going dancing—a thing she adored.

Mrs. Linmer was her hostess and had expressed an indirect wish for them to remain at home, so there was very little Melanie could do. But she couldn't refrain from looking up at Irving out of reproachful blue eyes and saying,

"Why, Irving, it was your idea for us to go over to Ellingham. And now you say you'd rather write letters!"

"Now, honey," Irving protested in his serious way, "I only suggested going out to Ellingham on account of the way *you* said you'd like to go dancing, and I recollected my friend Drew had mentioned this concert and dance to me earlier on."

Melanie turned away, shrugging her shoulders.

"Goodness—don't go on about it so. I'm sure I don't care one way or another." She yawned, covering her mouth with a small white hand. "I feel as if I'm covered with all the dust of Norfolk from the drive this afternoon, so I'm going off to bath and change." She moved to the door. "Bye, everyone."

As she brushed past Stevie she gave her a hard little stare for a long moment. A stare that held a sort of vindictive challenge in its pale blue depths. As if she said aloud to Stevie, "You didn't want us to go to Ellingham, did you? I suppose because *you* couldn't come. It's through you my plans for the evening are spoiled. Be careful I don't spoil some of yours next time!"

CHAPTER THIRTEEN

THE door closed behind Melanie. Stevie gazed after her in blank dismay.

She thought with distress, Why—Melanie dislikes me. Really dislikes me. She thought I was interfering. And I was, in a way. I hoped that because we couldn't all go along to the concert the idea would fall through and it would save Charles' face. I was trying to help him. If only he had been able to tell Melanie the truth she would understand. She wouldn't expect the same of him as she does now.

It was all very difficult. Even David was looking at her as if she were an intentional spoil-sport.

She had said good-bye to Mrs. Linmer. It was more than time to go. She turned and said good-bye to the others. Charles was last. He walked into the hall with her and down the steps, frowning as he did so.

"I'm afraid Melanie's definitely off me. I wish—I wish I could explain why I seem such a crab at times." He shook his head. "It would be a terrible shock to her. I don't think she'd get over it."

Stevie gave him a puzzled glance.

"How do you mean?"

Charles shrugged.

"It's complicated. Melanie's such a darling. She's had a wonderfully happy life. An only child—doting parents— bags of money. She's been cherished and protected— cushioned against all the snags of life. I've never wanted her to be any different." He gave Stevie a wry smile. "It sounds a bit silly, but you know the rhyme?—'Goldilocks, Goldilocks, wilt thou be mine? Thou shalt not wash dishes nor yet feed the swine.' Well, that's rather how I feel about Melanie. I want her to go on being happy in *her* kind of way. No shadows—no snags. I'v known her all my life, you know. There was a gap during the war when we were both growing up. She came back to England to stay with us after it, and she was—as she is now. She knocked me out cold, I must admit. I think she—sort of went for me a bit too. Then I had this smash-up and everything's been short-circuited. But if I told Melanie why, the whole relationship would be thrown out of gear. She'd have to be fussing around me and I'd be the dependent one." He shook his head.

"It's not in character, is it? What you'd call bad casting."

Stevie was silent. She agreed with Charles. It wasn't quite in character. And yet—and yet? Wasn't loving sharing? Wasn't it a sort of partnership—a pooling of good and bad and no obligation or sacrifice on either side? Not when two people loved one another utterly—equally?

She thought sadly, I love you, Charles. With all my heart. If I were the girl you cared for I'd want to stand shoulder to shoulder with you. And perhaps, because I'm the sort of person I am, whose life has already held the snags and shadows you speak of, you wouldn't mind it being like that. You'd never feel I had to be shielded and cherished.

But then, Stevie amended with a pang of bitterness, I'm not the kind of girl you ever would fall in love with. I'm too ordinary, too down-to-earth. Too much one of the crowd. The everyday crowd who have to live and work and plan and budget and face sickness and grief and deal with their problems, and manage to hope and dream and always, no matter what, carry on.

"It's only for a month or two more," Charles went on. "Then I hope I'll know—one way or the other. After the operation, I'll try to make it up to Melanie then."

Pity filled Stevie. Pity for Charles, and following it, a quick resentment. Make it up to Melanie! Because he couldn't fall in with her every plan, do all she wished him to? It made Stevie's heart ache.

David came up to them.

"My car's round the back, Stevie. I left it there earlier on. Good-bye, Charles. Expect I'll see you next time I'm down. I return to London tomorrow."

Charles shook him by the hand.

"Yes. We'll look forward to seeing you again. Good-bye. And—good-night, Stevie."

His smile seemed warmer, more friendly, as it lingered on Stevie. He gave them both a brief salute and went back into the house.

Neither Stevie nor David spoke very much on the brief run back to Whitegates. Stevie was lost in a confusion of thought. She had a longing to get away from everyone. To think over all the day's happenings. The shattering discovery that she was in love with Charles; the terrible problem that faced Charles and his difficult relationship with Melanie, whom he loved. And yet—she didn't want to have to think at all.

She made milking an excuse and plunged into the midst of the work, persuading Miss Mabel to return to the house to resume supper preparations. In cap, overall and gumboots Stevie dashed about the yard, helping Sam, the farm-hand. They finished the milking between them and Stevie assisted with the cleaning and sterilizing, and finally set to vigorously brushing up the yard, while Sam took the cows back to the meadow.

Lisa came out to stand and stare at her in amazement.

"Darling—what energy! I can't bear to see you. Are you trying to make up for lost time?" She added, "How did you enjoy your afternoon with David?"

Stevie stood the broom up in the shed corner and pulled the milking cap off her hair. She said over her shoulder as she walked away,

"David went to Norwich with Carole and Melanie and Irving. We missed each other."

Lisa came up behind her.

"Oh, what a shame! Then you never went sailing and had the walk over to Bracklesey for nothing?"

Stevie shook her head.

"I went sailing. With—with Charles." She explained briefly what had happened.

"How extraordinary," was Lisa's comment. "I think it was too bad of David not to let you know. But I'm sure it was Carole's fault—don't blame David too much. Poor Stevie—I can see you've had a horrid afternoon."

Stevie, hanging up the white milking overall on a hook, turned in surprise.

"What makes you say that?"

Lisa smiled sympathetically.

"You look hot and tired and very preoccupied. And whenever you have one of these furious bursts of energy and start turning the world upside down, I know there's something on your mind."

Stevie walked towards the house.

"You're imagining things, Lisa." She added matter-of-factly, "I wonder where Keith is. He may want me to go out this evening on a ride."

Keith was in the small room he used as an office, making out Milk Marketing Board returns. He shook his head at Stevie's question.

"No, I shan't need you, Stevie. I'm only taking Mr. Elliott, from the hotel. You go off and enjoy yourself with David."

With David. Everyone persisted in linking her with David. It was natural enough. It was through David she and Lisa had come here in the first instance.

Stevie pulled off the navy jeans and linen blouse and threw a dressing-gown over her shoulders. As she walked into the bathroom, with its sloping white ceiling and gay black and white curtains and fittings, she thought incredulously, "It's only a few days ago that David kissed me. Only a little while ago that I thought I was falling in love with him."

What happened when you fell in love with someone and it was quite hopeless from the start? You couldn't go on like that for ever, but how would you stop? How would you be able to get over it so that you could start afresh with someone else?

It wasn't possible. I *couldn't* stop loving Charles, Stevie thought desperately. But I must. I must try, because it's all absolutely useless and people don't pine away and die of despair in this day and age. You just have to go on and make something of your life.

The echo of Keith's words came back—With David. Could you make something of your life with David? Supposing that he loved you. Would it be fair to him?

Whatever happens I've got to try and wipe the image of Charles out of my heart. I've got to stop thinking about him, remembering him.

It was one thing to resolve. Quite another to go down, washed and changed, and on the surface of things cool and calm-looking enough, to eat supper. To join in con-

versation and jokes and topics that were suddenly as unreal and remote as conversation about Mars.

Miss Mabel's bright blue eyes, which Stevie sometimes
thought could see round corners and through brick walls,
surveyed her.

"You look tired, Stevie." She smiled with unexpected
softness. "I think that's the first time I've ever made that
remark to you, isn't it? It's usually reserved for Lisa. But
tonight Lisa looks blooming and you have shadows beneath your eyes. No—I don't want any help with the
washing-up. I don't want any help with anything. David
—take her out into the garden and make her sit down for
once."

There was nothing for it but to walk with David into
the garden, filled with evening sunshine.

Instinctively Stevie led the way towards the herb garden. There was a worn sundial here that had long ceased
to record any passing hours, and a rickety wooden seat.
Dwarf box edged the paths and wound in and out like a
tiny maze, separating the patches of sage and rosemary,
balm, lemon thyme, mint, parsley, tarragon, chives, basil
and lavender. Catmint and marigolds splashed blue and
gold amidst the more sober foliage of the herbs. It was a
fragrant spot. Sheltered, filled with sunshine, it held an
atmosphere of soothing peace and quiet.

Stevie sat down on the wooden seat, stifling the sudden
sigh of heartache. David stood beside her, fumbling for
his pipe.

Stevie put out a hand of protest.

"Please, David. Not here. Do you mind? It—it spoils
all the lovely herby scents and smells."

David gave her a surprised glance. He sat down on
the seat.

"You're not still annoyed with me, are you?"

Stevie looked round at him. She said gently,

"I haven't been annoyed with you at all, David. You're
imagining things."

"You don't seem yourself somehow. I feel it's my fault.
Because of this afternoon."

Stevie smiled.

"You've got a guilty conscience, David. That's what's
wrong."

111

David smiled in sudden relief.

"I believe I have. When I met Carole I shouldn't have gone back to the Manor House with her like that. Not before going on to Whitegates first and leaving a message for you. But I only went for a drink in the first place. Carole said, 'Come back and have a sherry before lunch' and I thought I'd plenty of time. And then they persuaded me to stay for lunch. And the next thing was I'd agreed to go to Norwich." He frowned. "I believe I was a bit flattered. It's a gorgeous house and Carole's—very attractive."

"I understand," Stevie said. "Don't worry about it, David." She reached a hand out to the straggling bush growing beside the seat and broke off a sprig. "It doesn't matter."

David's blue eyes were serious on her own.

"Don't say that, Stevie. I'd rather it mattered. I want to feel that what I say and do," he smiled ruefully, "even if sometimes it's the wrong thing, counts with you."

Stevie crumbled the stiff green leaves in her fingers, smelling the aromatic scent of them. She thought, "Rosemary—that's for remembrance." Remembrance of Charles and his black eyes smiling at her and the feel of his shoulder against hers as he helped her steer the boat, and the touch of his hand, and his mouth setting in rigid lines of strain, and his casual manner and the way he made so light of a heavy burden. *Charles*—Stevie thought.

"When I say Carole's attractive, I mean, generally speaking," David went on, as if in explanation. "To me, she isn't and never will be as attractive as you are, Stevie." He said, on a rising note of surprise, "*Stevie?*"

Stevie turned her head.

"Yes, of course. Thank you," she said quickly, apologetically.

His arm came round her waist.

"Please, Stevie. May I kiss you again."

He didn't wait for her assent or for Stevie to express the sudden sense of protest that rose in her. His hold tightened—his face came close to hers.

A late bee hummed in the lavender close by. It rose to zoom heavily through the golden air on its homeward way. Stevie could almost hear the sound of its wings as it sailed over their heads. She thought detachedly, It can never be more than this with David and me. A kiss that doesn't mean anything, an embrace that doesn't stir. I love Charles and I can never love anyone else, and that is all there is to it.

She freed herself, saying gently,

"I'm sorry, David. Please—I'd rather not."

David stared down at her out of eyes very blue and intense.

"Stevie—you know how I feel about you. In a little while my job will be better. I'm set for some promotion and then I shall be in a position to—to make things clear and definite." He broke off as if uncertain how to go on.

Stevie put a hand out.

"Don't say any more, David. I'd prefer you not to. Let's leave everything—just the way it is."

David's expression was an odd mixture of disappointment and relief.

"You know I go back to London in the morning," he said.

"I hope to come down again for a weekend quite soon, but in any case, I've arranged to have my two weeks' summer holiday at Whitegates. I spoke to Aunt Mabel and Keith about it. Keith said it would be quite convenient to them, and as it's in July I'll be able to help with harvesting and so on." He paused, as if waiting for Stevie to make some comment.

"It will be fun. To have you here, David," was all Stevie could think of to say.

"Perhaps we can talk about this again," David went on slowly. "Everything should be settled at work by then——"

Stevie didn't answer. July seemed suddenly a long way ahead. Time to be lived through. Time to be endured. And the time too when Charles' six months might be nearly up and he would be faced with the verdict upon his eyesight. She stood up.

"Let's go back to the house, David. It's your last evening. I'm sure Keith and Miss Mabel want to see something of you, too."

CHAPTER FOURTEEN

WHITEGATES settled down to an after-the-holiday lull. It was welcome enough, but after the rush and excitement of the Whitsun weekend, with the occasion of Carole's birthday dance and the influx of holiday visitors causing matters at the riding school to be somewhat hectic, life seemed very much of an anticlimax.

Especially so to Stevie. She found herself longing for an encounter with Charles. To see him again—to speak with him. She found herself checking the horses to their slowest walking pace as she took them up or down the lane where she had first met Charles. Unconsciously hoping that his big grey car would come roaring along from the direction of the Manor House. When the tide was out she made it an excuse to ride along the shore, as if she might find Charles there, seated at his easel painting, as she had discovered him that day in April.

There was no sign of Charles. It was extraordinary how, when she had been seeking to avoid him because of that queer antagonism she had felt for him, he had appeared at every turn! And now, when she longed so much to see him again, he seemed to have evaporated into thin air.

Perhaps he was ill? Perhaps he was away? There was no one to answer these questions, and if there had been, Stevie would have felt unable to ask them outright.

As the last few days of May drifted into June the Whitegates household seemed to spend more and more of their leisure time on the shore. This was on Judy's account. She adored building sand castles and paddling about in the shallow blue waves, and her one daily demand was, "Can we go on the sands today?" When school was over she raced down to the beach, and Lisa, her invariable companion, packed a Thermos of tea and some sandwiches and accompanied her, with Taffy making a joyous third. Stevie took to walking down after milking was over and as the days warmed into true summer the three of them essayed a brief, teeth-chattering bathe or two from the small beach hut which stood under the lee of the cliff and which belonged to the farm.

One Sunday Judy invited along two small friends and Miss Mabel joined them, sitting on the soft sand outside the hut as unconventionally dressed as ever in an incongruous dirndl skirt patterned with all the colours of the rainbow, and bare legs in rope sandals stretched out in front of her as she knitted briskly away at a pair of socks for Keith.

It was a golden day. The tide was exactly right for swimming. The children scrambled out of their clothes on the beach, while Stevie and Lisa undressed more decorously inside the hut. Then, hand in hand, the five of them went racing across the ridged sands into the dancing blue sea.

It was cold, as the first shock of that east coast ocean always seemed to be, but in a second or two they were hardened to it, and while the children jumped and splashed and screamed with laughter and delight at the water's edge, Stevie and Lisa swam more purposefully around.

There were a couple or so other people bathing and neither of them took any notice of the man swimming towards them until Keith's voice said at Lisa's side,

"You might have waited for me!"

Lisa gasped—whether with surprise or pleasure, or the mere effect of a wave threatening to submerge her, no one could say.

"We didn't know you were coming. You said at dinner time you wouldn't be able to."

Keith smiled, wiping spray away from his brown face as he trod water.

"It was too good a day to miss. I left my form-filling and accounts for another time. I hope you packed enough tea. We're going to need it after all this. Come on—I'll race you to the boat out there."

Keith's powerful crawl soon left Stevie and Lisa panting in his wake. Lisa was not a strong swimmer and Stevie, although competent, was out of practice. They plodded slowly on to the boat and hung on its side to get their breath before the swim back. A weather-beaten face grinned down at the three of them.

"Reckon you ain't in trainin' for swimmin' the Channel."

Stevie smiled.

"We certainly aren't." She added, "I hope we haven't scared all your fish away."

The old man broke into a hoarse guffaw.

"Won't beat the catch oi got now—will oi? Two marmaids and a gurt whale! Hee—hee—hee."

The boat rocked with his merriment. After a few more of such sallies Keith pushed gently off the side and the two girls followed him. This time Keith swam more slowly, keeping alongside Lisa, and Stevie drew ahead.

Judy was waiting for her.

"You said you'd hold me—so's I could float. Peter can float all by himself. Look!"

Stevie supported Judy to enable her to be suspended on the water. Peter floated on his own account, crying boastfully, "Look at me! Look at me! Floating *properly*," while his sister Jean, who was only five, rolled about in two inches of water, perfectly content not to compete.

The children were reluctant to leave the water, but Stevie felt that the warm day and the bright sunshine might tend to make them overdo it, and she said at last,

"We must get dressed now. It's nearly tea-time."

She looked over her shoulder and saw Lisa and Keith swimming around and laughing together. She was reluctant to break in on their obviously happy companionship. She thought,

"Lisa will see we've gone and follow in a few minutes."
She said aloud,

"Come on—let's see who reaches the hut first."

Miss Mabel received their dripping onslaught with calm, holding out towels and wraps.

"Come along, Jean. I'll rub you down."

Peter dried himself. Stevie rubbed Judy and hurried the two little girls into the hut, so that they could dress as quickly as possible, while Peter dived behind the hut to struggle into his shirt and shorts.

Miss Mabel began unpacking tea things. She glanced away to the sparkling band of water.

"How long are those two going to be?"

Stevie came out of the hut, fastening up the skirt of her cotton dress. She frowned.

"Lisa ought to come in. She'll catch cold." She moved forward to give them a hail, when she saw that Keith seemed to be supporting Lisa in the water. She gave an ejaculation and ran towards the sea. She reached the water's edge as Keith, half holding, half carrying Lisa, came splashing through the shallow waves to the shore.

Lisa's face looked white and pinched, but she smiled at Stevie.

"Don't w-worry," she chattered, "it's just a h-horrible attack of c-cramp. No, I'm all right, Stevie. Don't hold me—you'll g-get so wet."

Stevie caught the blue-white hands in hers, clasping them between her own.

"Oh, darling—you stayed in too long. Let Keith help you over to the hut and I'll rub you down and get you a hot drink."

Keith lifted Lisa up in his arms.

"It was my fault. I didn't realize." He looked down at her with a glance in which anxiety was mingled with some other, softer emotion. "Hang on," he said and loped quickly across the sands towards Miss Mabel and the children. Stevie came on behind them, and when Keith deposited Lisa gently on her feet she hurried her sister into the hut, where she rubbed Lisa's slender body down as briskly as she could with a sun-warmed towel.

"You are an ass, you know," Stevie remonstrated fondly. "It's only your second swim of the season, and you've stayed in over an hour."

"W-we were having s-such fun," Lisa protested.

Miss Mabel poked her thin brown face round the door.

"Put this extra woolly on, child. I don't need it. Tea's all ready."

The colour came back into Lisa's face as she sipped the piping hot tea that Miss Mabel had brewed on the Primus stove. Everyone was wildly hungry and in no time at all sausage rolls, tomato sandwiches, cheese scones, gingerbread, fruit tarts and chocolate biscuits had disappeared.

117

Peter and Judy were all set for a game of rounders and besought their elders to play. Miss Mabel put down her knitting.

"My goodness—not much chance to digest that meal! All right, Peter. Stevie, will you play too? What about Lisa?"

Keith answered for Lisa. He put out a big brown hand to ease the cardigan more closely over slim shoulders, saying,

"I don't thing Lisa should play. We'll have a walk along the shore instead with Taffy."

Stevie turned her head to watch them walk away together. For the first time she had a definite conviction that Keith was attracted to her sister. She had glimpsed the expression on his face a little while back. There had been a protective tenderness, a loving regard in that look.

"Come *on*," Peter urged. "We want you to field with Jean and Miss Mabel."

Stevie moved tractably in the direction Peter waved her to. She thought how surprisingly young and active Miss Mabel looked as she raced across the sand after the ball Judy had hit, dirndl skirt flying about her agile legs, her razor-edge profile biscuit brown above the white linen blouse she wore, her eyes as azure as the blue sea beyond.

Judy was caught and plump little Jean went in to bat. Her hits were more spasmodic and did not extend very far. There was a lot of slithering about on the sand and much laughter. Stevie, in a momentary lull, glanced to where the two figures walked in the golden distance. Two figures paddling in the rim of sea, somehow very close together. She screwed up her eyes. Were they hand in hand? For a moment it had seemed like it.

The ball bounced towards her. She sprang forward and was immersed in the game once more.

CHAPTER FIFTEEN

IT was past seven by the time they had packed up the tea things and tidied and locked the hut up. The sun, sinking in the west, had moved from their patch of shore and the cliffs cast a long shadow over the rumpled sand

and the stout fortifications of a castle Keith had helped the children to build.

They straggled up the narrow path, carrying towels and swimming suits and baskets and water-bottles, a weary, untidy, but immeasurably happy party. Keith walked beside Lisa with Judy on Lisa's other side. Miss Mabel and Peter conversed seriously together. Stevie brought up the rear with Jean, whose tired little legs plodded at snail's pace along the rough road.

A car hooted. A long-drawn-out, somehow familiar, hoot that went ta-ra-ra-rum, Stevie's heart seemed to leap like a Jack-in-a-box out of its placid lethargy. She turned her head at the same time as the others in front did. Everyone halted in their stride.

The big grey car pulled up alongside and Charles smiled at them.

"So this is where you've got to! We called at the farm but it was deserted. Most unusual, even for Sunday."

Stevie stood a little in the background, looking at Charles through thick brown lashes that endeavoured to hide her eager awareness of him. He looked very well. There was no sign of tiredness or strain on the lean brown face. He seemed gay and happy. As happy as the smiling Melanie beside him.

"Did you want to see me?" Keith asked Charles.

Charles lifted one hand from the steering wheel in a careless gesture.

"It was on Melanie's account actually. She wants to carry on with some more riding lessons." He turned his head. "Don't you, poppet?"

Melanie gave him a charmingly sweet smile before addressing Keith.

"Yes—I want to learn to jump. Charles and I hope to hunt next winter, and although I know that's ages away, I thought if I started now I'd be sure to be really proficient by then." She turned a beguiling glance on Keith. "Wouldn't I?"

Keith nodded politely.

"You should be."

"I'll come along tomorrow morning," Melanie stated in her autocratic way. "It will be convenient, of course?"

Keith inclined his head.

"We'll fit you in," he said with slow courtesy.

Melanie smiled.

"Lovely!" She surveyed them all and there was amusement in her glance. Stevie saw that Melanie was dressed as if for dinner. She was wearing a little cape of silver-blue platinum mink, delicately soft and silky, over a buttercup yellow organdie dress. Crescent-shaped gold ear-rings gleamed in her small ears. Above the exquisitely tinted oval of face her smooth hair shone in the evening sunshine. A drift of expensive Jacques Fath "Canasta" perfume floated towards the group standing in the roadway.

Stevie was suddenly very conscious of their combined effect upon Melanie. Of their hot, sunburned faces and bare legs and arms, gritty with sand and dried salt water. She was aware of Miss Mabel's lumpy dirndl skirt and wild grey hair; of Lisa wearing her red cardigan with Miss Mabel's bright yellow one tied shawl-like over her shoulders. Of the three children in crumpled dresses and shorts, and lastly, of herself standing there in the washed-out cotton frock, with her usually smooth hair blown into disarray and not a speck of make-up or lipstick on her skin.

Melanie's blue eyes rested thoughtfully on Stevie before she spoke to Charles.

"Come along, darling. We mustn't hold up the caravan." She added for their information, "Charles and I have a dinner date over at Lady Colwall's and we mustn't be late. Good-bye, everyone."

Charles smiled. A friendly smile that embraced them all with impartiality.

"Cheer-oh, folk."

The throbbing engine roared into life again. The car leapt forward and was gone down the road in a flash.

A hot sticky hand tugged at Stevie's.

"I's tired."

She lifted Jean up against her shoulder.

"You're nearly home, darling." She pressed her face against Jean's round cheek and thought,

He didn't look at me. Not at me. But why should he? I didn't expect him to. He looked well. I'm glad he looked well.

Stevie's heart felt as heavy as the little figure in her arms. He's happy with Melanie. They're going to hunt next winter. Perhaps when they're married, Melanie means. She's so beautiful. And so perfectly dressed. That lovely fur cape and the dress under it. She has—everything.

I don't envy her any of her possessions, Stevie thought sadly. i only envy her Charles' love.

And that I could never have. Even if he didn't love Melanie he wouldn't care for me. He'd love some other girl like Melanie. Rich and beautiful and successful.

She sighed so heavily that Jean opened big blue eyes of surprise to stare up at her. And Stevie felt as if all the simple happiness of the golden day had fallen into shadow.

Peter and his small sister were returned safely to their parents on the way back to Whitegates. In a few minutes the rest of the party had reached the farmhouse. Judy was bundled off to bed while Stevie and Lisa, after tidying and freshening themselves, went downstairs to help prepare supper.

Lisa was very quiet as she spread Marmite on cream crackers and poured milk into a beaker for Judy's tray. Stevie, although immersed in her own wistful thoughts, became aware of her silence.

"Tired?" she asked as she shook lettuce out in a muslin cloth.

Lisa turned on her with unexpected sharpness.

"No, I'm *not* tired. Why does everyone think I'm always tired or ill or something? Do I have to be fussed and fidgeted over all the time?"

Stevie stared at her sister.

"I'm sorry. I thought perhaps—I thought you'd overdone things a bit swimming."

"I simply had cramp," Lisa retorted. "If *you* had cramp, or—or Keith had, no one would bother. But because it's *me*—" Her grey eyes filled with tears. She broke off.

Stevie felt only amazement at Lisa's outburst.

"But you know you have to take care, darling—" she began.

"If you knew how sick I am of it all!" Lisa cried. "Of being delicate and cosseted. It—it spoils every-

121

thing. I can't—" She broke off and, seizing Judy's supper tray, rushed out of the kitchen.

Stevie stared after her in bewilderment. What had gone wrong? Lisa had seemed so happy with Keith this afternoon and Keith had seemed to show very plainly his attachment for her. They had obviously not quarrelled. Then why had she flown off at such a tangent just now?

Miss Mabel came into the kitchen, her untidy coxcomb of silvery hair smoothed down, a clover-coloured linen dress on in place of the skirt and blouse.

"Lisa seems in a hurry to give Judy her supper. She raced past me on the stairs like a whirlwind. Is something the matter?"

Stevie shook her head.

"I don't know. She seemed a little upset over something."

Miss Mabel nodded her head as she spooned coffe into the percolator.

"Perhaps she's tired."

Stevie couldn't suppress a wry smile.

"That's part of the trouble. She said we all fuss over her too much. She seems to be awfully tired of being told she's tired!"

Miss Mabel smiled too.

"It's difficult, isn't it? Yet what are we to do? Lisa isn't very robust and she does tire quickly. Naturally, we all try to take care of her."

"I know," Stevie agreed. "And you've been wonderful, Miss Mabel. No one could possibly have been kinder. Lisa's a different person since she came here."

Miss Mabel switched on the hot plate. She looked thoughtful.

"Something's worrying the child. Do you think she wants us all to feel she's perfectly fit and strong? But why?" She gave Stevie a sharp look. "You're not thinking of leaving us, are you? Not tired of the farm life and your job?"

"Oh *no*," Stevie cried fervently. "We love it here." She went on impulsively, "We only wish we could stay for ever."

"My dear child, as far as I'm concerned you can!" Miss Mabel smiled. "Your company's meant a great deal to

122

me. Always wanted daughters. Wanted sons too. Three of each would have been nice!" She shrugged her thin shoulders. "Never even found a husband." She turned her head to look at Stevie. "But you and Lisa will find them. You'll marry and have your own homes."

"I shall never marry," Stevie said quickly. "Lisa—perhaps—" She hesitated.

Miss Mabel gave her a quizzical smile.

"Never? What about David? He's a cautious enough young man, but I should think by this time he's given some indication as to how he feels about you."

Stevie hoped that the glow of sunburn hid her sudden blush.

"I—I like David very much," was all she could bring herself to say. She was thankful that Miss Mabel's keen eyes had failed to detect where her true feelings lay. That was her secret. The hidden ache and longing for Charles that filled her heart.

Miss Mabel shook her head.

"I've a feeling that both of you are bound up with Whitegates."

She said no more, but walked into the larder and came out carrying some cold veal and ham pie.

Later that evening, however, she made a further reference to Lisa. Lisa had gone upstairs and Stevie was just preparing to follow. Keith was in his small study-cum-office dealing with the forms he had neglected to finish earlier on.

Miss Mabel opened a drawer in the old walnut bureau.

"You've seen a photograph of Lois, haven't you?"

Stevie nodded.

"Yes. The one in Judy's bedroom. She looks very sweet. And very pretty."

Miss Mabel shuffled through some snapshots.

"It's not a true likeness. Too much of the studio portrait about it. These are Lois as she really was."

Stevie gazed down at the smiling girl sitting on the low wall, standing beside a pony and trap, kneeling on the grass holding a Labrador puppy. She was puzzled at Miss Mabel's sudden introduction of the subject, and puzzled, too, by something else. A sense of having seen this oval face before, these big gentle eyes.

"They're alike, aren't they?" Miss Mabel said.

Stevie turned her head.

"They?"

"Lois and Lisa. Can't you see it? Keith sees it. More plainly every day."

Stevie's glance returned to the snapshots. Yes—they were alike. The same graceful build and dark hair; the same eyes and smile.

She said slowly, "There is a resemblance."

Miss Mabel took the snaps from her and replaced them in the drawer. She closed it up.

"I think Keith is in love with Lisa. Oh, not just because they look a little alike. But because they're the same type. It's nat. al enough. People always follow a pattern."

Stevie was too intrigued by the latter part of Miss Mabel's statement to express wonder at something she herself was already conscious of.

"A pattern?" she repeated.

"Just a theory of mine," Miss Mabel answered. "I've seen it happen again and again. A man is attracted by one type of girl and that's the sort of girl who always will attract him. Or vice versa. If the marriage ends—they lose their partner or it fails in some way and they separate, one thing you can be sure of: In a few years' time they'll be trying all over again—with the same type of person."

Stevie felt oddly depressed. For a moment she wasn't thinking of Lisa and Keith. She was thinking sadly that if Miss Mabel was right then Charles would never be in the least likely to fall in love with someone like her, Stevie. If Melanie refused him, he would automatically fall in love again with someone identical to her.

But I know that, Stevie assured herself. I said so—only this evening. And it's fantastic to have any kind of hope in your heart. Melanie isn't in the least likely to refuse Charles—unless—unless—She paused, thinking of the shadow that hung over him. No—it can't happen. I'd a million times rather he married ten Melanies than that he should lose his eyesight.

She was recalled to present matters by Miss Mabel saying,

"You're very serious, Stevie. Don't you think it would be a good thing?"

Stevie hesitated.

"I'm—not sure, Miss Mabel. Not on Keith's account—he's tremendously nice. But on Lisa's. Is she—would she make a suitable farmer's wife? Is she strong enough?"

They stared at one another. Miss Mabel said slowly,

"Maybe Lisa's wondering that too? It could account for her behaviour tonight. Silly girl. She mustn't let that worry her. Keith's not a poor man—they could afford sufficient help around the house when I'm pensioned off!" She smiled. "Judy loves her. Now that *is* important. Well, it isn't for us to settle these sort of affairs. Off to bed with you, Stevie. Good-night."

"Good-night, Miss Mabel."

Lisa was having a bath. Stevie slowly undressed, thinking over Miss Mabel's conversation. And hearing the echo of her words, "I've a feeling that both of you are bound up with Whitegates," repeat themselves again and again before she fell asleep.

CHAPTER SIXTEEN

THE next morning Melanie appeared for her jumping lessons. Stevie was dreading to see Charles and yet longing for him to bring Melanie in his car, and so perhaps linger a little while and talk with them all. And with her, Stevie. But Carole ran Melanie down and the morning after Melanie walked down on her own.

The following two mornings Melanie missed coming, and then on the Friday when she was due to appear Keith asked Stevie to take the lesson.

"Just let her go over the low jumps in the school a few times. To give her confidence. Don't raise them higher than I've fixed them." He added, "I want to run over to the horse sale at Stanton—I hear there's some good stuff coming up."

Stevie's heart leapt as she heard a car turning into the yard, but when she forced herself to look round, it was to see Irving clambering out of his big Buick to open the door for Melanie.

He grinned at Stevie.

"Say, can I hang around for the hour? I guess Miss Mabel'll find a job for me if I go ask her, huh?"

Melanie eyed Stevie with disfavour.

"Oh dear—isn't Keith here? I have great faith in him— he's such an expert."

It wasn't encouraging, but Stevie managed to smile pleasantly as she brought Shannon forward for Melanie to ride. They waved good-bye to Irving and trotted off in the direction of the school.

"Isn't Irving a scream?" Melanie said. "He absolutely haunts me, you know. He's supposed to be over here on business, but it's just an excuse to follow me over to England. And he comes trailing down to Hedburgh and poor Aunt Margaret has to keep inviting him to stay. Charles, of course, gets frantically jealous." She smiled. "Not that he need be, I tell him. Irving's such a ponderous, puddingy old thing, while Charles is quite definitely the answer to the maiden's prayer." Her blue eyes stared intently round at Stevie. "Don't you agree?"

Stevie bent her head to adjust her stirrup leather.

"He is—very handsome," she answered in an even voice. "Shall we go over the bar first?"

The bar was laid flat on the ground, not raised at all, and this was taken at the trot so that pupil and horse gained confidence together as they went over it. After a round or two Stevie instructed Melanie to hold the reins loosely in one hand and to hold the front of the saddle with the other while she went over the first low jumps.

"That's fine. Don't forget to lean forward as Shannon takes off, and tighten your grip. Don't point your toes down."

Melanie succeeded in taking the jumps without mishap. She said breathlessly as they rested in between,

"I feel rather noble enduring all this on Charles' account. I hope he appreciates my efforts."

"You mean, Charles asked you to learn?" Stevie could not resist enquiring.

Melanie pushed a stray tendril of golden hair back under her hat.

"Well—not exactly asked. He said he hoped to hunt next winter, and I thought it sounded fun. I should hate to be one of those dreary women who peer at everything out of car windows. I like my entertainment first-hand, don't you? Besides, I think if you've got to live some of the time in the country, you should be able to join in the life going on there." She turned her smoke-blue eyes on Stevie. "Charles has to live here a certain part of the year under his godfather's will."

"Yes," Stevie answered in a low voice. And if Charles lived here, of course Melanie would do, too. It was all sealed and settled in Melanie's eyes. She was already planning her life.

"I wanted Charles to teach me to jump, but he said Carole's horse Diamond was too difficult for me to ride. I can't understand why he hasn't bought some horses of his own. He probably will have done by next winter. He had a car smash last year, you know, and that put things back a bit."

"Yes—I heard he'd had an accident," Stevie said. "Perhaps he still—still feels some of the effects," she added slowly.

"Oh no," Melanie said airily. "He's quite all right again now. But it seems to have left him rather lazy and un-bothered." She frowned. "I hope he peps up again soon. He used to be an absolute dare-devil." The frown changed to a smile. "I adore that streak in him—it's sort of exciting. I'll have to see if it's still there one of these days."

Stevie couldn't bear to listen to any more. She said quickly,

"Shall we go round again? Let your hands go easily with Shannon's head. Try not to pull or jerk the horse's mouth."

At last the lesson was over, to their mutual relief. Melanie, becasue she soon wearied of concentrated effort; Stevie, because she had a dread of listening to further conversation and confidences.

There was no sign of Irving.

"I expect he's in the house," Stevie said. "Will you come through, Melanie?"

They went into the house and discovered Irving sitting on a stool in the kitchen talking to Lisa. Between his knees was a colander and on the table in front of him a basket of peas.

He smiled.

"My time's not been wasted, you see. I've been shuckin' peas for Lisa here, and enjoying a real good gossip. Makes me feel like I was back home in Mom's kitchen in Colorado."

Melanie wrinkled her nose up in kittenish scorn.

"Don't sound so dismally homespun, Irving. It's most putting-off. I'm ready," she stated flatly.

Irving tipped a handful of peas into the colander and stood it on the table. "Sure hate not to finish 'em for you, Lisa honey."

Melanie's blue eyes flicked at his casual endearment. She said,

"Oh, come on, Irving," and turned away.

At the same moment there came a tremendous noise from the yard outside. A clattering and banging, mingled with a horse's neighing that rose almost to a scream. For a moment the four of them were arrested in amazement.

"Say—what in heaven's name is going on out there?" Irving ejaculated. They rushed to the back door and halted abruptly.

In the stable yard, kicking, plunging, rearing, bucking, was a black tornado of a horse. He had evidently just come out of the van which was backing swiftly away through the gates. Holding on to the reins with all his not inconsiderable strength was Keith. For a moment he seemed to hang suspended off the ground as the great horse reared almost upright. Then, as it crashed down, he regained a foothold and with grim determination pulled at the reins, speaking as quietly and soothingly as he could to the horse.

The watchers in the doorway held their breath. They dared not take a step forward lest they startle the animal afresh. Irving whispered,

"Guess if I hadn't parked that bus of mine right over the far side he'd pound it to tintacks."

Gradually Keith gained some mastery over the horse. He succeeded in guiding it into a loose-box, where he slipped the rein and freed it, closing the door upon it with incredible swiftness. His speed was necessary. Form inside the stable came the most awful sound of clattering hooves and splintering wood and a wild neighing. Then quiet, broken only by restless pawings and scrapings.

Irving stepped forward.

"Say—what've you got there? The original bucking bronco? We sure had a ringside seat of the rodeo from here."

Keith mopped his forehead.

"Phew!" he whistled. "That horse is practically jet-propelled." He wiped his wet hands, scarred red with the pull and pressure of the reins, on a handkerchief.

Lisa was staring at him with apprehensive grey eyes.

"Oh, Keith—I was so terrified." She shuddered. "A horse like that is mad and dangerous."

"Have you bought him?" Stevie asked.

Keith nodded.

"Dirt cheap—he's supposed to be a bad 'un. But he's a magnificent brute really. That set of tantrums he's just indulged in is merely on account of the ride here in the horse van. It was worse getting him in the thing than out." He smiled slowly. "But I had some help the other end. He'll settle down all right and I intend to re-train him to better ways."

"I reckon you've got a full-time job on," Irving commented.

Melanie had said nothing, only paled with fright.

"Well, *I* certainly shouldn't care to ride him," she remarked.

In a few minutes Melanie and Irving left and Lisa returned to the house, while Stevie went on to give another riding lesson.

CHAPTER SEVENTEEN

KEITH re-named the new horse "Demon". He had been christened "Roy", but as he did not respond to any name whatsoever, Keith said he would name him afresh and that "Demon" certainly suited him better than the original appellation.

At first only Keith had any dealings with the horse. Demon tolerated him, allowing him to enter the stable with food and water while he watched him with a rolling white eye, sometimes turning on Keith with a flashing hoof or tossing his head with bared teeth as if about to attack him. But gradually he stood more still at Keith's approach, and the time came when Keith was able to mount him and ride off some of his ferocious energy, so that the animal returned sweating and wearied to his stable to assume a further docility.

Slowly, Demon grew accustomed to Stevie too, so that when Keith was away she was able, with great wariness, to deal with him. Apparently, from what Keith said, the horse had undergone much ill-treatment and this had turned him into the fierce, bad-tempered brute he appeared to be on first arrival.

Certainly he was a superb creature, with a black coat that began to shine like rich satin under the better food and care, and with mighty shoulders and powerful flanks that bespoke a hunter of the finest class.

Melanie was still coming for her jumping lessons. Sometimes Keith instructed her but frequently Stevie took over, and she had to endure Melanie's constant references to Charles, and her proprietorial ways and manners when he put in an appearance.

It wasn't easy. Sometimes it was a form of refined torture that set poor Stevie's nerves on edge, but there was nothing she could do about it, and it came to the point when she felt she would rather not set eyes on Charles than have to go on suffering such misery. Sometimes, indeed, she wondered if Melanie did it on purpose. As if she had a suspicion of Stevie's feelings and was determined to let her know that she, Melanie, was the one Charles had chosen.

But she did know that. Better, perhaps, than Melanie, who was unaware of the reason for Charles' procrastination. Perhaps that was the reason Melanie was anxious to assert her dominion over him, Stevie thought. She has to reassure herself of Charles' love. She doesn't know why he is unable to ask her to marry him.

Whatever the reason, one afternoon Melanie had been particularly trying.

"When I'm married, I hope to have a flat in town," she informed Stevie. "Hedburgh's quite amusing in the summer, but I'm sure it's deadly in the winter. Of course, we shall be here for the hunting and for shooting parties and all that. Charles wasn't living here last winter. Were you? Oh no, of course, you were working in London. Did you like it? I should hate a job in an office."

She quickly changed the subject.

"I expect we'll go to the States for our honeymoon. Poor old Irving—won't he be shattered? Charles hasn't been to America yet. He's been all over Europe, of course. Racing and all that."

It went on and on. Melanie and Charles and Charles and Melanie until Stevie had to bite her lip to stop herself crying aloud,

"Please. Stop. I don't want to hear any more. I can't bear it."

At last the lesson was over, and as they came into the stable yard, there was Charles' big grey car and Charles himself sliding out of the front seat, while Carole sat smiling at them from the back.

Charles' smile included Stevie.

"Well, how did things go?"

Melanie shrugged.

"It's getting rather dull. Too much repetition. I don't think I shall come any more." She looked at Charles. "I'll wait until you buy yourself a string of hunters, darling, and then I'll come and ride them for you."

Charles didn't answer. Carole leaned forward over his shoulder and addressed Stevie.

"When is David coming down again? Irving's friend at Ellingham asked us over to another concert, and I thought it would be fun to go when he was here."

"I think he is coming down on Friday," Stevie answered slowly. "His holiday starts next week."

Charles grinned at her.

"Careful! She's after Superman. Don't say I didn't warn you."

Carole smiled gaily at Stevie.

"Stevie doesn't mind. Do you, Stevie? Every girl for herself in these hard times!"

Stevie had to smile back as she shook her head.

"I'm sure David would like to go," was all she said.

They were interrupted by the appearance of Keith riding through the gateway on Demon. He slid off the horse's back and tied him up, saying,

"Don't bother with him, Stevie. We're going out again soon." He walked past the group by the car. "Good afternoon, everyone. Sorry I can't stop just now, but I've an urgent telephone call to make."

Melanie stared across to Demon.

"Gracious! is that the horse that nearly kicked the place to pieces a few weeks ago?"

Stevie nodded.

"Yes. He's coming on very well."

Melanie turned to Charles.

"You should have seen him—he was positively murderous. No one could get near him."

"No one can now," Stevie said. "Keith's the only one who can ride him. He looks quiet enough at the moment, but he's as wild as ever underneath."

Melanie tossed her head slightly.

"Charles could ride him—couldn't you, Charles?"

"I doubt it, if what Stevie says is true. Though he certainly seems quite tractable from here."

"Stevie exaggerates," Melanie said. "I agree he was a fiend the day he arrived here, but he seems thoroughly broken in now." She moved towards the horse before Stevie could warn her. "Hello, Demon. You're friendly now really, aren't you?"

Demon suddenly reared and plunged, tugging at the fastened rein and baring his teeth, so that Melanie leapt back behind the others in quick fright.

Stevie said nervously, "Please don't go near. He's better left alone. Strangers excite him."

Melanie came forward a pace between them. She stared up at Charles.

"Why don't you ride him, Charles? I dare you."

Charles met the speculative glance from the kitten-blue eyes. He said slowly,

"Don't be silly Melanie. You heard what Stevie said."

Melanie laughed—a hard little laugh.

"Don't tell me you're afraid. I wouldn't have believed it of you, Charles. One of the things I've always admired most about you is your courage." She half turned away. "You're growing weak-kneed in your old age."

Stevie's heart seemed to miss a beat. Melanie surely couldn't mean what she said. To dare Charles to ride Demon! Whatever happened he mustn't. Demon was beyond control. And with Charles' eye trouble—the handicap of a sudden blackout—it was a challenge impossible for him to accept. She said quickly,

"Keith will be coming back any moment. I think we ought to move away. Our voices are upsetting Demon."

What she said was true. Either the excited clamour of their voices, or Melanie's approach a few moments ago, had set him off, and he was tossing his head incessantly and pulling against the reins in an attempt to free himself.

Melanie looked first at Stevie and then at Charles.

"Stevie's nervous for you, Charles. Why don't you do something about it? Ride the horse. Then I'll know you aren't nervous as well."

Melanie and Charles stared at one another. It was as if Melanie were seeking in some way to demonstrate her power over him. Trying to make him prove himself to her, and at the same time prove his love for her.

Charles' mouth was set in a firm line. His black eyes were opaque and expressionless as he looked back at Melanie.

Before he could make any further move the disaster happened. Demon snapped one of the reins and with a wild plunge was free. He kicked and bucked and then tossed his head high as if deciding whether to bolt through the gate, jump over the car, or plunge into their midst.

Melanie screamed. Carole ducked on to the floor of the car. Charles sprang forward with a shout, but Stevie was ahead of him. She had to be. She had to get Demon before Charles did.

Demon knew her and he hesitated, rolling his eyes and stepping sideways. How she ever managed it, Stevie never knew. He was a tall horse and difficult to mount at the best of times. Love and fear seemed to lend her wings. Somehow, incredibly, she clutched at bridle and saddle and with one breathless spring landed in the saddle. She seized the two unbroken reins and pulled hard at Demon's mouth.

There was no stopping Demon now. Bit between his teeth, Stevie's weight and hold no more than feather-light against his massive strength, he was away. Through the gate and down the lane. A second gate leading to Keith's fields stood open and he swerved through this and pounded on at a breakneck speed. Stevie let him have his head. It was useless to waste her strength in a vain endeavour to check him. The only thing to do was to sit down in the saddle as tightly and as firmly as she could and try to stay on.

Mangolds went flying through the air as Demon's thundering hooves tore across them. A hedge of thorn barred the way to the next field, but the horse took it in his stride as if it were merely the bar lying on the ground of the riding school. He was over and down the other side and across the half-cut crop of lucerne while Stevie was still getting her breath.

It was hard going. Demon had an enormous stride that seemed to bounce Stevie about like a ship at sea. But she hung on. Gradually his pace slackened and at last, when she pulled at his head, he answered by swerving in the direction she had indicated. Another quarter of an hour's riding and she had him across the fields and headed in the direction of the stable.

Stevie felt exhausted. As if she had just ridden a Grand National winner round Aintree. She had difficulty in getting her breath, and her arms and shoulders ached with the efforts she had made. But Demon's mad gallop had eased to a canter and when they reached the lane he slackened to a trot.

She saw the grey car approaching, but it pulled in to the side before Demon had time to resent the noise of the engine. Charles got out and came towards her.

He said in a curt voice,

"For God's sake, get down."

Stevie's gasp was almost audible. She didn't know what she had expected of Charles. A flippant, "So you're all in one piece!" or a normal, "Thank goodness you didn't

have an accident," or even a brief, "Thank you, Stevie."
She certainly had not expected this white-lipped rage, this
look of cold anger.

She hesitated.

"I can't—Demon might—"

"*Get down.* I'll cope with the brute."

He seized the bridle and Stevie slid off the horse's
back. The drop seemed interminable and as she landed
on her feet, her knees seemed to sag under her and give
way. She lurched towards Charles. His free arm came
about her waist. He held her tightly against his side while
with the other hand he restrained Demon. Stevie's face
was against his shoulder. In the midst of the faintness that
misted consciousness she was aware of warmth and delight. Charles was here. Holding her within the fold of his
arm.

His voice said,

"You utter little fool. You might have been killed."

Smelling salts or sal volatile couldn't have been more
reviving than the icy chill of Charles' voice. Stevie freed
herself—stepped back a pace.

She stammered,

"I had to—I did it—" She broke off, unable to go on.

"I know. You did it for me. Very noble. But when I
want a girl to break her neck on my account, I'll ask her
to."

Stevie met his black stare. She was too unutterably
weary to feel indignation. But she wanted Charles to
understand. She said,

"But Melanie—I thought she would—you would—"

Charles' black eyebrow shot up in its characteristic way.

"My dear girl, because *you* dash off into heroics on the
slightest provocation, don't think *I* should. Not for
Melanie or any other woman living have I the least intention of playing the false hero. You take too much
upon yourself. As usual. You're still the interfering girl
who always thinks she knows best." He gave Demon's
rein a tug. "Can you walk to the house? I may add, the
search party is out for you. Keith has gone tearing off on
some other horse in an endeavour to pick up the bits and
pieces, and I perforce set off in the car."

Stevie was absolutely stunned. Stunned and miserable. She had only been thinking of Charles. She had been so frightened that Melanie might goad him into a reckless action that she had, as he had just expressed it, "risked her neck" for him. And far from being grateful, he was furious. And here was Keith dismounting from Caesar's back to stride over and say,

"Stevie! What on earth possessed you? Why didn't you hang on to Demon and yell for me?"

Poor Stevie. All she could do was glance at him and mumble something about Demon being excited. Thinking it was the best thing to do.

The best thing to do. With Charles looking at her in a way that made her feel she couldn't have done anything worse!

Fortunately, to the rest of them, it was a five minutes' wonder. Charles, without another word to Stevie, went into the house to collect Carole and Melanie. After saying good-bye to Miss Mabel the three of them disappeared in the car.

Miss Mabel and Lisa made some anxious enquiries as to how Stevie felt and then left her in peace. Keith, shaking his head disapprovingly, said,

"It was a silly thing to do, Stevie. Not a bit the sort of thing I'd expect of you," and strode off to the stables to see Demon and the other horse.

Stevie's knees managed to support her up the stairs. Once inside the bedroom, she flopped down on to the edge of Lisa's bed, feeling suddenly weak and shaken. It was the reaction, of course. Reaction and an awful sense of despair at Charles' wrath.

Heroics, he had called it. Looking at her in icy rage. She had never seen him like that before. Cold with anger.

She felt like bursting into tears. Because now she had destroyed all sense of friendship and understanding between them. It hadn't been very much. Just a casual liking on Charles' part. But it had meant everything to Stevie. What on earth had possessed her to do such a thing? In the cold light of reason it appeared both absurd and dramatic. Leaping on to Demon's back like that. As if she were some novel heroine.

Reason hadn't entered into it. It had been done on impulse. The impulse to protect and shield Charles, because she loved him.

She felt unutterably depressed. She had made a fool of herself and Charles just about hated her, and it was the end of everything.

CHAPTER EIGHTEEN

DAVID arrived on Friday evening for his two weeks' holiday. He looked pale and tired. As if the summer heat in London had exhausted him, or as if he had been working harder than usual.

"I've never looked forward to my holidays so much," he told Stevie. "I've certainly earned it this year." He smiled at her. There was an air of quiet triumph and self-satisfaction about him. "Wait until you hear about it." He added, with a meaning look, "You know, it concerns you just as much as me."

Stevie turned hastily away. She was in no mood to listen to David's confidences. Her mind was too much preoccupied with its own problems.

She said, "Wasn't that Miss Mabel calling? Excuse me a moment, David."

David stretched his arms, yawning slightly.

"What I have to tell you will keep. This isn't the time or the place." He smiled again. "Carry on, Stevie."

Stevie fled from the room, to find that Miss Mabel was indeed calling.

"It's Carole, dear. Something about a concert at Ellingham Camp." She pushed the receiver into Stevie's unwilling hand.

Stevie wanted to refuse there and then. She *couldn't* go. She just couldn't. And be in a party with Charles again and have to face his unfriendly look. And see him smiling at Melanie. Loving Melanie.

The difficulty was, the invitation wasn't merely for her. It included David and Lisa and Keith. She began mumbling something to the effect that she would like to go but wasn't quite sure if she was free when David came out into the hall. He lifted an enquiring eyebrow.

"Carole? Aunt Mabel said it's about the concert. Shall I speak to her? Sounds like a good beginning to the holiday."

Stevie's heart sank as she heard David entering with obvious enthusiasm into Carole's arrangements. She heard him say,

"I'd better have a word with Keith. Hold on, will you?"

Keith, curiously enough, raised no objection, but Stevie was surprised to discover that Lisa was against the project.

"I don't want to go one scrap," she whispered to Stevie. "What excuse can I make?"

Stevie looked at her. For a moment she forgot her own opposition to the plan.

"But—Lisa—why not? Carole says they are having some well-known guest artists down for it, and afterwards there's to be dancing. It's the sort of thing you like." She added, "And Keith wants to go."

Lisa turned away.

"That's why. I mean—it's because Keith is going that I don't—" She broke off.

Stevie followed her into the kitchen.

"You haven't quarrelled with him, have you?" she asked incredulously.

Lisa shook her head.

"No, that would be impossible. I *couldn't* quarrel with Keith." She hesitated. The violet-grey eyes filled with distress. She shook her head again. "I just don't want to be where Keith is."

Stevie stared at her in amazement.

"But I thought you were in love with him?" she blurted out.

Lisa's soft mouth trembled. She said in a low voice,

"Yes—I am. I've been in love with him for weeks." She averted her face. "Oh, it's all so hopeless, Stevie."

Stevie put a hand on her sister's arm. She said gently,

"Lisa, it *isn't*. It can't be. Because I'm sure that Keith cares for you in return."

Lisa shook her head, blowing her nose on a minute handkerchief.

138

"It's no use, Stevie. At first I thought—I hoped, that Keith did like me. But now I can see it wouldn't be any good. And I'm doing my best to prevent us from being thrown together all the time."

"But why?" Stevie demanded. "Where is the obstacle? If you've fallen in love with Keith and he looks like falling in love with you in return—what's the objection?" She smiled at her sister. "It sounds perfect to me."

"No," Lisa said. "It wouldn't do. I'm not cut out to be a farmer's wife." Her usually gentle voice sharpened into bitterness. "You've all pointed out enough times to me how weak and delicate and useless I am."

Stevie caught her hand.

"Lisa—you're being cruel. We've only tried to help you take care of yourself. And after all—Keith knows you're not"—she hesitated—"strong. If, with that knowledge, he's still in love with you and wants to marry you, then that's surely the end of the matter."

"You make it sound very simple," Lisa said. Her voice was suddenly weary. "It's presumptuous of me—of us, to think Keith might even want to marry me. But because I feel that perhaps he does like me, then—then I must try and check the whole thing while it's at the beginning."

"You're just being a martyr," Stevie said roundly. "It's absurd and unnecessary. Pull yourself together, Lisa. You're not entirely decrepit yet."

Lisa turned her head to look at Stevie. She said slowly, "You once asked if I thought you were interfering. I said 'No' then. Well, I'm saying 'Yes' now. I think you're interfering and officious and I wish you wouldn't be."

She turned on her heel and left the kitchen.

Stevie stared after her in consternation. Now Lisa was upset, and she was only trying to help her. Lisa was taking the whole thing too seriously. Why didn't she just sit back and let things work themselves out instead of trying to head Keith off? She would only hurt herself and him as well in the process.

She felt like running after Lisa to tell her so. Or like going to Keith to tell him how Lisa felt. She wanted to help—to put things right.

Stevie's mouth twisted in a wry smile.

Would she never learn? Not to try to help people. Not to interfere. She had tried to help Charles and it had wrecked their new-found friendship. She wanted to help Lisa and she was called officious.

David walked into the kitchen looking pleased with himself.

"It's all fixed," he informed her. "We're to be at Ellingham by seven to have time for drinks in the Officers' Mess before the concert. Irving is staying at the Manor House for the weekend so they are using his car and we're to meet them at the camp." He looked at her. "What's the matter? Don't you want to go?"

Stevie hesitated. What could she say—what excuse could she make? And upstairs there was Lisa trying to get out of it too.

"I wasn't sure—Miss Mabel might want me—" she began.

"I never heard such nonsense," a brisk voice said behind David's shoulder. "Since when has Miss Mabel been a spoilsport, may I ask?" Miss Mabel's bright blue eyes quizzed Stevie as she walked across to the kitchen dresser. "My dear child, of course you want to go to the concert. If you didn't go, you'd ruin the start of poor David's holiday. Wouldn't she, David?"

David nodded, unperturbed by the battery of Miss Mabel's teasing glance.

"She would, indeed."

There was nothing else for it, except to submit with good grace and hope fervently that somehow she would not have to encounter Charles at too close quarters.

Apparently Lisa felt the same and could find no real reason for staying behind, and so the next evening the four of them set off in Keith's car for Ellingham.

The party from the Manor House had arrived before them and were waiting in Irving's big car outside the camp gates, so that they could all go in together under Irving's escort. Ellingham was an immense straggling camp with endless-seeming runways stretching out towards the wooded horizon and a collection of huts and buildings assembled around what had once been a big private house known as Ellingham Grange.

As soon as they were inside the Mess a tall young man, wearing the uniform of a Major of the United States Air Force, came forward and greeted Irving. Irving introduced him as Drew Hurstein and in a few minutes they were in the centre of a gay laughing crowd of American Air Force officers—several of them accompanied by their very attractive wives.

Stevie couldn't bring herself to look at Charles, although she was very conscious of him standing among the group. Her glance was caught and held by Melanie, who had never looked more beautiful. Tonight she was wearing black—a short sleeveless frock of Chantilly lace. Her slender neck and arms looked alabaster-white against its cobwebby folds, and the fabulous hair gleamed brighter than ever in dazzling contrast. She looked the essence of everything that was chic and charming and delectably feminine.

Obviously, several of the American officers were of that opinion. They clustered round Melanie like bees round the proverbial honey pot. Charles, deep in conversation with Drew and his wife, showed no apparent resentment of this, and when, in a little while, the party made their way to the huge hut where the concert was about to start, Stevie observed that Melanie sat in the middle of four of the Americans, while Charles sat between Drew's wife and another American girl. Stevie was seated beside David with Carole on David's other side, while on Stevie's right hand sat Irving and Lisa next to him. She leant forward and was surprsed to find that Keith was not sitting next to Lisa but was on Carole's other side. Lisa must have arranged that deliberately.

The concert was excellent. The hut seemed to literally shake and tremble with the great shouts of laughter which emerged from several hundred lusty American throats. Irving gave his deep slow chuckle and Stevie could hear Lisa laughing in unison. She could also hear Lisa talking. In between the acts Lisa engaged in what was, for her, very animated conversation.

141

David turned his head to lift a questioning eyebrow at them. He smiled as he whispered,

"Those two seem to be very taken up with each other."

Stevie looked along the row. She felt a pang of uneasiness at the way Lisa was smiling up at Irving. Was she trying to flirt with him? That sort of behaviour was so unlike Lisa. And Irving was responding in somewhat heavy solemn fashion. Smiling back at Lisa through the thick glasses and addressing her as "honey" and baby" with every other sentence.

Stevie turned to look in the opposite direction and saw Keith sitting very stiff and upright and, despite the uproarious laughter and applause, staring straight ahead of him with a marked frown on his brown forehead. She felt sorry for Keith. He was obviously not enjoying himself and Stevie couldn't help feeling that this lack of enjoyment had something to do with Lisa.

CHAPTER NINETEEN

WHEN the concert was over the party went back to the Mess, which was held in what had been the Great Hall of Ellingham Grange. It was a huge wide room with a raftered ceiling and an immense stone fireplace. A buffet supper was being served at one end, while in the centre a space had been cleared on the polished oak floor for dancing. A radiogram with amplifier was playing music from a current musical show.

A tall American boy called Rick had attached himself to Carole and she appeared to have momentarily lost interest in David. David invited Stevie to dance. Lisa was dancing with Irving and she looked more excited and animated than ever as they danced round together. Her usually pale face was flushed with colour, her big eyes sparkling with eager vivacity. She looked gay and pretty, but nevertheless Stevie felt like shaking her. Especially when she looked across the room and saw Keith standing by the long buffet table, holding a sandwich in one hand and scowling blankly at the wall opposite without making any attempt to eat.

When the dance was over Stevie excused herself and went over to Keith's side. She smiled hesitantly.

"Are those sandwiches nice?"

Keith seemed to bring himself down to earth with an effort.

"These—oh yes—very good." He gazed at the still uneaten sandwich as if he had never seen it before.

Stevie shook her head gently.

"You haven't tasted it. Come on, let's put some food on a plate and go and sit down over there." She started to make a selection from the deliciously appetizing array of rolls and patties and sandwiches before her. "Will you have coffee, Keith?" She didn't wait for an answer, but put the piled plate in his hand and picked up two cups of coffee.

Keith followed her quite meekly to the seat against the wall. He sat down with Stevie. He picked up a patty and then put it back on the plate.

"What's got into Lisa tonight?" he demanded abruptly. "She's never been like this before." His voice sounded cross and bewildered. "I can't understand her."

Stevie looked down.

"She's in an odd mood," she agreed.

"Have I done something to offend her?" Keith went on. "She wouldn't sit beside me at the concert, and she's just ignored me all evening." He shook his head. "Of course, I know that fellow Darrell likes her. Perhaps Lisa likes him. I don't know. But even so, is that any reason why she should be unfriendly towards me? What have I done?"

Stevie met his stare. He looked so puzzled and hurt that her resolve not to say anything or interfere evaporated. She said slowly,

"It isn't Irving Lisa likes. It's you."

Keith frowned.

"I don't understand. If Lisa likes me why should she behave as if she hated the sight of me?"

Stevie took a deep breath.

"It's awfully complicated. And very difficult to explain. And it's really none of my business and Lisa will be furious with me for saying anything." She paused and looked at him. "The truth is, Keith, Lisa is frightened you might fall in love with her."

Keith stared. He frowned.

"Frightened? But why? Why shouldn't I?" He stopped abruptly. "Oh, I see. You mean—there isn't a chance for me and she's trying to tell me so."

Stevie shook her head.

"She's trying to put you off her, Keith, but not because there's no hope. Because she's in love with you."

Stevie's heart seemed to stop beating as she waited—her eyes on Keith's face. She had betrayed Lisa's secret. Lisa might never forgive her. But if, as she believed, Keith was in love with her sister, then somehow, now that she had spoken, things might be put right between them.

Keith said slowly,

"Lisa's in love with me?" He shook his head. "I can't believe it." He looked across the room to where Lisa and Irving were deep in conversation together. "Do you mean she's trying to make me jealous?"

Stevie shook her head quickly.

"No—no. Lisa isn't like that. She wouldn't act so meanly, or so childishly." She paused, endeavouring to choose her words carefully. "Lisa feels that she must try to put a barrier between you and herself. She's frightened that if you fell in love with her and—and it's serious, she wouldn't be fitted, I mean—she isn't physically strong enough to make you a good wife. You're a farmer, Keith, and a farmer's wife should pull her weight and help in a hundred ways about the place. Lisa might never be able to do that. You have to face the fact that she *is* delicate and hasn't much stamina and quickly over-tires." She broke off, aware of someone standing near by. She looked up and met Charles' black eyes fixed upon her. He looked quickly away again and went on talking to the man beside him.

Keith put down the plate of untouched food. He stood up. He was smiling his rare and unfamiliar smile.

"That's a load off my mind," he told Stevie. "If what you've told me is really true, and I'm just going to find out, I shall be eternally grateful to you, Stevie. Thanks. Excuse me now—I'm going over to Lisa to have this out with her."

144

He turned and strode across the room. Stevie watched him speak to Lisa, incline his head towards Irving, and take Lisa's arm in his. Lisa appeared to be protesting, but Keith moved away towards the doorway with her arm firmly held.

If only it would all come right, Stevie thought. And Lisa wouldn't hate her too much for revealing her secret. She stood up, and at the same moment Charles turned from the man he had been speaking to and came face to face with Stevie. He looked down at her. His smile was as mocking as ever it had been.

"If it isn't little Miss Fix-it! I hope you've arranged everything quite satisfactorily with poor old Keith? I saw you were busy giving him a lot of motherly advice."

Stevie's cheeks flamed. She said hotly,

"I suppose you've been listening to other people's conversations."

Charles raised a sardonic eyebrow.

"Not at all. But I'm not so obtuse I haven't noticed Keith brooding over Irving's heavy rush, or Lisa doing her best to encourage him. Then I observed you took over and the next minute Keith leapt across the room as if the Angel Gabriel had been whispering in his ear." He shrugged lightly. "One and one make two and add up as usual to Miss Stevie Fix-it."

He waited for Stevie's angry words of protest. He wasn't quite sure why he was baiting her in this fashion. Lately he'd come to like Stevie a lot. Even when he'd flown off the handle the other afternoon at her extravagant gesture of riding Demon he had come later to see that she had meant well. Too well, Charles thought. He didn't want anyone to risk their neck on his account and that was precisely what Stevie had done.

It wasn't in Charles' nature to say, "Look—I rather blew my top off the other day. You put the absolute wind up me—racing off like that. You might have been killed. I'm sorry I was so rude. Forgive me. Is everything 'as we were'?"

He wanted to say something like that to Stevie, but he couldn't quite bring himself to. And because she'd been too engrossed with David to as much as say good-evening to him and then she'd suddenly got all wrapped up in Keith and *his* troubles, Charles used the sardonic approach to divert Stevie's attention to himself. He smiled. She certainly was a little Miss Fix-it, and yet, in a way, this very attitude of hers to things and people amused him.

Stevie didn't smile in return. Her hazel eyes, usually so clear and steady, fell under Charles' gaze. It was as if she were trying to hide something from him. Charles was puzzled. He wanted Stevie to flash back at him as she had done so often in the past. Instead, she stood there, looking suddenly small and defenceless, without a word to say for herself, and he was aware of a sense of compunction and regret.

He said hesitantly,

"I was only joking. Would you—care to dance, Stevie?"

Stevie shook her head.

"No, thank you," she answered very quietly. "And you weren't joking at all, Charles. That's the way I always appear to you, I know. A—a Miss Fix-it." Her mouth seemed to tremble. "An interfering Miss Wurple." She turned away because she was suddenly aware of the hateful betraying tears in her eyes.

"*Stevie?*" Charles' voice was aghast. "Look—I've hurt you in some way. I didn't mean—" He broke off because Stevie had hurried away out of earshot.

He stared after her, feeling several shades of a cad. What was all that about? Had he sounded more sarcastic than he'd intended? Had he sounded unkind? It was the last thing in the world he would ever be to Stevie. He pictured her standing there a minute ago. So neat and compact. Sturdy. With the wide cheekbones that swept down to the small square chin and the hazel eyes that always looked at him so honestly and so directly, hidden by the short thick lashes.

"I didn't mean anything," Charles told himself again. "I must explain."

Melanie came drifting towards him, her lace dress floating out behind her.

"Oh, there you are, Charles. I'm sure this is our dance." She glanced up with self-conscious awareness at the two tall officers on either side of her. "I've been telling these very persistent boys that you've already staked a prior claim to me."

Charles glanced absently at her, registering Melanie's obvious loveliness, the petal-fair skin set off by the filmy lace, the blue eyes glowing with pleasure and self-satisfaction. Melanie throve on admiration and tonight she had had her full share.

"Yes—of course. Certainly. If you want to dance," Charles began.

A tiny frown puckered Melanie's smooth brows.

"Darling—if I want to? You mean surely that you want to?"

"Yes, of course," Charles repeated mechanically. He put his arm about Melanie's waist. He was still thinking of Stevie. What on earth had he done to bring that "stricken deer" look to her face? He'd called her "Miss Fixit" and he'd said he hoped she had arranged things satisfactorily for Keith. What else? Nothing she could take serious offence at, surely? He'd have to find her and apologize.

Melanie pulled back to stare at him.

"Charles! I've asked the same question twice. Have you suddenly gone deaf or something?"

"I'm sorry," Charles said hastily. "I was thinking about something. What did you say?"

Melanie's voice was chill.

"I said, do you think Drew's wife is pretty?"

Charles frowned.

"Drew's wife? Oh, the girl in the red dress? Yes—she is rather. Very good figure."

"I said pretty," Melanie chided. Her blue eyes opened wide to stare up at Charles. "Prettier than me, Charles?"

Charles stared down at her. He looked at the pointed oval face and the smoke-blue eyes and the shining aureole of hair. He had a sudden recollection of the Queen in Disney's film, *Snow White and the Seven Dwarfs*. Melanie wasn't in the least like her, but the rhyme echoed in his brain,

> Mirror, mirror on the wall,
> Who is the fairest of them all?

He was always thinking of Melanie in terms of nursery rhymes. Odd. Perhaps because she *was* rather like a character out of a fairy tale? Beautiful and fascinating and not quite real. Melanie resembled the Queen in *Snow*

147

White in one instance at least. She would always want to be regarded as the fairest of them all.

He said the words without thinking.

"*You* are the fairest of them all."

Melanie's eyes flickered for a moment. Then her face broke into a radiant smile.

"Why, Charles, how sweet. Really? Am I ? To you, anyway, I hope."

"To everyone," Charles said gallantly.

Melanie snuggled closer against his shoulder in a melting kittenish way.

"You needn't be jealous of any of these Americans. I'm only flirting with them. I much prefer you."

Charles didn't answer for a moment. Then he said slowly,

"That's very—dear of you, Melanie."

Melanie glanced into the long gilded mirror as they danced past it. She moved her head slightly this way and that.

"We make a handsome pair, Charles. Don't you think so?"

Charles looked at their reflections. At the tall dark man and the beautiful blonde girl in the filmy black dress. They looked like an illustration in a shiny magazine. Handsome enough, Charles acknowledged to himself, but, again, not quite real.

He looked down at Melanie. She had never appeared more lovely. A symphony in black and white and gold. But even as he acknowledged her charm Charles felt a queer detachment. As if here were gazing at Melanie through the wrong end of a telescope. There she was. A tiny figure. Quite perfect, but unreal. And very far away.

He shook his head quickly as if he were shaking away some image—some hallucination.

Melanie's voice said crisply,

"Well, really, Charles! You appear to have gone mad. What are you doing? Nodding and grimacing in the most crazy fashion!"

Charles brought himself back.

"I'm sorry, Melanie—" He broke off as someone tapped him on the shoulder.

"Say—excuse me! I guess you've danced with this young lady quite long enough."

It was one of the Americans. Charles smiled good-humouredly and relinquished Melanie.

He looked purposefully about him. Where was Stevie? He wanted to put things right between them before the evening ended.

He smiled to himself as he saw Keith and Lisa dancing together in what seemed to be most perfect accord. They looked so quietly happy and content that Charles thought, "I bet little Miss Fix-it fixed that! Bless her. I'll tell her so, when I see her."

"Stevie?" Carole said in answer to his enquiry. "I saw her standing by the door over there a few minutes ago."

The door led into a stone passageway. It was empty, but another door farther along stood half open— a ray of light falling from it into the passage. Charles took a few paces along and put his head round the door in vague curiosity.

He said abruptly,

"Oh—sorry! Excuse me!" and jerked back.

He strode quickly back the way he had come, feeling all kinds of a fool. Feeling embarrassed and, in some curious way, chagrined.

He tried to laugh the sensation off.

"Nothing to be surprised about," Charles told himself. "I've known all along the fellow was keen on her. Why—I teased her about it one day." He shrugged characteristically.

He couldn't dismiss it as easily as all that. The sight of Stevie and David standing so close together in that little room had affected him peculiarly. David had been holding one of Stevie's hands in his and staring down at her very intently while he spoke with great seriousness.

"I believe the fellow was proposing to her," Charles thought frowningly.

Well—what was his objection to that? It was an ideal, a to-be-expected ending. Stevie with David and Lisa with Keith and—and if everything went well, himself with Melanie. Perfect. Happy ending for everybody. Oh—must find someone for poor old Carole, Charles thought with giddy levity. Of course. Irving. Splendid. He'll do for

Carole. "Every Jack must have his Jill," Charles mused. There he went again—nursery rhyming.

He felt slightly punch-drunk. As if someone had delivered a blow that left him dizzy and light-headed and not entirely sensible.

I only hope Superman is good enough for her, Charles thought. I suppose he is. Because Stevie—Stevie deserves the best.

David went on speaking as if the sudden appearance of Charles' head round the doorway had made no interruption.

"My dearest Stevie, I've come to care for you very much. And, if I may say so, I think we're ideally suited. We're neither of us frivolous-minded and we should both take a thing like marriage seriously, and so would be bound to make a success of it." He paused, looking down at her with a grave blue stare. "Please say you'll marry me."

Stevie had difficulty in bringing her thoughts back from Charles to David. The unexpected sight of him had jarred her into unrest again. No matter what he said or what he did she loved him. He would never know how much his unkind teasing had hurt her. *Miss Fix-it.* She was a figure of fun to Charles. Someone he laughed at, despised perhaps?

She *wouldn't* think about him. She would do everything she could to put him out of her heart. She would think of something else. Of someone else. David.

David was asking her to marry him. It was a tremendous compliment he was paying her. The seriousness with which he regarded the occasion showed in his somewhat punctilious phrases.

Stevie hesitated, staring down at the hand David held in his own. For a moment she longed to say "Yes." As she would once have done, before she met Charles. She would have been eager and happy to marry David. He was all that she admired still.

But—love? You couldn't marry a man when you loved someone else with all your heart. Even when that someone could never care for you and it was all quite hopeless. It wouldn't be fair.

David said quietly,

"You're taking a long time to think it over, Stevie."

Stevie lifted her glance to his at last. She said,

"I don't know quite what to say, David. I'm honoured—very honoured that you should care for me in this way, and that you should ask me to be your wife. But—I—can't say 'yes'."

David's jaws seemed to fall apart.

" *'Can't'* ," he echoed. "But, Stevie, what do you mean? You like me, don't you? We've always got on so well together. Our tastes—our outlook on life, are similar. Why do you say *'can't'* like that?"

Stevie shook her head.

"I'm not in love with you, David."

David's smile held renewed confidence.

"You mean you haven't fallen in love with me? But Stevie, my dear, with two people such as you and I a romantic notion like falling in love is of secondary consideration. It's much more important to have a deep and sincere regard for one another; to have mutual tastes and values; to know that together we can build a good and lasting relationship and make something worthwhile of our lives."

Stevie's hazel eyes regarded him uncertainly. It sounded fine and splendid. It sounded the only sort of marriage that a girl who hopelessly loved someone else could ever hope to contract. If she could never care for another man in quite the way she cared for Charles, wasn't this the answer?

Stevie wavered. The thought of a future life with David was tempting. And yet?

She heard herself asking the question,

"Are you in love with me, David?"

David nodded.

"Yes—I think I am. I'm sure I am. Oh, not in any silly heart palpitating way, of course." He smiled. "That sort of thing is all very well in novels, but in real life it's different. You don't lose every shred of common sense and intelligence you have just because you fix your emotions on someone. You love wisely and discriminatingly." He put his hand under her chin and tilted her face up gently. "I love you, Stevie, because I know you inside out. As I told you once before, I know your faults and failings as well as all your many virtues. I'm quite certain you would make any man an excellent wife. Capable —level-headed—intelligent—attractive and kind. Everything a man could wish for."

Stevie's eyes fell under his look. She thought a little sadly, "That's not true, David. That you know me inside out. I don't think somehow you will ever be able to read my heart. Even if I married you and we lived together for a lifetime."

They shared many things, as David had said. Tastes and viewpoints; values and ideas. But something intangible they did not share. Some essence. A magic that united two people with an invisible bond. It was there or it wasn't. If it was, then everything else fell into place. Differences of temperament, of mind, of blood, even of race, didn't matter. You were still together in some enchanted way. If it wasn't there, then with all your many sharings you had constantly to strive to get close to one another and you remained for ever a little apart.

Stevie said slowly, almost reluctantly,

"Thank you, David, for all the nice things you've said to me. I appreciate them and I think there's a great deal of truth in what you've told me. But I'm not sure of myself. I'm not *certain* enough to say 'yes'."

"You don't have to decide right away," David answered. "I can't really expect you to. Any sensible girl likes to think around a big question such as I've put to you. If it's only to make sure she's doing the right thing." He smiled reassuringly at Stevie. "*I* know. So don't worry, Stevie, my dear. I'm down here for two weeks. We'll be together every day. I'm sure at the end of that time you'll have had a real chance to weigh things up and decide—" He paused with his head a little on one side as he looked quizzically at her, "In my favour, I hope."

Stevie smiled hesitantly back at him.

"That's very sweet of you, David, and very considerate. Perhaps—perhaps my mind will clarify itself when I'm with you."

Lisa was waiting for her when she and David rejoined the rest of the party. She smiled at Stevie—her violet-grey eyes starry with happiness. Her hands squeezed her sister's as she whispered,

152

"It'll all come right. Keith's been—wonderful. And—and so have you, Stevie. Thank you." She added, "We don't want to tell anyone until we've talked to Miss Mabel and Judy."

Stevie squeezed her sister's fingers in response.

"I'm so happy for you, darling. Are you—engaged?" Lisa nodded breathlessly.

"Yes. But—oh, don't say anything yet, Stevie. Here's Carole."

She raised her voice to make some ordinary remark to Stevie.

Stevie looked after her as she moved away. Darling Lisa. Oh, she was so pleased about it all. It was strange to think that tonight the two of them might have become engaged, if she had felt the same way about David as Lisa felt about Keith. Her glance instinctively wandered in the direction of Charles. There he stood, tall and very handsome. Would the day come when she would no longer feel that ache and sadness of longing?

One day he would marry Melanie. If all went well with his eyes, and Stevie sent up a silent prayer that he would make a perfect recovery. When he married Melanie they would live at the Manor House. The thought of it was almost enough to drive her into David's arms. To decide there and then to marry him and go off and live in this new job he had been telling her about which meant promotion and a move to Birmingham. Only she had to consider David too. She had to be fair to him.

Miss Mabel was fast asleep in bed when they all returned home, so nothing was said until the morning. Even David was unaware of Keith's and Lisa's engagement until he came down at breakfast to find them all kissing and laughing and chattering in the kitchen while the kettle boiled over and the bacon sizzled in the pan.

"It's quite perfect," Miss Mabel declared. She pulled off her blue-rimmed glasses and dabbed at her eyes. "Oh dear, how silly to be tearful over something so absolutely joyful. That's the way of women. Weeping at weddings and stoic-like at funerals."

"Who's talking of funerals?" David remarked. "Congratulations, Keith old man, and Lisa, what about a

153

cousinly kiss? We'll be almost related after you're married."

Judy had been told first thing. Lisa had gone in to help her dress and Keith had accompanied her and together they had broken the news to her. She had been ecstatically happy and excited.

"You're going to be my second Mummy. Like Bridget had. Bridget *loves* her second Mummy, and although she's awfully nice she isn't nearly as nice as you are, Aunt Lisa. Oh, goodness! What'll I call you? 'Cos you won't be an aunt any more, will you?"

Lisa smiled, combing the straight brown hair back into neat plaits.

"We'll have to think of another name. Whatever you want to call me, darling. Perhaps after Daddy and I are married you might feel you'd like to call me Mummy. We'll wait and see, shall we?"

Judy hopped up and down on one leg.

"Gosh—I'll be able to be a bridesmaid!" She hugged Lisa and dashed out of the room and down the stairs to inform Miss Mabel that she was to be a bridesmaid like Bridget had been and like Celia had been at Celia's sister's wedding, and would she be able to wear a silk dress with frills right down to the ground as Celia had done?

Keith, as usual, was the quietest member of the party. But he smiled in perfect content and his gaze rested on Lisa with such warm and loving affection that Stevie felt, as Miss Mabel had done, an emotional pricking of tears behind her eyelids. She quickly covered them up by rescuing the bacon before it burnt and busying herself frying eggs and fingers of bread.

Judy insisted on putting matters on a practical basis.

"When'll you be married? Will you be married next week, p'raps? I'd like a pink dress—not pale but sort of deep—an'—an' *sumpshus*."

"Next week's a bit too soon," Keith stated. He smiled at Lisa, "Not that it wouldn't be all right by me, but I suppose there are things to be arranged." He looked across to Miss Mabel. "I thought the end of August. After harvesting. I daren't take more than a week off, but we could fly to somewhere like Jersey for our honeymoon."

Miss Mabel gazed up at the ceiling, calculating dates. "Let's see. It's July 14th now. In about five weeks? Just time to have the banns called and fix everything."

"What are banns?" Judy demanded.

"Nothing that concern you, young lady," Miss Mabel answered. "Eat your breakfast up and off to school. Or we shan't buy you that 'sumpshus' pink bridesmaid's frock, will we, Lisa?"

Lisa followed Miss Mabel into the kitchen as they cleared away the breakfast things. Stevie heard her saying,

"Miss Mabel—I want to do everything in the world to make Keith happy. I—I know I'm not really suitable to be a farmer's wife, but Keith wouldn't listen to my objections."

Miss Mabel put the teapot down in the sink and turned round to face Lisa. Because Lisa was tall she had to reach up to her as she cupped Lisa's face in her two thin hands.

"Child, you're talking nonsense! Couldn't be *more* suitable. I knew this was going to happen from the start. Wanted it to." Her bright bird's eyes twinkled up at Lisa. "Don't mind admitting I helped pull a string or two. Threw you together whenever I could." Her voice changed as she added more seriously, "Keith's been very lonely, Lisa. I saw him growing quieter, more withdrawn with every year. Then you and Stevie came here and it all changed. He needs you, child."

Lisa hesitated.

"And—and you don't think it matters that I—I'm not very capable or practical or—or hard-working?"

"Matters!" Miss Mabel echoed. "Why, it's ideal." She smiled brilliantly. "Now I shan't be out of a job, you see!"

"Oh, Miss Mabel darling, bless you!" Lisa leaned down and they hugged one another.

Stevie smiled from the recesses of the larder. It was all going to work out well. It warmed her heart to feel that Lisa and Miss Mabel were so fond of one another and such good friends.

CHAPTER TWENTY

DURING the next few days she found herself a great deal in David's company. Although it was his holiday and he had no great liking for farm work, he undertook various jobs so that he could be with Stevie. The weather was gloriously warm and in the late afternoon of each day they went swimmig together. David's pallor changed to pink and then to an even tan. His face filled out again. He looked more rested.

Only once did he refer to his proposal. Speaking of Keith's engagement he said,

"I hope you'll feel you want to keep it all in the family, Stevie. Very nice and convenient, you know. If you marry me you'll be linked with Whitegates and Lisa for the rest of your life."

Miss Mabel had said something like that. "I've a feeling your life is bound up with Whitegates," she had told Stevie. Was that true? Stevie sighed. It would certainly solve a whole lot of problems.

"We must have a little party to celebrate the engagement," Miss Mabel said. "Don't you think so, Keith? It would be nice to ask Mrs. Linmer and the Manor House people down and Mr. Pollitt and his wife and Miss Burton and Mr. Dodgson—"

"Whoa there!" Keith ejaculated. "Go easy, Aunt Mabel. I've all my farm work to get cleared up."

"Well, we must do something," Miss Mabel protested. "Perhaps as it's such a short engagement we can make it a party to welcome back the happy pair from the honeymoon. Would that be better?"

"Let Lisa decide," Keith said. "I'm not for any kind of party at any time."

Lisa voiced the opinion that with so many plans on hand it might be advisable to leave celebrations over until the end of the summer, so matters were left like that.

Stevie was walking one of the horses down to the forge a morning or two later when someone smiled and nodded at her from across the road. She recognized Mrs.

Linmer. She returned the greeting and was prepared to pass on, but Mrs. Linmer crossed over to her side.

"Good-morning, Stevie. May I say how delighted I was to hear of your sister's engagement to Keith Arnott? Would you please give her my best wishes for her future happiness and my congratulations to Keith."

Stevie smiled. "Thank you," she said. "I will tell my sister."

Mrs. Linmer fell into step with Stevie.

"When is your sister to be married?" She enquired.

"In about five week's time. Mr. Pollitt is calling the banns on Sunday. Everyone will know then."

Mrs. Linmer smiled.

"Everyone knows now! Villagers have a sort of bush telegraph. Oh, here we are at Fred's." She hesitated, looking at Stevie. "Do you have to wait for him? Your horse, I mean."

Stevie nodded.

"Yes. About a quarter of an hour. I see Fred is busy at the moment."

Mrs. Linmer gave her a direct look from the dark eyes that were so like Charles'.

"If you have time to spare, would you care to have a cup of coffee with me at the Magpie?"

Stevie felt vague surprise at Mrs. Linmer's friendly gesture, but she also felt pleasure. She liked and admired Charles' mother.

"Thank you very much, Mrs. Linmer. I should like to. I had better just explain what is wrong to Fred and tie Shandy up and then I'll be free to come with you."

They walked from the end of the street where the forge stood up the slight incline to the black and white façade of the Magpie Tea Rooms.

It was pleasantly full with a few local people and a considerable influx of holiday visitors. Stevie was conscious that several eyes followed her as she came in behind Mrs. Linmer and they sat down together. She was thankful that today, instead of blouse and jodhpurs, she was wearing a pale blue linen dress, which was clean if not very new.

"Did you enjoy the concert at the American camp the other night?" Mrs. Linmer enquired as she poured out Stevie's coffee.

Stevie nodded.

"Yes, it was most enjoyable. Some excellent artistes from London came down for it."

Mrs. Linmer smiled ruefully.

"We seem to have been submerged by American officers since last Saturday. Three came over on Sunday. One to see Carole—a tall boy. Rather attractive." She frowned. "Rick, I think his name is. And two came over to see Melanie. Of course, Melanie always gets on very well with Americans, having lived over in the States for several years. Her father is at the Washington Embassy, you know."

Stevie nodded again.

"Yes, Carole told me."

Mrs. Linmer was still frowning. She stirred her coffee thoughtfully.

"Melanie is a dear girl. Quite—quite one of the family. And she's remarkably pretty. Charles is very fond of her, you know."

Stevie stared down at the digestive biscuit on her plate.

"Yes—I—I imagine he is."

Mrs. Linmer sighed.

"I suppose I'm being silly. Mothers are like that. But I can't help wondering sometimes if Melanie is the right one for Charles." She added quickly, "Or, indeed, if Charles is the right one for Melanie."

Stevie said nothing.

Mrs. Linmer glanced up at her.

"You must forgive my talking to you like this. Perhaps it's because of your sister's engagement. I started thinking" —she smiled with unexpected wistfulness—"as mothers will do. I—worry about Charles because, you see, he hasn't been well. He—he had an accident. And I feel— oh! it's so important that the girl he loves should be understanding and sympathetic and—strong. Melanie is none of those things." She broke off.

Stevie looked at her. She said gently,

"Perhaps—if Melanie were given the chance to know the truth about Charles she would alter. She would be understanding and—sympathetic. Anyone would be."

Mrs. Linmer stared at her.

"The truth?" she repeated. "Do you mean that *you* know what is the matter with Charles?"

"He told me a little," Stevie said in a low voice. "Because of circumstances. He had had two blackouts when alone with me. He told me about the car smash and about—his eyes."

Mrs. Linmer went on staring at the girl opposite her. At the clear hazel eyes in the smooth sun-browned face. She was greatly surprised to learn that this girl was the one person Charles had confided in, except herself. And yet, looking at Stevie, her surprise ebbed. She had a feeling that here was someone you could talk to. Someone whom you could rely upon.

She said slowly,

"Then you and Charles must be—great friends?"

Stevie felt the colour come up. She looked away, shaking her head.

"No, not really, Mrs. Linmer. It was just—circumstances. That day when we went sailing he told me, because he had to."

"I remember," Mrs. Linmer said thoughtfully. "I remember how he brought you back for tea and then later Melanie wanted you all to go to the concert. And you—you made an excuse." She looked at Stevie. "On purpose, I think. Thank you, my dear. It's curious, but I had the feeling that evening that you had helped Charles." She sighed again. "Perhaps it is wrong of Charles not to have told Melanie the truth. It's very chivalrous and quixotic of him to wish to see how things turn out, but is it fair to Melanie?" She added, "You know he wants to marry her?"

"Yes," Stevie said in a low voice. "Yes—he told me that."

Mrs. Linmer gave her a puzzled glance.

"And yet you say you and he are not great friends? I can't believe that."

Stevie didn't answer. The quarter of an hour had grown to twenty-five minutes. She thanked Mrs. Linmer for the coffee and said that she must leave her to go and collect Shandy from the forge.

Mrs. Linmer walked out with her and halfway down the street they parted, both subconsciously reluctant to do so, and both of them aware of having established a curious intimacy.

More than once during that day Stevie thought of her meeting with Charles' mother. She admired her immensely. She had a charming, almost royal, dignity and yet she was friendly and kind. She was beautiful too with a beauty that made no attempt to hide the years, but only to make the most of the particular age she had reached.

The remembrance of her words stayed in Stevie's mind. "Then you and Charles must be great friends."

It had started out that way. Charles had seemed to like her, to want to talk to her. It had seemed, after that time at Bracklesey, that they had drawn close together. Oh, not in love. The love was only on Stevie's side. But in friendship and liking. And then she had abused Charles' confidence by rushing off on Demon because she was so frightened he might risk himself. Had she made him feel a fool? Impinged upon his sense of manhood? Was that the reason he had turned on her so angrily? He had called her interfering and then, the other night, he had named her Miss Fix-it.

Only when she was alone dared Stevie relax and admit to heartache and loneliness. The rest of the Whitegates household were so happy with plans and arrangements that she could not mar Lisa's bright day by letting her see how unhappy she often felt.

Being alone was a luxury these days. There were so many people coming and going. Always someone with her, David particularly. Sometimes it was difficult to keep the mask from slipping and not reveal sadness and despondency.

She snatched at the chance to take an evening ride and persuaded Keith to go with Lisa and Miss Mabel to friends of Miss Mabel's for supper one evening. David too, although he protested.

"Please, David. Do go with the others. I—I'll come with you another day."

"That's a promise," David said. "D'you hear, Keith? If Stevie takes these people tonight, will you let her off tomorrow or the next day to come out with me?"

Keith nodded.

"Gladly. *I* don't want Stevie to overdo things. Not to-morrow, because I really do need her, but the day after."

Yes, Stevie thought again, being alone *was* a luxury. She had deposited the party from the evening ride back at the Cliff Hotel and was now walking the tired horses up the road which led from the sea past the church and so to Whitegates.

Old Tom had long since gone home. Stevie unsaddled the horses and rubbed them down before watering and feeding them. There was something immeasurably sooth-ing about working with animals. They were companion-able and yet there was no intrusion. She could let down her guard and think of Charles and remain silent save for an occasional sigh and no one would remark upon her, or expect an answer to conversation or some smiling interest.

Swallows flashed and darted against the evening sky. A thrush called from a tree in the nearby garden. Trixie, Miss Mabel's cat, picked her way carefully over the cobbles and greeted Stevie plaintively before sitting down to wash an already spotless white paw.

Stevie bolted the stable door and walked over to the saddle room carrying one of the saddles. Trixie followed her with upright tail. A shadow fell across the doorway and Stevie glanced up.

Her heart seemed to stop beating with her held breath. She remained sitting very still and upright on the stool, holding a duster in one hand, as she stared in surprise at Charles.

CHAPTER TWENTY-ONE

CHARLES smiled uncertainly, almost apologetically.

"Hello, Stevie."

Stevie let out her breath and her heart started beating once more.

"Hello." She added very quickly, "I'm sorry. Everyone's out. There's no one here—if you want to see Keith, I mean."

Charles shook his head.

"No, I don't want to see Keith. I came to see you." He turned a box over. "Mind if I sit down?" His lean length doubled itself up on the upturned box.

Stevie didn't know what to say, so she went on rubbing at the saddle with the cloth in her hand.

"I'm afraid I offended you the other evening," Charles said. "I'm sorry, Stevie. I was only joking, you know."

Stevie looked up at him and met a glance so intent and direct that she looked as quickly away again.

"I came along later to find you and apologize," Charles went on. "But you were rather engrossed with—David." He bent down to scratch Trixie's head. His voice sounded muffled and far away. "Are you going to marry him?"

Stevie stared down at her shadowy reflection in the gleaming brown leather. She said abruptly,

"I thought I was the only one who interfered in other people's business?"

Charles straightened up. He laughed.

"So you haven't lost all your bite? I'm glad. And I stand rebuked. By the way—I was very happy to hear the news about Lisa and Keith. I did congratulate Keith, but haven't seen Lisa. Will you convey to her my good wishes?" He gave her a warm and unexpectedly friendly smile. "I mustn't say anything about 'fixing' things, or you'll blow my head off again."

It was difficult to resist Charles' charm.

"I did try and help them," Stevie admitted. "And I'm glad now."

"I came along to be helped too," Charles said.

Stevie looked across to him in surprise.

"You came to be helped? In what way?"

Charles picked Trixie up on to his knees. He shrugged.

"Oh—I dunno. I think I felt like one of your pep talks. You know how you used to lash out at me. Play the man, Charles! Brace yourself! Buckle on your armour! That sort of thing."

Stevie's look was puzzled. She was aware suddenly of something troubled in Charles' manner, despite his smile and flippant talk.

"I don't think I understand. You mean you came specially here to see me—to talk to me?"

Charles nodded. "That's it exactly. Just wanted to talk to you. I was mooching around at home like a lost soul when it came over me suddenly. 'I'll go and find Stevie and talk to her. She'll do me some good.'"

"Thank you," Stevie said. "I will if I can, Charles."

Charles smiled, but there was a lost and lonely quality in that smile.

"I feel better already. Just to see you sitting there like that. Sane and calm and competent. And courageous, too. I feel in need of all those qualities at the moment. You're the only one I can talk to, Stevie, because you're the only one who knows what it all adds up to. This eye business. Oh, of course my mother knows! But I can't talk to her. She's too concerned, too worried about the whole thing. Now with you it's different. You know how things are with me but you don't care. I mean, you're naturally very kind and all that, but you're not particularly involved. You're detached and impersonal."

Stevie felt the knife turn in her heart. She bent down and rubbed at the saddle with renewed energy. Don't care, she thought, when I care so utterly! To Charles I'm detached and impersonal and indifferent. And because I seem all those things to him, it helps.

She said calmly,

"I see. Well." She raised her eyes and looked across at him with an even steady look. "Tell me what it is that's worrying you?"

Charles' black eyes fixed themselves on her. He was no longer smiling and his voice sounded grim.

"I leave for London tomorrow morning. To see the specialist again. And to fix a date for the eye operation."

Stevie seemed to freeze into stillness. She went on staring at Charles. The back of her hand lifted against her mouth as if to silence the cry that filled her heart. Because she was frightened that she would reveal to Charles how she felt about him she rose abruptly and

163

walked across to hang the saddle on one of the pegs against the wall.

Now her tell-tale face was out of Charles' range. Without turning she said,

"I'm sorry, Charles. It's a—horrible thing hanging over you. Your mother knows, of course?"

It was extraordinary to hear her own voice sounding so reassuringly calm.

"I haven't said much. I can't stand any flap and tears. Not that Mother isn't wonderful—don't think that. But she takes it all to heart so." Charles' voice changed. "God—it's a relief to talk to you, Stevie! I've sometimes felt I couldn't keep up the act much longer."

"I think I understand," Stevie said. Too well. She knew too well how difficult, how almost unendurable it was to present a façade of happiness over a desolation of spirit. "When—when do they expect to operate?"

"The date isn't fixed yet. When I saw the specialist a few weeks ago he told me he didn't think the pressure on the nerves would clear without an operation. It's apparently rather tricky. If it doesn't come off"—Charles shrugged— "I've had it, as far as my eyes are concerned. When I go up tomorrow I shall hear just how good or how bad things are."

Stevie turned to look at him. She said slowly,

"With all my heart I hope things will go well, Charles."

Their glances met and held. Charles' dark eyes were very serious and intent as he stared at her. He uncoiled his long height from the upturned box and came over to stand beside her.

"Bless you, Stevie. I know you mean it. I believe you always mean what you say, don't you?" He smiled slightly. "And say what you mean! You're that sort of a person. Sincere and very real."

Real, Charles thought, looking down at Stevie's smooth brown head. Yes, Stevie's a real person. So real and true—that Melanie seems unsubstantial and imaginary by comparison. But it's Melanie I'm in love with.

For a moment he was puzzled. I *am* in love with Melanie, Charles insisted silently. She only seems shadowy to me because I've kept her outside all this trouble. And because she hasn't shared it with me she appears distant and unreal at times.

Stevie glanced up and met his frowning look.

"What is it?"

Charles went on frowning.

"It's struck me, for the first time, I think, that perhaps I haven't been very fair to Melanie. I should have told her about my eyes. Let her know the complications and the risks. I feel I've—shut her out, in some way."

"Yes," Stevie said in a low voice. "I think you have. I should feel it was so if I were in her place. If you love someone you want to share everything that happens to them. The good and the bad things. You *want* to help, with all your heart."

Charles was arrested by the intensity of feeling in Stevie's voice. Although she spoke quietly there was a tremulous warmth in her speech that caught his attention. He said slowly,

"Is that how *you* feel about someone, Stevie?"

Stevie's clear candid eyes were suddenly veiled by the short thick lashes. For a moment she was silent. Then she nodded.

"Yes—that's how I feel."

Charles almost whistled. Was she really so much in love with Superman—with David? he amended.

He said gently,

"And if it were—" He stopped abruptly. Stevie had chewed him off once for asking questions about David and herself. It would be better not to mention names. "If it were the man you're—in love with, you'd rather know all the facts? Even if it meant that you'd faced with a difficult choice?"

Stevie turned her head.

"Choice?" she echoed. "If you really love someone there's no choice left. Whatever happens to them is just part of things. You accept it as happening to you, too."

Charles gave her a long look.

"Even—blindness?" he asked.

For the first time Stevie glanced at him directly.

"Would you stop loving Melanie because she was suddenly faced with blindness? Could you?"

165

Charles was silent. It was difficult to visualize himself in such a relationship with Melanie. He loved her for her prettiness and charm; for the fact that she was glamorous and gay. He had known her as a child. She had returned from America an enchanting young woman who easily outshone all the other girls Charles knew. He was aware of a childish streak in her nature, but it had seemed rather appealing. In delightful contrast to the outward sophistication of dress and manner. He had been inclined to pet and spoil her; to shield her from the more unpleasant aspects of life.

He was suddenly aware that, in comparison with Stevie's conception of love, his regard for Melanie was a juvenile fancy.

If Melanie were faced with some disastrous handicap could he share it with her? Would she—*could* she share it with him?

Charles knew the answer. He must have known it all along. Instinctively. That was why he had never told Melanie the truth about his accident. Because she was incapable, by temperament and upbringing, of facing up to it.

He looked down at Stevie's hand resting on the edge of the shelf. For some reason he couldn't account for he took it up in his own. He stared at it. A small hand, firm and strong and sun-tanned. The rounded nails were neat but unvarnished. There was a callous under the base of one finger.

A workaday little hand, Charles thought. A very different hand from Melanie's slender white one, with its long painted nails and baby-soft texture. Yet when he held Stevie's hand in his he had the curious impression of holding on to something tenacious and reassuring. A lifeline. A guiding hand in the dark.

In the dark, Charles thought grimly. That's just about it. Only it will never be my hand Stevie holds in the dark. It will be another man's. David Arnott's.

He said slowly,

"No, of course I shouldn't stop loving a girl if she were faced with some ghastly trouble or illness." He added, thoughtfully,

"Not if I loved her enough."

166

If I loved her enough, Charles thought. There's the rub. What I feel for Melanie isn't adequate. Not for the big things of life. I can see that now. That's why we never shared this eye business.

But I shared it with Stevie.

He looked down at the brown hand in his own and was filled with a queer tenderness. *Stevie,* he thought. There's something about her that draws me all the time. I'm closer to her than I am to anyone else I know. Even my mother. It's extraordinary, I want to be with her. When I'm worried sick I come looking for her.

What's the matter with me? Charles demanded silently. I'm supposed to be in love with Melanie. And Stevie's given her heart to David. I can see that by the way she spoke just now. She's head over heels in love with the fellow. It—it seemed to shine right through her.

He gave an abrupt sigh, and as Stevie glanced at him in a questioning way, he said,

"I'd better be on my way. Thanks—thanks for helping, Stevie."

Stevie's hand was still in his. The hazel eyes that looked up at him were gravely intent.

"Please let me know what happens. Will you?"

Charles nodded.

"Of course. You've been a darling, Stevie. Wish me luck."

Stevie's eyes were suddenly over-bright.

"I do. All the luck in the world."

Charles stared down at her for a long moment. He felt as if he couldn't look away from those clear eyes. He bent his head with an abrupt movement.

" 'Bye, Stevie."

His mouth rested for a moment on the lips beneath his in an intended light kiss. And lingered. The brief pressure deepened. His hold on Stevie's hand tightened; his other arm came round behind her shoulder. The soft mouth under his own seemed to answer and respond to him, and suddenly the two of them were lost in a long, intense and apparently endless kiss.

It was a dizzying moment. When at last they drew away from one another there was a look almost of bewilderment on both their faces.

Charles said unsteadily,

"Stevie—?"

Stevie half turned away. She didn't want Charles to say anything more. She didn't want him to apologize or say he was sorry. She just wanted him to leave her now whilst she could still feel his arm about her and the echo of that strange, unexpected, but magical kiss pounding through her veins.

Her voice was almost a whisper.

"Good-bye, Charles."

She heard the stable door creak after him. His footsteps sounded over the cobbles. She heard a car starting up in the lane.

Stevie leaned against the ledge. She said aloud on the breath of a sigh, "Oh, Charles."

She had never in her life been kissed like that before. She had never experienced such breathless rapture, the heady and spontaneous response which she could no more have checked than a flower could stay its petals unfolding in the warmth of the sun.

Why did he kiss me like that? Stevie asked herself. She realized that Charles had only intended a friendly but casual salutation of farewell. But something had happened to him. To them both. Stevie felt her cheeks warm. Was it because she had responded too warmly, too eagerly? It had seemed to her that Charles' embrace had deepened as quickly and as suddenly as her own. She couldn't remember. She couldn't dot the i's and cross the t's of something so confusing and so wonderful.

Was it very wrong of her? To have allowed Charles to kiss her like that when he belonged to Melanie? It shouldn't have happened and yet—she couldn't regret it. Always—for all her life through she would have the remembrance of his kiss. For one breathless moment she had lived a dream. As Charles' lips had touched hers she had answered his kiss as if he loved her as deeply and utterly as she loved him.

But it was only a dream. It could never become reality. Never? Stevie thought despairingly. If anything went wrong, if the operation failed and Charles became blind, then he would not marry Melanie. Might it be possible that he would ever turn to her, Stevie? He liked her. He

168

confided in her. They were friends. There might be a chance of a place in his life.

No—Stevie cried from the bottom of her heart. No, Charles *must* recover. I couldn't bear it for him, otherwise. I would rather a million times never see or hear of him again than that he should lose his eyesight. I want him to be made whole. To be able to marry Melanie, because that is what he wants, and for them to be happy always.

She left the saddle room and walked across to the house. The colour had faded out of the evening sky. A luminous blue dusk shrouded the stables and roof tops. One palely glittering star hung in the green-streaked west. Stevie paused.

She thought, I shall never forget tonight. I shall never forget the moment when Charles kissed me.

The next day was particularly busy, as Keith had hinted to David. Stevie was thankful. She didn't want time in which to remember that it was today Charles would be in the train *en route* for London. That it was this afternoon he was seeing the specialist. That by now he might know the worst.

He couldn't really know the worst until after the operation. But he would have some idea. When would he be returning, Stevie's anxious heart demanded. Tomorrow? The day after? Would he telephone and let her know the verdict? Or would he call down and tell her?

Two days dragged past. Three days. Stevie felt taut with anxiety. She was tempted to make some excuse to call at the Manor House and see Charles' mother. Surely Mrs. Linmer would have heard by now. Perhaps Charles had forgotten his promise. He couldn't know how much it meant to her to know what the specialist had told him.

Only the fact that the rest of the Whitegates household were engrossed in Lisa's and Keith's wedding plans allowed Stevie's strained manner to escape notice.

CHAPTER TWENTY-TWO

LISA and Miss Mabel were making some rearrangements in the house. Decorators were coming in to do over the big room where Lisa and Stevie slept together. This was to be Lisa's and Keith's bedroom. Judy was moving into Keith's bedroom and Stevie was to have Judy's room. The small study which Keith had used as an office was being re-papered and painted to make a charming little "den" which Lisa and Keith would be able to use whenever they wished to be on their own.

Lisa was thrilled and happy with all the plans.

"You're sure you don't mind moving out?" she asked Stevie anxiously when they were discussing the rearrangements. "This is the biggest bedroom, that's why Keith thought"—she hesitated—"we should like it." She looked at Stevie. "You know the other room is to be yours— always."

Stevie put her arm about her sister.

"Darling, thank you. It's wonderful of you and Keith. But this is your home and your life. I'm not really part of it. Not any more."

Lisa's grey eyes were troubled.

"Of course you are. I don't want you ever to go away, Stevie." She hesitated. "That is—unless you—you marry someone."

Stevie turned to the drawer she was emptying of things.

"I shan't marry anyone."

"There's David," Lisa said slowly. "Aren't you—I thought—Oh, Stevie, it would be so perfect. For all of us."

Stevie placed a pile of underclothes on the bed preparatory to carrying them into Judy's room. Judy was sleeping with Miss Mabel so that Stevie could move into her room while the big bedroom was being redecorated. Lisa was to sleep in the spare room when David left after the weekend.

For a moment she longed to confide in Lisa. To say, "I can't marry David because I'm hopelessly in love with Charles." She dismissed the impulse. It would only worry and distress Lisa. In her sensitive sympathetic way she would grieve for Stevie, and it wasn't fair to trouble her so soon before her wedding.

She said lightly,

"One engagement in the family is enough for the present. Don't worry about me, Lisa."

"Well, this is your home for as long as ever you want it to be," Lisa declared. "Keith promised me that."

Stevie walked towards the door with the pile of clothing in her arms.

"It's very dear of him. But—we'll have to see how things go."

She was thinking of Charles. Of staying on at Whitegates, with Charles married to Melanie living at the Manor House. So near. So immeasurably far away. I don't think I should be able to stand it, Stevie thought sadly. I'll have to go away. Get a job somewhere else.

When she came down the stairs after completing the removal into Judy's old room, she found David waiting for her.

"Stevie, do come out with me. Keith says there's no more riding this afternoon. And I never seem to get you on my own for more than five minutes."

Stevie hesitated. She had been purposely avoiding David this past week, but his gaze was almost wistfully beseeching on her own.

"I was going over to Bassett with some gilts for Mr. Roach. Didn't Keith mention it?"

David shook his head.

"No. But can't I go with you? We'll drive over together."

Stevie smiled.

"I'm taking them in the cart. It's slow, and not particularly elegant. Do you still want to come?"

David wrinkled up his nose at the thought of trundling along in the old float with a bunch of squealing pigs netted in behind him, but he nodded his assent.

"If it's the only chance I have to talk to you, yes."

Miss Mabel glanced up over her glasses at them when Stevie explained their errand.

"Mind you take your macs. It looks like rain and the wind is blowing a gale."

171

Stevie harnessed Toby between the shafts of the cart, while Old Tom, after much manoeurvring, managed to get the six Essex gilts into the back and net them securely over.

They rumbled slowly out of the gate and down the lane to the main road leading to Bassett. David perched himself on the dusty corner seat, while Stevie stood, leaning against the high front of the cart with the reins in her hands. Behind them the pigs protested loudly at their prospective journey.

Stevie looked round at David.

"Don't say I didn't warn you! I'm afraid this is a primitive outing." She shook her head. "It doesn't seem a bit like you."

David dusted down the knees of his flannel trousers.

"You're quite right. I told you before I was a townee at heart. I'm beginning to hope Bassett isn't very far."

"Four miles," Stevie told him.

"At this rate? We shall be all night getting there."

Stevie glanced up at the sullen grey sky. The fine weather had broken overnight and all day a squally wind had blown off the sea, bringing an occasional spatter of rain in its wake and seeming to deny the tranquil July days that had gone before.

"Miss Mabel was right. It's a real summer gale. And very overcast out at sea. It looks as if it's going to pour."

She chucked encouragingly at Toby, who quickened his sturdy pace a little.

David bent his head, cupping his hand to light his pipe.

"I've only tomorrow and Sunday left of my holiday," he remarked. "It seems to have gone quickly. Next time I'm down will be for Keith's wedding. I'm to be best man."

"Yes," Stevie said. "And Judy and I are to be bridesmaids."

David puffed at his pipe for a few minutes in silence.

"You know what they say. About one wedding making another. I wish it could be true of you and me, Stevie."

Stevie turned her head.

"Please, David, I'd rather you didn't talk that way."

"You said you'd think it over," David urged. "And give me an answer before I went back. You know how I feel about things. I don't care if you're in love with me or not. I feel so certain that we could be happy together."

Stevie looked up the flat wide road ahead. Her voice was wistful.

"Do you David? I—I wish I could feel the same."

And marry you and go away from Hedburgh and never see Charles again. Forget him for ever.

Impossible. She could never forget that enchanted moment when he kissed her. Or the rapture they had seemed to share. She didn't want to forget it. It was the most wonderful thing that had ever happened to her.

I couldn't marry David or any man, feeling as I do, Stevie thought on a sigh.

"Why not?" David persisted in answer to her last remark. "It's only a question of time, Stevie, I'm sure."

For the second time that day she had a sudden impulse to reveal her secret. To tell David the reason why she could never marry him. Something stayed her. An instinctive awareness that David would not understand. He would think her inclined to over-romanticize her feelings.

Stevie turned Toby's head towards a small thatched white house set back from the road.

"This is Mr. Roach's smallholding," she said. "Would you mind opening the gate for me, David?"

They drove in through the gateway up the rutted track. David stood by somewhat helplessly while Stevie and Mr. Roach unloaded the young pigs amidst a cacophony of gruntings and squealings. Then Mr. Roach insisted on showing them all his newly-built sties and the up-to-date henhouses he had recently acquired.

"Pigs an' poultry," he affirmed roundly. "Can't miss with 'em. One helps t'other."

It was impossible to refuse Mrs. Roach's offer of a cup of tea, although Stevie sensed that David was impatient to be off and away. He said as much when at last they managed to make their escape and set off in the cart again.

"These homely sessions are a bit much, aren't they? I thought Mrs. Roach would never stop talking."

"She likes company. They haven't been there very long. Mr. Roach comes from somewhere in the North. He was due to retire and they decided to take that little place near the coast. They hope to serve teas and things next summer."

David rolled his eyes.

"Heaven help them." He turned his collar up. "Here comes the rain."

Stevie pulled a plastic hood out of her mackintosh pocket.

"I don't think it will be much. The wind is too strong. I think we'll go back the coast road—it's quicker, only very bumpy. That won't matter now the pigs are out."

"This is grim," David scowled. "I wanted to have a serious talk with you, but who can concentrate in the teeth of a seventy-mile-an-hour gale?"

"It's not as bad as all that," Stevie protested. "Though the sea looks awfully rough."

"Words fail me when I contemplate the English summer," David said. His voice changed. He put his hand over one of Stevie's holding the reins. He looked down at her rain-swept face under the red plastic hood.

"Stevie, you didn't answer my question. If—if you aren't sure enough to say you'll marry me, why don't we have a trial engagement? Lots of people do, and I think they're a good idea. Don't you?"

Stevie shook her head.

"No, David, not really. I've always felt that when two people are in love, they know it. Overwhelmingly. Without the shadow of a doubt. A trial engagement isn't necessary."

"But not everyone who plans to marry is necessarily madly in love," David stated flatly. "Look at the French— they arrange a marriage so that all the factors involved are covered. Family, background, money, and so on. It's very sensible and practical. All this 'I-can-only-marry-the-love-of-my-life' is schoolgirl stuff."

Schoolgril stuff, Stevie thought. Is it? Perhaps David's right. Perhaps I'm not nearly as sensible and practical as I'm supposed to me. I couldn't marry without that sureness of heart. That feeling of love and certainty. If I can't marry Charles I'd rather be like Miss Mabel and never marry anyone.

She said slowly,

"Everyone has a different point of view on these things. Mine is the schoolgirl one, as you put it, and I'm afraid I can't alter. With all my heart, I'm sorry, but—it's no, David."

She broke off, to stare out to sea.

"David—look! What's that out there? That flash against the sky. It's a rocket or something. Why—it's a distress signal!"

CHAPTER TWENTY-THREE

STEVIE jerked Toby to a standstill and they both stared out across the white-crested waves to where they could see a small ship of some kind tossing and rolling in the rough sea in seemingly helpless fashion. Again the gun-metal-grey sky was torn by a sudden flash of light, whilst above the tearing rattle of the gale the siren shrieked eerily.

David whistled.

"It's definitely in trouble of some kind. There's a lifeboat at Hedburgh, isn't there? We'll see it put out in a few minutes."

Stevie shook the reins, calling out to Toby to get on.

"Yes—it's launched farther down. Past the Ship Inn. We'll go along there and see if there's anything we can do. Sometimes they need a hand with the sending off."

Toby's smart pace soon brought them into Hedburgh. Stevie tied him up outside the Ship Inn and hurried with David to join the crowd of people gathering beside the lifeboat station.

The wind buffeted at them as they stood there. The rain spattered down intermittently with each fresh gust. The tide, rolling in with a rough sea, had not yet reached the lifeboat runway. Willing hands helped the carriage down on to the beach and into the first flurry of waves.

"It's a fishin' smack out there," someone told Stevie and David, with a jerk of his head in the direction of the ship. "The *Silver Queen*. Dunno quoite what a' gone wrung. Must a' shipped water in some way."

The crew were scrambling into the lifeboat. Someone called and shouted above the whistling wind to the knot of people on the shore. A man shouted back.

Stevie watched the boat pitching in the fast-running sea, the deep throb of its engine mingling with the roar of wind and waves.

"What's the matter?" she asked the old man who had first spoken. "Is something wrong?"

He frowned, shaking his head without answering. He splashed forward to call out to the boat.

A woman's voice said to Stevie's shoulder:

"They're short of the crew. One's my husband—he's sick in bed, and another man is away inland. They're asking for a volunteer—"

The lifeboat waited, rocking at the water's edge. Stevie looked round at the faces beside her. None of the fishermen was here. Women, boys, children, a couple of very old men, some holiday visitors, made up the watching throng. Her glance returned to David—their eyes met.

"What is it?" David asked.

Stevie looked away.

They're asking for a volunteer. Oh—surely!" She broke off. "Not that *old* man!" She stared in consternation at the hobbling figure of the man who had spoken to her. He was hanging on to the edge of the lifeboat while the captain shook his head and gesticulated refusal with his hands. "He can't go—he'd be a liability. They want someone young, someone who's used to sailing—" Stevie broke off—her eyes wide on David's face.

She could see the battle going on within him. It was written in his frowning look and narrowed eyes. He was weighing up the risks. Calculating the chances as he was apt to calculate any unexpected action.

"It's no good being foolhardy," David began, when the murmur of the crowd stopped him. There was another shout. Stevie turned her head. A tall figure seemed to force a way through the group at the water's edge. Stevie heard herself cry out as she recognized the wide shoulders and that unmistakable black head.

"Charles! No—no—you can't—" Her voice was carried away by a fierce gust of wind. She saw him splash through the waves—catch at the edge of the boat. A hand came out to help him over. The old man stepped back—waving an arm in salute and encouragement.

The throbbing engine rose to a loud crescendo. The bow of the lifeboat turned towards the open sea. In a few seconds it was beating its way steadily in the direction of the distressed ship.

Stevie stared after the lifeboat, her heart sinking in dread. As the distance between the vessel and the shore widened it became impossible to distingish any member of the crew; difficult even, through the curtain of driving rain and spray, to see the boat itself as it rose and fell admist the swift waves of the incoming tide.

Charles must be mad to take such a risk. And how had it happened that he was at the lifeboat station at that particular moment? When had he returned from London?

Stevie screwed her eyes up in a desperate effort to keep the boat in sight. She had the superstitious feeling that while she could see it her glance, her thoughts, the prayer that was in her heart, would somehow keep Charles, and with Charles the other members of the crew, safe from hazard.

David's voice said above her head,

"That was Linmer, surely?" His voice seemed to hesitate. "Decent of him to volunteer. But I suppose he knows the crew, probably been out with them before."

Stevie didn't turn her head, because she had to keep on staring out across the tumbled sea to that tossing boat, grown unaccountably small and vulnerable-looking. She thought bitterly, "Don't make excuses, David. Whether Charles knows the crew or not doesn't enter into it. You hesitated—and were lost."

Stevie bit on her lip—pushing her clenched hands deep down into the pockets of her mackintosh as if to steady herself. To prevent herself from suddenly turning on David. Railing at him. Crying, "If anything happens to Charles, it will be your fault. Why didn't you volunteer? You're fit and strong and you've been used to boats all your life."

She checked herself—blinking her eyes against the rain on her lashes and face. It wasn't David's fault. He had acted as he would always act. Weighing up chances, calculating the odds. Deliberating whether a risk were worth while or not. It was typical of David all through and one couldn't blame him. Nor term it cowardice exactly. It was more an inherent caution. But there were moments in life when to pause and consider overlong was to lose the chance of saving someone from danger. Sudden, unexpected moments, when the only thing to do was to act with split-second courage. As Charles had done, handicapped though he was.

The boat was lost to sight. Stevie went on staring in a fixed stubborn fashion at the place where it had been, willing it to appear again before her vision. She heard voices behind her; David's voice mingling with other people's in a murmur of sound quickly lost beneath the whistling wind and crash of waves.

Someone tugged at her arm.

"Stevie—what happened? Have you been here long?"

It was Carole—a scarf tied over her dark hair, the collar of her camel coat turned up. Stevie gave her a brief distracted glance before turning back to the self-imposed vigil. She said,

"There's a fishing boat in trouble out there. The lifeboat is on its way to them." Now she felt impelled to look round at Carole. "Charles volunteered to go with them."

Carole's dark eyes widened.

"*Charles!* But how—I mean—he's away! In London. How could he—?" She broke off. "Oh, heavens! Stevie —I hope he'll be all right."

Even Carole didn't know the real danger. The threat of such strain and effort upon Charles' eye trouble.

Stevie gave a sudden gasp of relief.

"Oh—there's the boat! Away to the right—do you see?" She felt rather than saw Carole's nod.

"Yes, I see it. And look—that must be the fishing boat. They've nearly reached it. Melanie, did you hear what Stevie said? Charles has made up one of the lifeboat crew and is going out there to the rescue with them."

Melanie. Stevie turned her head again and saw Melanie standing on Carole's other side. Tendrils of spun-gold fair hair blew from under her woollen cap across the pale oval of face. She frowned plaintively, her blue eyes narrowing to follow the line of Carole's pointing finger. She said, as Carole had done,

"But I thought Charles was in London. I suppose he got off the afternoon train and joined the stampede down here." She gave a sudden little laugh. "Really, doesn't he do the craziest things? That's Charles all over."

The cool tinkling laugh sounded oddly clear through the jangle of wind and waves and voices. Stevie couldn't bear to hear it. So untroubled and inconsequential. Just as a moment ago she had nearly turned on David, now she wanted to turn on Melanie. "You don't understand," she longed to say. "You've no conception of the difficulties Charles is fighting under. This isn't just some terrific joke—one of Charles' amusing escapades."

Calm down, Stevie told herself. Don't get so steamed up. It won't help Charles out there. Everything will be all right. It—it's got to be.

She took a deep breath and felt better. Her fixed gaze never left the space of wild grey sea, although by now it was almost impossible to distinguish the lifeboat or to make out what was happening.

Melanie shivered.

"Do we have to wait here? It's fearfully cold." She looked about her. "Couldn't we go inside the Ship Inn? We can see everything quite well from the windows."

"Good idea," David said. He glanced at his watch. " They're open, too. What about it, Stevie?"

Stevie shook her head.

"I'd rather stay here. But you go, David. Take Melanie and Carole."

David hesitated.

"Why don't you come? There's no point in hanging around here. You're getting soaked to the skin, Stevie."

Stevie shook her head obstinately.

"No—I'm all right. I—I'll come in a few minutes. Go along, David. There's no need to wait with me."

"Well—*I'm* certainly going," Melanie stated flatly. "Come on, Carole."

David lingered a moment or two at Stevie's side as the two girls walked away. Then, after another murmured protest, he left her and followed them.

Stevie didn't move. It was impossible to explain, but she had a wild conviction that she must remain on that exact spot, staring with unwavering vigilance in the direction of the lifeboat until she saw it return to shore once again. Until she saw Charles safely back at Hedburgh.

It was absurd and irrational. But she had to go on standing there whilst the minutes dragged past and the people about her made every kind of conjecture as to what they could see and what they couldn't see and what was supposed to be happening.

A sigh went through the watching crowd. It became a rumble, then turned into a sudden roar. Someone shouted,

"There they are!—coming back towards shore."

A little cheer went up.

Stevie felt a moisture that was something more than rain or sea spray on her cheeks. She tasted the salt of her own tears on her lips, unaware that she had been crying with relief. She wiped the back of her hand against her face while her heart cried, "Charles! Oh, Charles, my darling—"

CHAPTER TWENTY-FOUR

THE laden lifeboat made slow and difficult progress towards the shore. Although the tide was an incoming one, the strong wind buffeted the boat remorselessly, as if determined to do battle to the last. Gradually it drew nearer. Soon Stevie could distinguish the crowded figures in it and then, in a few minutes more, it was running aground with eager figures rushing into the water alongside it to give assistance.

Stevie still stood there like someone laid under a spell. She watched the rescued fisherman, huddled in blankets and coats, being helped ashore. She watched the crew greeting people in the crowd. And at last she saw, splashing through the water, his black seal's head wet and flattened down, his face drawn and white above the borrowed oilskin, Charles.

The spell was broken. Stevie started forward. Her voice was almost a sob as she said his name.

"Charles!"

He turned his head in her direction and as Stevie moved towards him with a sudden unsteady gait, she heard Melanie's and Carole's voice crying in echo of her own voice,

"Charles!"

They came hurrying down the steps from the Ship Inn with David at their heels and intercepted him before he reached Stevie.

Carole hugged him despite his dripping clothes.

"Oh, Charles—you are the limit! We were all having heart failure. When on earth did you get back?"

Melanie linked her arm through his.

"Darling—imagine you dashing off like that! Whatever came over you? But I think you're simply heroic and I love you for it." She reached up and kissed him.

Across the space of wet sand Stevie watched them. She saw Charles give a queer set smile down at Melanie and his sister. He said something to them both. He looked chilled and immeasurably weary, but Stevie felt only thankfulness that he had come to no apparent harm despite the strain he had undergone.

As she looked across at the little group she felt suddenly lonely.

"I don't belong there," Stevie thought. "Melanie and Charles. They belong together. And Carole belongs to them both. He doesn't even know I'm here. When he heard me call he thought it was Melanie."

David had come across to her.

"What's the matter, Stevie? You look like a stone statue." He reached out and caught her hands in his. "Why—you're frozen. You should have waited in the inn with us."

Charles heard David's voice and looked round to see David clasping Stevie's hands between his own and bending solicitously towards her. His glance met Stevie's. He didn't smile, only stared across at her. Then he moved towards her and David.

Stevie freed her hands from David's. As Charles approached she managed to smile. She said slowly,

"I'm glad you're safe, Charles."

Charles gave her a long steady look.

"Thanks, Stevie." He addressed David. "I wonder if I could come back to the farm with you and dry off a bit? I'm afraid if I turn up at home looking like a drowned rat it's going to alarm my mother unduly. She hasn't been too fit and I don't want to upset her."

"Of course," David said quickly. "You look pretty well all in, old man. And Stevie is soaked through. She *would* stand out here all the time instead of sheltering at the inn as we did."

Charles turned his head to look at Stevie again. But all he said was,

"My teeth w-won't stop c-chattering. Let's go."

"Goodness—yes!" Melanie interposed. "You're turning blue before my very eyes, Charles."

The party straggled up the cliff path to where the pony and float were tied up.

"Pile in," David said. "It's quicker this way."

Stevie took the reins up between her numb fingers and gave Toby a sharp flick. The stout little pony started along the road at a brisk pace, with the cart in which David, Carole, Melanie and Charles stood huddled together, rattling noisily along behind.

"This is an absurd idea," Melanie cried. "You're dripping all over my feet, Charles. Do hurry, Stevie."

They were at the farm in a few minutes. As the cart banged to a halt on the cobbles Miss Mabel appeared at the back door to stare at them all in momentary consternation.

"Charles, my dear boy, what has happened to you? Come along in to the kitchen fire." She reached up two thin hands to pull off the wet oilskin as he went through the door.

As Charles moved forward he seemed to stagger. Stevie saw David's arm come about his shoulders—Miss Mabel catch at one arm. She stared after him in swift fear. Carole said,

"Poor old Charles—he looks quite groggy. I'd better go in and help." She went quickly in, followed by Melanie.

Stevie began mechanically to undo the traces fastening Toby to the shafts of the cart. There was nothing she could do. Everyone was helping Charles. And poor Toby was wet and tired. Before she did anything else she must unharness him and give him a rub down and some food.

When she came into the kitchen twenty minutes later she found Charles seated beside the Aga stove, clad in a pair of Keith's flannels and an old sport jacket belonging to him. Melanie was sitting beside Charles, smoking a cigarette. Carole was helping Lisa cut bread and butter, while Miss Mabel made tea. Keith was apparently still up on the fields, as there was no sign of him.

"I'd no idea all this was happening," Miss Mabel was saying. "Of course, we heard the alarm going off at the lifeboat station, but"—she nodded her head towards the jewel-glow of newly filled jam jars—"I was making jam and Lisa was helping me. We didn't dare leave it and I knew we couldn't do anything." She smiled. "Not like our hero Charles here. And doubtless David, if he'd been there in time."

David stared out of the window as if he hadn't heard, and Stevie felt sorry for him, knowing that indeed he had arrived at the scene in time, but had hesitated when the call came. Perhaps if Charles hadn't put in an appearance at that particular moment David might have volunteered. It was kindest to give him the benefit of the doubt.

"But how did you come to be there?" Melanie demanded of Charles. "You were supposed to be in London. When did you get back?"

Charles smiled up at Lisa as she handed him a cup of tea. "Thanks, Lisa." He looked round at Melanie.

"My train arrived at Bassett about five and Frank Tuddenham gave me a lift up to Hedburgh. I called in at home but no one was there, so I dumped my bag and was on my way down to Whitegates. That siren affair went suddenly whooping off like a mad thing and everyone started hurrying down to the shore, so I joined the throng. That's all."

Stevie listened to Charles' deep easy voice without looking at him. She wondered for a brief moment if he had intended calling at Whitegates to see *her*. To tell her the specialist's verdict. He had promised to let her know. But it was unlikely that he would come so promptly. As if she were one of his first thoughts. After all, he could not know how much everything that concerned him mattered to her.

Melanie shook her head at Charles, dimpling into laughter.

"Darling, you do look quaint in your borrowed finery! Your hands and wrists stick out from Keith's jacket like an orphan Oliver Twist or something. I never thought you were so much larger and longer than he is."

Charles did look amusingly unlike himself as he sat there with a good four inches of leg between trouser end and socks, and, as Melanie had observed, a length of tanned wrist extending out of the tweed sleeve to grasp his cup.

Charles grinned ruefully.

"It's jolly good of Keith to lend these things to me." He glanced up at Miss Mabel. "I hope he won't have your blood for such a kindly deed. I'll return them just as soon as I can."

"Don't worry a scrap," Miss Mabel said. "Keith would have offered them himself if he'd been here. Are you warmed through now? I must say you look better. I thought you were going to collapse on my hands when you came in through that doorway."

"I'm fine!" Charles said. His eyes moved to find Stevie, but Stevie had withdrawn to the far end of the kitchen and did not see his glance.

"We really ought to be getting back," Carole said. "Mummy will be wondering where we are. I said we'd be in for dinner and it's after six now. Miss Mabel, I hope we haven't interrupted all your arrangements? It has been good of you to let Charles change and rest here before going home."

"No trouble at all, my dear," Miss Mabel returned briskly. "He did look rather an unnerving sight, didn't he?"

Melanie stood up, holding out a hand to Charles.

"Come on, scarecrow. It's time you went home and made yourself look respectable again. And I want to talk to you."

Charles straightened up somewhat stiffly. Stevie heard him say,

"I want to talk to you too, Melanie."

Stevie put the cup back into its saucer with a sharp clatter. Her hand trembled as she gathered up Lisa's plate and her own and the nearby cups and saucers. She hurried out into the scullery with them and stood for a

184

moment staring down at the cold white porcelain of the empty sink.

"I *want to talk to you, Melanie*," Charles had just said. That could only mean one thing. That the specialist's verdict was favourable. That—that he felt free to speak to Melanie. To ask her to marry him.

How could you feel so glad and thankful and yet so utterly miserable all at once? How could you feel as if Charles' reprieve was the clash of prison gates closing in on all your hopes—your happiness?

She could hear their voices from the kitchen.

"I'm awfully grateful to you, Miss Mabel," Charles was saying. "I'll return Keith's things as soon as possible."

Miss Mabel called, "Good-bye—"

Stevie turned quickly from the sink as someone came into the scullery. It was Lisa.

"Oh, Stevie, there you are. They've gone."

"I'm—I'm just going to wash the tea things," Stevie mumbled. She hurried back into the kitchen and started gathering the rest of the cups and saucers together. David had left the kitchen. Miss Mabel had gone to shut up the hens.

I never even said good-bye to him, Stevie thought. I wanted to speak to him but I couldn't. I don't suppose he even noticed I wasn't there, when he and Melanie and Carole left. He's forgotten all about his promise to let me know what happened. It's natural enough. He has more—more important things to discuss with Melanie. He wouldn't have said, "I want to talk to you" to her like that unless it meant that he was no longer handicapped. Or would he? Oh, she wished that he had told her the specialist's verdict.

CHAPTER TWENTY-FIVE

STEVIE had washed up the crockery and was putting it away when Keith came in. He kissed Lisa, saying with unexpected humour,

"I met my sports jacket walking up the lane towards me and it turned out to be Charles! He told me what had happened and I gave him and the two girls a lift back to the Manor House. He put up a good show going off in the lifeboat like that. I heard from Sam Bailey that the *Silver Queen* has gone down, so they only just got them off in time."

Stevie sneezed and went on sneezing.

"You've caught cold," Lisa said. "You ought to have changed your wet things when you came in."

"I'm all right," Stevie protested. She sneezed again. "I think I'll go up and have a hot bath, if there's any water."

"It's piping," Lisa said. "I'll put a match to the sitting-room fire and you can come down and sit by it." She looked through the kitchen window at the chill summer evening outside.

"It seems more like October than July."

The glow from the hot bath didn't seem to reach to Stevie's heart. Even the log-fire crackling in the pleasant sitting-room failed to warm her cold being. She sat huddled in one of the chintz-covered armchairs while Miss Mabel remonstrated with her and urged her to go to bed.

"Take a couple of aspirin with hot milk. You'll be as right as rain in the morning."

David stared at her gloomily.

"I warned you, Stevie. You would hang around in that pelting rain. Absolutely asking for it."

Stevie felt like bursting into tears. The prickle in her nose and the sudden watering of her eyes was something more than the effects of another sneeze.

"I'll go in a few minutes," she said.

Lisa and Keith went off to their "den" to arrange furniture and measure for curtains. Miss Mabel, with a final shake of her head, said,

"Now do take my advice and pop off upstairs. You don't want to be ill with double pneumonia just before Lisa's wedding, do you?"

Lisa's wedding. Only a few more weeks and the turning point in Lisa's life would be reached. And the end of something in Stevie's. Things would never be quite the same again between them.

She felt more than ever like crying. I mustn't be morbid, Stevie told herself. It's all so wonderful for Lisa and I'm really awfully happy for her. It's just feeling miserable and low when everything is turning out so perfectly for everyone else that does it.

David paced about the room—his hands in his pockets, his unlit pipe between his teeth. He said abruptly, "Stevie—"

She looked up.

"About this—this afternoon. When I asked you to marry me. Was it absolutely final—your 'no', I mean?"

Stevie hesitated. Was it? It would be such an easy way of escape. Away from the constant sight of Charles and Melanie living together at the Manor House. Away from that lonely sense of dwelling on the fringe of other people's happiness—Lisa's and Keith's.

She shook her head.

"I'm sorry, David. It's final."

He didn't answer. He pushed the empty pipe into the pocket of his jacket and moved towards the door. As he pulled it open he almost collided with someone on the threshold. Stevie heard him say abruptly,

"Oh, hello. Come in." He held the door open and Charles came through carrying Keith's jacket and trousers over one arm. He looked towards Stevie, who had half risen from her chair by the fireside, and back to David standing in the doorway. He said lightly, "I came to return these," and held the clothes out towards him.

David took Keith's neatly pressed things and laid them over a chair back.

"I'll get Keith. He's only in the next room."

Charles made a brief gesture.

"Don't trouble him. I—I'd like a word with Stevie first, if I may."

David shot him a quick look. He said,

"Certainly. Stevie will find Keith for you if you want to speak to him."

"I'd like to thank him for the loan of the jacket," Charles said. He added, "Later."

The door closed behind David. Charles came over towards the fireplace to where Stevie stood, her usually smooth hair ruffled from the recent bath, her face flushed pink above the blue woollen house coat.

He smiled, but before he could speak, Stevie sneezed.

187

"Excuse me." She pulled out her handkerchief and said in a muffled voice. "I'm sorry. I think I'm getting a cold. Would you like to sit down?"

Charles shook his head. He looked his usual immaculate self in a smooth green tweed suit with spotless linen at neck and cuffs and a striped club tie knotted under his firm brown chin.

"I'd rather stand. D"you mind?"

Stevie subsided suddenly back into the armchair.

"No, I don't mind." She gave him a puzzled stare. "You wanted to—to see me?"

"I wanted to see you very much," Charles said gravely. "In fact, it was to see you that I came down to Whitegates earlier on this afternoon. I promised." He paused. "If you remember."

Stevie stared down at the tight ball of handkerchief in her hand.

"I remember." She added almost inaudibly, "I thought —perhaps you'd forgotten."

"No, I hadn't forgotten. Only—things got mixed up a bit. That lifeboat business. And then there were far too many people around for me to get a chance to speak to you."

"Yes," Stevie said. She thought, "He's come to tell me what the specialist said. To tell me that it's all right and that he's going to marry Melanie." To put off the dreaded moment she said quickly,

"It—it was a risky thing to go off in the lifeboat like that. You told me once you didn't believe in playing the false hero for anyone."

"I don't," Charles answered. "Only that was rather different, wasn't it? No one was daring me to do something. It was a sudden emergency one just had to rise to."

That's like you, Charles, Stevie thought. You took the chance. David—so worthy, so admirable, so splendid in every way—wavered. It's just the difference between you both.

"You haven't asked me what happened," Charles said gently. "Don't you want to know any more?"

Stevie looked up and met his intent black stare. She said bravely,

"Yes. I want to know. Please tell me."

"I think I'm more or less in the clear," Charles told her quietly. "There is to be an operation, but Mr. Walderbroke says it will only be a slight one. He's distinctly pleased with the progress I've made, and says I'll be able to go back to work by about Christmas time."

Stevie let out a sigh.

"Oh, I'm very glad—very thankful for you, Charles. It's wonderful news. Your mother will be so happy about it all." She hesitated, forcing herself to ask the question. "And—and Melanie? It will be all right for you and—Melanie?"

Charles shook his head slowly.

"No—as a matter of fact that doesn't come up any more. My first thought when I walked down Harley Street after seeing the old boy was, 'Now I can marry Melanie'. And my second thought was, 'But I don't want to'."

Stevie stared at him in amazement.

"You—don't want to?" she echoed.

Charles shook his black head a second time.

"No. Queer, isn't it? I think I must have been falling out of love with Melanie for quite some time. I suppose you might say from that particular moment when I started to fall in love with someone else."

Stevie couldn't speak. She felt submerged by a fierce choking emotion that seemed to start at her toes and work up through her entire being. She wanted to laugh and cry and shout out all at once. Instead, she sneezed.

Charles cocked a black eyebrow.

"Bless you! Here, take this." He held out a spotless white linen handkerchief and pushed it into Stevie's resisting fingers. His hand closed gently round her own. He pulled her up slowly out of the armchair.

"Stevie—what about you, and—Superman? He's always hanging round you and looking as if he's on the point of making the most formal of declarations."

Stevie couldn't stop the smile that touched her lips.

"I'm not in love with David."

Charles put his other hand out and tilted her face up to his.

"I rather thought you weren't. Ever since—the evening I kissed you."

189

Stevie felt her flushed face grow a deeper pink.

She said protestingly,

"That isn't—I didn't mean—" She tried to look away from Charles' black gaze.

"Darling," Charles said, in a quiet deep voice that Stevie had never heard him use before. "Darling, I love you with all my heart and soul. I love everything about you. I love you because you're pretty and you have beautiful eyes, and when I take you in my arms like this something within me goes 'zing!' and I want to kiss you without stopping. And I love you for other things too. Because you have courage and common sense and you will try and boss me around a bit and because you have a quality of stead-fastness I value very deeply." He smiled. "I even love you with a shiny pink nose and a cold coming on. Will you marry me, Stevie?"

Stevie felt his arm tighten about her. She opened her mouth to say something. To answer with all the rapturous delight that was flowing through her. All that came out was a muffled sneeze.

Charles brushed her hair with his lips.

"Poor poppet. Does that mean 'yes'?"

Stevie nodded her head.

"Yes. Charles—is it all really true? I can't quite believe it. But—" she hesitated. "What about Melanie? She's in love with you. Won't she be hurt and unhappy?"

Charles smiled, shaking his head.

"I doubt it. I doubt if Melanie is in love with anyone very much as yet—only herself. I did sort things out a bit with her this evening, just to remove any misapprehensions. We had a little talk. I don't think she took it too much to heart. I've a feeling she'll settle down with old Irving in the end. They'll probably be very happy. He's lashings of money and he's just the sort of doting Yankee who'll get a kick out of lavishing it all on a lovely decorative piece of goods like Melanie. They're made for one another." He drew her close up against him. "We are too, Stevie. I can't get along without you." He bent his dark head to hers.

It was everything she'd ever dreamed of coming true. A beating joy, a surging delight. And beneath all the ecstasy the deep warm consciousness of something real and true and everlasting. Something essentially right and harmonious.

"We belong," Stevie thought, her arms tightening about Charles' neck. "We shall always be together in our hearts. That's the way it should be."

A long while after she said softly,

"You'll catch my cold, Charles."

"Who cares?" Charles said. "We might as well start off right from the beginning. Sharing everything." He frowned. "You won't mind too much about this eye business? I feel I'm on top of it all at last, in spite of the proposed operation."

"I thought you said we were going to share everything?" Stevie chided him lovingly.

Charles kissed the cupped palm of her hand. He sighed. "Yes—that's the perfect part. I feel I shall never mind what happens with you beside me." He added, "Mother's going to be very happy about all this. She thinks a lot of you, my darling. She fairly sings your praises."

"Does she?" Stevie said wonderingly. "But I'm so ordinary and everyday."

"Don't fish," Charles said. "You're good and beautiful and quite, quite perfect. Lots of ordinary everyday things are. Kittens and primroses and new bread and honey and spiders' webs in the sun and 'radiant raindrops couching in cool flowers'. Now I've started quoting Rupert Brooke! You see the effect you have upon me."

He hugged her in a sudden embrace. "Oh, dearest, I love you so much."

"I love you too," Stevie said.

The door opened suddenly and there stood Lisa and Keith. Their startled expressions changed quickly to one of pleased happiness.

"Why—Stevie—Charles!" Lisa began.

"*A-tish—oo!*" Charles ejaculated in reply.

THE END

Harlequin Romances

TITLES STILL IN PRINT

〜〜〜〜〜〜〜〜〜〜〜〜〜〜〜〜〜〜〜〜〜〜〜〜〜〜〜〜

TO OUR DEVOTED HARLEQUIN READERS—

FOR INFORMATION ON FORTHCOMING NEVER-BEFORE-PUBLISHED
HARLEQUIN ROMANCE TITLES, WRITE TO:

HARLEQUIN ROMANCE BOOKS
DEPARTMENT Z
SIMON & SCHUSTER, INC.
11 WEST 39TH STREET
NEW YORK, N.Y. 10018